One
Small
Town

'False face must hide what the false heart doth know'

**William Shakespeare
(MacBeth)**

Chapters

How much can you get away with in one small town?

CHAPTER 1

Hello Goodbye

In accordance with her wishes no one was present at the cremation of Mrs Marjorie Edge. Mrs Edge lived in a small English town and had previously informed what few friends and relatives she possessed that she had bought for herself a 'Cremation Without Ceremony'. Her arrangements were carried out on a dismal, grey November day,

The death certificate would record that Mrs Edge died of heart failure. She was 81. She had 3 close relatives and they were all in Perth, Western Australia throughout that November. Her son and daughter-in-law because they lived there and her grandson Andrew Edge because he was visiting his parents.

The three of them learned of Marjorie's demise when Andrew's phone rang. His grandmother's solicitors in England who were also the executors of her will broke the news to Andrew. In well-practised sympathetic tones the voice of Miss Audrey Hinstock expressed regrets on behalf of Lapley & Hinstock and reassured Andrew that the matter of Mrs Edge's estate could be held in abeyance until his return to England. Andrew in turn broke the sad news to his parents.

"So do we go back to England?" asked Andrew's father Greg

"Would seem a bit odd if we didn't" offered Vanessa, Andrew's mother

"What would we be going back for exactly? There's no funeral to attend, we all knew ma had done this, the arrangement is a cremation without mourners. It seems, I don't know, wrong in some way but it was ma's decision. What do you think, Andy?"

"Grandma told me she'd bought this cremation plan. I'd never heard of it before but she told me she went into a local funeral directors and asked them 'If I said I want a David Bowie would you know what I mean?' and they said 'yes we know exactly what you mean and it's one of the plans we offer'. Gran told me the man then said 'they're becoming very popular' then realised what he'd said. But gran started laughing and took all the details home"

"It can't be wrong if it's what Marjorie wanted. It's just that until fairly recently no-one had heard of it" Vanessa said

It was the death of David Bowie and his cremation without a ceremony, without religion nor music nor a congregation which had triggered a surge in interest in this kind of non send off.

"And Marjorie didn't do religion" continued Vanessa

"Well let's be honest, when was the last time any of us was inside a church? Whichever funeral we last attended. And we're all thinking the same thing, when does the booze up start?" Greg said then continued

"It's not as though we have any function to perform back in England. The solicitors will sort everything. And we all know the contents of ma's will - Andy here is the sole beneficiary"

The three of them decided there was little point in returning to England for a non funeral and even if they had decided to make the trip there was little likelihood of getting flights at this busy time of the year at such short notice. So they opened another bottle of Australian wine and drank it sitting outside in the shade on a hot November night in Perth. They thought about and talked about their late matriarch.

Andrew returned to England two weeks later on two Emirates flights - Perth to Dubai then Dubai to Birmingham. He got a train from Birmingham Airport to Repton Magna where he lived alone and worked as a police constable. At the age of 37 Andrew was soon to discover he was to become a wealthy man.

His grandmother had been born in Birmingham and with her late husband George ran a successful antiques business in one of that city's wealthier suburbs. On retiring from their business the couple bought and moved to 22 Station Road Market Repton to the north of Birmingham. Marjorie was widowed at the age of 79. She lived alone at 22 Station Road until her final wishes were carried out two years later. She had been in good health, slim with short, straight well cut grey hair and always dressed simply but stylishly. There had been no history of heart problems.

When Andrew got home after his 4 weeks leave from work he was greeted by a pile of post behind his front door. Most of it went straight into the bin.

He noticed an envelope marked 'Lapley & Hinstock Solicitors Market Repton'. The letter within expressed deepest condolences on the loss of his grandmother and asked him to make an appointment to visit their offices to discuss the finalisation of the late Mrs Edge's affairs. He rang them. Miss Audrey Hinstock would see him next day. On that next day he was told what he already knew - he was sole beneficiary under his grandmother's will. He was to inherit 22 Station Road Market Repton, all its contents and money on deposit in various savings and bank accounts amounting to over £180,000 net. The figures involved came as a surprise and shock to Andrew.

The following day Andrew reported for duty at Repton Magna police station. The only people he had so far told of his inheritance were his parents and one close police buddy he'd known for nearly twenty years who agreed to keep the matter confidential. His parents in Perth WA asked him if he now intended quitting his job. Andy replied he had no such intention. His parents had now been in Australia for 16 years through his father's work. When they left the UK they asked their son to go with them but Andy was then in the first year of police training and wanted to make a success of his chosen career. 16 years later and still a uniformed constable may not be regarded as a successful career to some high flyers. Andy Edge thought differently. He enjoyed his position as a reliable, experienced senior constable.

But in that November Andy Edge had decisions to make on what to do with 22 Station Road Market Repton. He would seek help, get some impartial advice. He thought he knew the right people to ask.

CHAPTER 2

This Is Your Land

County Repton occupies rich, red, fertile land midway between Liverpool and Birmingham. It became wealthy as over the centuries more and better travel and transport links were built. Rapidly expanding cities to the north and south needed supplies and the high quality beef, poultry and dairy comestibles provided by County Repton were feeding millions by early Victorian times.

Four north-south routes running parallel through County Repton all played their part in its wealth creation. First in 1777 came the opening of The Trent And Mersey Canal. The railway line opened in 1840. The A34 trunk road of 1935 passes through the county on its way from Manchester to Winchester and lastly since 1965 the M6 motorway on its route from the Scottish border to Rugby. Both Birmingham and Liverpool airports are easily accessible by rail or road.

The county has three major towns - Dainford in the north population 62,000, Market Repton in the middle home to 13,000 & its main town Repton Magna in the south where dwell another 210,000. The three towns are in a north-south line through the county and the canal, the railway line and the A34 trunk road pass through all three the M6 motorway passing them all to the west. When estate agents cannot think of anything complimentary to say about a property (although that rarely happens in County Repton) they will default to 'excellent transport links' - a euphemism for 'easy to get out of'.

Unless you are retired or have an interest in cows or trees there is nothing to keep you in County Repton which is why many of its over 30s are now working in Birmingham or Liverpool. Those who wish to commute make use of the surprisingly good train service with all three of the county's towns having well patronised stations.

The county used to have town councils, borough councils and a county council all of which were swept away when Repton Unitary Authority was created its HQ being in the county's largest town Repton Magna.

It also used to have its own constabulary until that too was abolished (or merged as some press release claimed) along with 3 or 4 other small traditional county constabularies when they all became part of Mid Land Police Service.

The wealthiest of the 3 towns is Market Repton sitting quietly and smuggly between its 2 larger neighbours. Its streets are lined with fine Victorian and Edwardian houses, cafes, shops and pubs.

It was in Market Repton where a bizarre sequence of events would soon begin to unfold.

CHAPTER 3

Money

There proved to be no complications nor delays in finalising the affairs of Mrs Marjorie Edge. Her solicitors Lapley & Hinstock were based in High Street Market Repton a short walk from 22 Station Rd where Mrs Edge had lived for 30 years. Her will was a simple matter with everything she possessed left to her only grandchild Andrew Edge. By the end of the following February the UK Land Registry showed Andrew was the owner of 22 Station Road Market Repton and his bank balance had increased by nearly 200,000 UK pounds.

Andy was a little over 6 feet tall, broad shoulders, robust build with no sign of an expanding waistline. He was clean shaven, had blue eyes and short straight black hair. Facially he was interesting rather than handsome. He lived in a traditional English 1930s semi detached house within walking distance of Repton Magna police station from where he worked. Like many of his neighbours he had replaced his front garden with a parking space for his car. Andy hated gardening. His garage contained his large, powerful motorcycle and all the accoutrements of bikes, bikers and biking.

Being single and without any family commitments Andy as usual had worked over the Christmas and New Year holidays so allowing a married police colleague to be with family and turkey dinner. He would call in the favour at a later date. In between dealing with the drunkenness, fights and domestic incidents ('someone won't stop throwing snowballs at my wall and it's making the dog bark') which nowadays make for a traditional British Christmas Andy thought about 22 Station Road Market Repton. On his first rest day in that February Andy drove the 12 miles north to Market Repton to keep two appointments.

His first visit was to the estate agents Spring & Fall whose offices were in the middle of Market Repton High Street. This business was run by two young men Ian Fall and Carl Ramsey. There was no Mrs/Miss/Mr Spring. They thought Spring & Fall looked and sounded better than 'Fall & Ramsey' or 'Ramsey & Fall'. Andy's appointment was with the aforementioned Mr Ramsey who looked vaguely familiar to Andy but he couldn't remember why.

"How can we help you, Mr Edge?" Carl asked once they were seated. Andy explained his recent acquisition of 22 Station Road just a short walk away and showed Carl a series of photographs of the property he'd taken with his phone.

"I've got to decide what to do with this house. It's too big for me to live in so I guess it's either sell or rent"

Professionalism prevented Carl Ramsey from shouting out the 'wow' which had lit up in bright neon letters inside his head as he studied the photographs of the beautiful detached Victorian home in one of the town's most prestigious streets.

"We'd be delighted to handle this for you. My advice would be to sell. It's a bit too big to attract the rental market we get here. But if you do want to consider renting you could divide the house into a couple of flats. That way you'd attract the well-off retired or given its proximity to the railway station the Birmingham or Liverpool commuters".

The two men discussed the pricing options should Andy decide to sell and also possible rental returns. The figures either way were eye watering to Andy who was paying a mortgage on his house and keeping two vehicles on the road on one constabulary salary. Carl handed Andy his business card and Andy agreed to return when he'd made a decision. They shook hands and Andy departed for his next meeting.

In Market Repton High Street directly opposite Spring & Fall Estate Agents stood Lapley & Hinstock Solicitors who had recently and surprisingly quickly concluded the matter of Marjorie Edge's estate.

Andy's next visit was to his friend Simon King who lived nearby within walking distance but Andy had parked his car in the small car park behind Spring & Fall so drove over to his pal's house.

Simon King was one of Andy's closest and oldest pals. The two had met 20 years earlier when they were both attending Repton Magna College. Simon was then doing the City And Guilds construction training course, Andy the public service course. Simon was now the boss and owner of a successful building firm the biggest and the best in the Market Repton area. He specialised in small construction projects, home extensions and conversions, garages, windows etc. He excelled at carpentry. His vans were a familiar site around town. Simon was divorced, lived alone and was a similar age to Andy. He was a little under 6 feet tall with a neatly trimmed beard and the hint of an expanding waistline. When his hairline started to recede he'd adopted the shaved head look. Like Andy, Simon owned a car but preferred to ride a motorcycle weather permitting.

The two men sat around Simon's kitchen table drinking tea as Andy talked about his visit to Spring & Fall and the decision he'd soon have to make. He'd told Simon some weeks earlier about his inheritance. Simon suggested the two of them visit 22 Station Road and he'd give Andy his opinion on the feasibility of creating two flats if that were his decision. They'd make this visit one day soon in daylight, being February it had now gone dark.

A short while later as Andy left Simon's home he asked Simon if he knew Carl Ramsey. Simon did. He'd done work at Spring & Fall's offices and was also the on-call builder for some of the rental properties they managed.

It being a Wednesday Carl Ramsey and Ian Fall were having their regular midweek post-work drinks in The Golden Lion a traditional, comfortable, red brick pub in Market Repton High Street. They jokingly referred to it as their weekly management and strategy meeting.

Ian Fall then aged 33 was tall, slim and fair. He was married, had two children and a dog and lived in an 8 year old house on the west side of Market Repton. One of hundreds of new houses built in the last 5 years with hundreds more to come. Additionally the busy trunk road running north-south was attracting businesses and workers to its expanding industrial estate. The future looked bright for Spring & Fall.

Carl Ramsey then aged 32 was short, stocky and dark haired. He was unmarried and lived alone in a flat in Repton Magna. In his spare time he worked as head coach for Dainford football club in the north of the county. Most days he drove to work but on Wednesdays he always caught the train to Market Repton so he could enjoy a couple or three pints in the Golden Lion with Ian.

Once installed in the pub with their first pints in front of them Carl told Ian about the day's most promising event, the meeting with a potential new client about 22 Station Road.

"I just walked along to have a look at it. I reckon if he sells we'd be asking upwards of 550k"

"Who is he ?"

"Big guy called Andrew Edge. Looks like a right thug but doesn't talk like one. He may sell but I put the idea in his head of doing flat conversions then letting. If he does I'd be interested myself. Move from Repton Magna and live here. Great position near the station and within walking distance of the High Street".

Meanwhile as Andy drove south back to his home in Repton Magna he felt reassured his friend Simon would help with his decisions on 22 Station Road. He also had a feeling that a very different issue was nearing its resolution. But just where had he seen Carl Ramsey before?

CHAPTER 4

Shapes Of Things

The following Sunday Andy and his friend Simon the builder met at 11am outside 22 Station Road Market Repton.

Station Road was a cul de sac. It was situated to the north of Market Repton High Street to which it was linked by a perfectly square park opened in 1840 the same year as the railway line and station. Terraces of large Victorian houses lined the 4 outer sides of the park with each house facing straight into the park. Station Road began where High Street ended, ran along the west side of the park and extended from its north west corner. The B9916 road north to Dainford ran from the park's north east corner. Beyond the park the west side of Station Road had no houses and was lined with mature trees behind which ran the railway line, the east side had a row of large detached Victorian villas. Number 22 was the last house before the Grade II listed railway station. Everything in sight, every tree, every railing, every brick, every chimney pot was within Market Repton's rabidly enforced Conservation Zone.

The two men got out of their cars and stood for a moment silently staring at the empty house which had been Andy's grandmother's home for 30 years. Andy was familiar with the property. He was 7 when his grandparents moved here from Birmingham. He and his parents had visited almost every Sunday until Andy's parents moved to Australia. Andy had continued visiting his grandparents regularly. His grandmother had lived there alone after her husband had died over two years ago.

Andy recalled the house had a collection of things that as a youngster he never understood, ornaments and small statues in startling styles and pictures on the walls he found alarming - dark figures against dark backgrounds. They were to be found in every room of the house. Then on his next visit he'd notice the pictures had been changed around or looked completely different as if his grandmother was never satisfied with how they were presented.

The house itself was of unusual design in that the main door was not in the centre of the double fronted structure but on the right hand side of the building's facade. Andy put his key into this door and he and Simon entered the wide hall, stepped onto the original Minton tiled floor and experienced a moment of stillness and silence. The hall went in a straight line to the back door. Midway a corridor off to the left gave access to the rooms on the ground floor. To the right a broad staircase rose to the first floor. The staircase was built against an external wall and two opaque glass windows gave light onto the stairs. Andy remembered that as recently as last Autumn pictures had hung on the wall between and either side of the two windows but now the walls were empty. Beneath the stairs a flight of steps went down into the cellar.

Andy picked up an accumulation of letters and junk mail which had fallen through the letterbox since his last visit. He would take them home and deal with them later.

"Where do we start, mate?"

"Upstairs first then work our way down" Simon replied.

They took an hour to do their initial survey, Simon taking photographs with his smartphone, making measurements with a laser ruler and jotting down details in a notebook. No structural alterations had been made since the careful and efficient Victorian workers had built the house. Simon was in awe of their workmanship. Solid brick walls everywhere and when he shone his torch into the loft space Simon observed that even the brickwork on the chimney stacks which could only be seen from within the loft had been perfectly finished. He took a photograph of a square patch of cement on one side of the chimney stack into which one of the craftsmen had written in finger width characters `MPJ 1842´. Simon looked at this transfixed as he thought about a man perhaps like himself proud of his workmanship who maybe even drank in one of the same pubs Simon did now nearly two hundred years later. Simon wondered if anything he had built would last as long.

The internal inspection completed the two men went outside. There were lawns and privet hedges back and front and nothing else. Andy's grandmother had kept the grass and the hedges cut but there were no bushes, shrubs or flowerbeds. No shed, greenhouse or garage. No tools, no lawnmower.

"Did your grandma have a car, Andy?"

"I don't recall ever seeing a car here". Thinking about this question a little longer Andy remembered his grandparents had had a succession of white vans with windowless side panels. Plain, white vans with no signage. Andy relayed this information to his friend.

"And after your grandad died?"

"Grandma continued driving around in a white van. The last time I saw her was in early October last year when I visited a few days before I left for my 4 weeks in Australia with mum and dad. She died while I was over there. I'm sure the white van was here then, parked on the drive at the side of the house"

"How old was she then, Andy?"

"80 or 81"

The two men quietly and separately considered the strangeness of an 80 year old woman owning and driving around in a white van.

"She must have engaged a gardener to keep the grass and the hedges neat and tidy. There's no sign of any gardening equipment here Andy so she can't have been doing it herself" Simon observed. Andy had never considered the issue before but agreed with Simon.

"Where's the white van now, Andy?" Andy had no idea.

"Are you still thinking about selling or renting?"

"Yes. What's your opinion on converting the place into a couple of flats, Simon?"

"Do-able. The house is solid and well built with brick walls everywhere. The unusual idea of a staircase at the side helps a lot. You'd have a shared main door and hallway, shared back door and the stairs leading up to a first floor flat. You'd need to create parking spaces. I'd do that at the back by getting rid of the back lawn. Flat dwellers generally aren't interested in gardening and flats don't have storage spaces for lawn mowers and all the other stuff you'd need. Leave the front lawn and hedges alone. Saves yet another battle with The Judd"

"What's 'The Judd', Simon?"

"Bloody busybody Hilda Judd. One of Market Repton's councillors. On every sodding committee going with her busybody nimby cronies. This entire part of town is in the Market Repton Conservation Zone. That means no changes are allowed to the external appearance of anything round here. Have you noticed there's no satellite dishes in sight? They're not allowed. They can't do anything to stop us ripping up the back lawn but if Hilda Judd or one of her network of informants sees any hint of a front lawn disappearing there'll be a penpusher with a clipboard and a stop notice round here in minutes.

I've noticed all your gran's windows are sash. If any of them need replacing it can't be with UPVC. Any conversion job would have to include replacement wood framed sash windows and they cost thousands each even if I made them myself. And then they have to be painted every few years.

If I were you I think I would go for the two flats idea. The rental market here is brill. And the station less than 200 yards away helps. Just what folks retiring and scaling down would go for. And I'd recommend top end fixtures and fittings especially in the bathrooms and kitchens. Get you the best rent possible. You'd be rolling in money if you weren't already. Fancy a pint?"

"Yes but can't" his pal replied. "I'm on duty 4pm til midnight tonight and the rest of this week. We'll have a pub session the week after. If I do go with the conversions idea what happens next?"

"You'd need to get plans drawn up by an architect. I could sort that for you. I've worked with a local architect Alice Wardell before on lots of similar jobs. She's a near neighbour of mine"

"I´m not going to arse about, Simon. I'll probably make the decision this week but I'm bothered about the nitty gritty of letting property. I don't know a thing about it"

"Most people don't. You don't need to. Engage a letting agent to do it all for you. They'll advertise, draw up the tenancy agreements, collect the rent, engage a gardener and a window cleaner and such like. Spring & Fall in the High Street would do it for you. And they have a first class builder on call to sort out any problems. That's me of course. You can stay in the background. Sorry, I mean you can keep yourself at arms length" .

Andy went back into the house to collect the pile of post. He also took from his grandmother's bureau in the sitting room all the personal documents she had kept there and put them in his car. He would go through them later at home. He locked up the house, the two men said goodbye and drove off to their respective homes.

As Andy was driving the 12 miles south back to Repton Magna he thought about his grandmother's white van. Its absence hadn't registered with him until his friend Simon mentioned it. So where was it now? Andy decided he would extract from his grandmother's papers the vehicle registration document for the van, take it to work later that day and see what the police computer system revealed about it.

Andy thought it would be better if a colleague checked the computer system for him to avoid any accusation he had used police facilities for a personal reason. During a quiet period of his Sunday evening shift Andy mentioned to his sergeant that his late grandmother's vehicle seemed to have disappeared. He produced the vehicle registration document and the sergeant said he would run the check.

"White Citroen Berlingo van. Registered keeper Mrs Marjorie Edge 22 Station Road Market Repton RE15 8EP. Was Mrs Edge your grandma, Andy?"

"Yes, sarge"

"According to our records the driving licence is still valid and current and nobody's told DVLA yet that she's died. You say the van's gone so do you want to report it as missing, Andy?"

"Not just yet, sarge. But I'll tell DVLA that grandma's died"

"When did she die, Andy?"

"November when I was visiting mum and dad in Australia"

"So the white van might have disappeared months ago. Perhaps your gran sold it"

"I'm seeing the solicitors who handled grandma's estate within the next few days. I'll ask them if they know anything about it".

CHAPTER 5

Up The Ladder To The Roof

One good thing about working the police 'late turn' is the time off during daylight hours, a real bonus during the British February. On the Monday morning after his sergeant had run the vehicle check on his grandmother's van Andy Edge phoned Lapley & Hinstock Solicitors in Market Repton and booked an appointment to see Miss Audrey Hinstock who'd handled and finalised the estate of his grandmother so quickly and efficiently. A meeting was arranged for Tuesday morning 11am.

The original Messrs Lapley (Samuel) & Hinstock (Eric) founded their legal practice in 1923 in the very offices in Market Repton High Street where Eric Hinstock's great-granddaughter was now a partner. Having any legal qualifications before calling yourself a lawyer was still a novelty in 1923. When the 20th century started anyone who deigned to give legal advice could call themselves a lawyer. It was not a requirement to undergo training or pass an examination. This alarming system gradually diminished after the first world war. Both Samuel Lapley and Eric Hinstock had attended law school which was where they met.

They met in 1920 at King's College London which at that time was one of only a few educational establishments in England possessing a law school. They met and within 6 months had decided on where they wanted their legal knowledge to take them. Three years later it took them to Market Repton. They were the first qualified solicitors that the town had ever had. Eric Hinstock's son and grandson followed in his footsteps.

For nearly ten years his great-granddaughter Audrey Hinstock had been a partner in the firm. There were no Lapleys left. Audrey's fellow partners were Brian Atchley, the senior partner, and Mrs Laura King.

Brian Atchley was aged 55 when Audrey and Laura both joined the firm a decade earlier. But now Brian's thoughts were mostly about his forthcoming retirement. The two women had expanded the firm's reach and, it seemed to Brian, never stopped thinking about ways to innovate, computerise and they said 'proactivise' the business. Proactivise was a word Brian had never heard before.

Audrey and Laura met at Nottingham Law School one September at the start of their three year law degree course. Audrey was short and plump with a round face and unflattering round glasses. Laura wasn't. Laura was 5' 7'' tall, slim, attractive and had shoulder length blond hair. They soon became friends. They talked about where they wanted their careers to take them in the future. They realised they had a lot in common. Laura learned her friend intended eventually to join what sounded like an unambitious small town family   practice. This didn't at first reconcile with the plans Audrey had talked about. But as Audrey had said 'you don't have to live in a big city to have big ideas'.

The 3 year law degree course is followed by a year doing the LPC or Legal Practice Course where students learn how to bring theoretical law into the real world. Next comes a 2 year training contract with a law firm. Here one can learn more about specialist areas of law. Audrey's 2 year contract was with a firm in Manchester specialising in family, land and inheritance matters. Laura meanwhile joined a large international firm of lawyers in Birmingham which specialised in corporate law. The two women seemed to have chosen quite different career paths. Then they brought their accumulated knowledge and ideas to Market Repton High Street.

When George and Marjorie Edge retired and moved home from Birmingham to Market Repton thirty years ago the senior partner of Lapley & Hinstock was Audrey's father. Her grandfather held a consultancy role. Mr and Mrs Edge engaged the firm initially to deal with the conveyancing work arising from their purchase of 22 Station Road. Once installed in their new home they turned to Lapley & Hinstock for all their legal advice. They got to know both Mr Hinstock and Mr Hinstock senior.

After Marjorie Edge was widowed she visited the offices of Lapley & Hinstock to have a new will prepared. There she met for the first time Audrey Hinstock who dealt with the matter for her.

"I hope you've inherited some of the special talents of your grandfather, Audrey" Marjorie had said

"Inherited 'em and added to 'em" Audrey had jokingly replied.

And now one Tuesday morning three years later Marjorie's rather large grandson was sitting in front of Audrey. After the meet and greet and the exchange of pleasantries Audrey asked in the nicest possible way how she might help.

"There's a couple of things bothering me. Do you know anything about my grandmother's white van? It's not at the house but the vehicle documents still show her as the van's owner"

"Sorry, Mr Edge but I can't help you with that. Under the terms of your grandmother's will it's technically now yours along with all her other chattels. But the van's missing you say?"

"It seems to be, yes. I visited the house last Sunday and the van wasn't there. And there's something else. I'm certain some of the pictures have disappeared from the walls. As far as you know has anyone got keys to the house?"

"Well, we certainly don't have any keys and I can't think of anyone else who might. Concerning the van and the pictures perhaps Mrs Edge sold them. How did you get into the house if you don't mind my asking?"

Andy explained his parents had held a spare set of keys to the house until they moved to Australia and since then Andy had kept them in case his grandmother had had a fall or any other emergency. But Mrs Edge was not the kind of person to have falls or emergencies.

"I don't know what to say, Mr Edge" Audrey continued. "As you know we were executors of your grandmother's will and that work is now complete. We also held a Lasting Power Of Attorney which enabled us to finalise all Mrs Edge's financial affairs. Our late client had already provided us with a list of all her bank and savings accounts and other investments which is how we were able to realise the capital and transfer the net amount over to yourself. We didn't need access to the house to do this"

Lasting Power Of Attorney? This was the first time Andy had heard mention of this.

"My grandmother never mentioned anything about a Power Of Attorney. Neither to me nor to my parents. What was that all about?"

"Usually it's a sensible step to think about when a will is made. Sometimes as people become elderly they may get a bit.....er.....frail and so nominate someone else to make decisions for them especially where large sums of money are involved"

"But wouldn't I be the obvious person to hold any Power Of Attorney?" Andy asked thinking that 'frail' was the last word he'd use to describe his grandmother.

"Possibly yes especially with your living nearby but if I remember rightly I think Mrs Edge mentioned she wished to avoid a conflict of interest"

"Conflict of interest? I don't understand"

"Well it's a service we offer. In fact it's one of our specialities and if a client asks about it we provide impartial advice. I prepared the final will so I knew that you were to be the sole beneficiary and in many cases like this you would be the obvious choice to hold a Power Of Attorney. But Mrs Edge made the decision and we complied with her wishes. The work's now completed as I say. Have you made any decision about 22 Station Road? Will you be moving in? And have you made a will yourself? As you now have substantial cash and property assets Mr Edge if you haven't yet thought about a will now may be a good time"

"I don't intend moving into the house, it's much too big for me. I'm thinking about converting the property into two flats and letting them. And no I haven't made a will yet but it's something I'll think about"

"Fine. If you need any help you know where I am. I'd be happy to help in any way I can. And across the road you'll see Spring & Fall Estate Agents run by Ian Fall and Carl Ramsey. Let me give you one of their cards. They not only sell properties but also offer a lettings management scheme. We have a number of mutual clients. It frequently happens that someone interested in one of their properties will just cross the High Street to us and engage us to do their conveyancing"

And at that moment Andy realised where he'd seen Carl Ramsey before. On a previous visit to Lapley & Hinstock's office he remembered seeing Carl coming out of one of their back offices.

Meeting over Andy was driving back to his house in Repton Magna pondering the words 'conflict of interest'. Could it be anything to do with his being a policeman? What and why? And did it really matter considering his grandmother's estate was now settled? But something about it rang a little alarm bell in Andy's head. He knew his grandmother would never do anything without good reason. She certainly wouldn't enter into a Lasting Power Of Attorney arrangement just because a solicitor had suggested it.

Like many police officers nowadays for a variety of reasons not least that of personal security Andy usually avoided mentioning what he did for a living. At no time had Audrey Hinstock asked him where he worked. And pondering also if he should now report his grandmother's white van as missing.

When Andy got home he made the decision and telephoned the Driver & Vehicle Licencing Centre in Swansea and gave them three items of information :

- The former registered keeper of the vehicle Mrs Marjorie Edge died the previous November

- He was now technically the owner of the vehicle

- The whereabouts of the vehicle were unknown

During that evening's 4pm to 12am shift Andy mentioned to his sergeant that he had decided to record the vehicle as stolen on the police computer system for insurance purposes if nothing else.

"Who are you entering as the vehicle's registered keeper, Andy?"

"Me, sarge"

"OK, Andy. But we both know what the chances are it'll ever be recovered" the sergeant replied. The two experienced officers exchanged a knowing look.

At that same moment the white van in question albeit displaying fake number plates was transporting stolen goods across Birmingham.

CHAPTER 6

Here Is The House

Andy had made another decision. He'd convert 22 Station Road into two flats - one occupying the whole of the ground floor the other all of the first floor. The large Victorian cellar could be used as storage space by the residents. He spoke to his builder mate Simon King about this and Simon contacted his architect friend Alice Wardell for whom jobs like this were a sideline. Simon and Alice had worked together before on similar jobs. By late Spring the architectural plans had been drawn up and approved. Work started in May.

Andy had agreed with Simon's idea of ripping up the rear lawn and replacing it with residents' parking spaces. Andy had also approached Spring & Fall Estate Agents, told them of the work underway and sought details of their let properties management scheme. Carl Ramsey had helped him, assured him they could handle all aspects of the letting including scrutiny and vetting of potential tenants, contracts and day to day maintenance including gardening and window cleaning. They could relieve Mr Edge of all the stress and legalities of letting the property. Mr Edge could simply sit back and watch the regular rental payments arrive into his bank account. Nothing could possibly go wrong. There was no need yet for Carl to inform his new client that Carl himself was interested in renting one of the flats.

Councillor Mrs Hilda Judd and her husband lived in one of the large terraced houses surrounding the small perfectly square park at the top end of Market Repton High Street. Their house was on the north side of the park from which vantage point Mrs Judd could observe vehicles and pedestrians using Station Road for the railway station, all the other houses around the four sides of the park and when the trees in the park were in their leafless months a good chunk of the north end of the High Street.

Mrs Judd was aged 67 and had shortish, straight brown hair for ease of maintenance. She was slim, 5' 4" tall and had a habit of standing very still when talking to anybody whilst holding unwavering eye contact. Mr Judd's appearance was of no consequence.

Staring out of her window one Monday morning in May Mrs Judd noticed Simon King's builders' vans driving past her house and turning right into Station Road. She put on a lightweight jacket for it was a warm day and marched along Station Road to investigate. She saw two vans at the end house, number 22, one parked on the drive to the side of the property and one parked on the street. She took three photographs with her phone.

Then she approached a young man with tattoos and a hi-viz jacket who was leaning against the van parked on the street while he tapped away at the screen of his smartphone and loudly asked him

"Where can I find Simon King?"

"You can't come on site, elf and safety like" the youth replied adding "who are you anyway and what do you want like?"

"I am Councillor Mrs Hilda Judd and I'm making sure whatever's going on here complies with planning regulations and the guidelines surrounding development and alterations to structures in the Market Repton Conservation Zone of which this entire road and all its properties are parts"

The young man had never heard so many big words in one sentence before and repeated the words his boss had drummed into him "you can't come on site, elf and safety like"

"Please tell Simon King I wish to speak to him now"

"Boss isn't here like"

"Where is he and when will he be back?"

"Gone home for his breakfast. Be back when he's had it like"

But at that moment a third van bearing the signage 'Simon King Builders' was on approach carrying the now breakfasted boss.

"Mrs Judd, how delightful to see you again. On your way to the station? Leaving town perhaps?"

"In your dreams. What are you vandalising today? This is Mrs Edge's house isn't it?"

"No, it was Mrs Edge's house it isn't any more"

"So whose is it now and what are you lot doing here?"

"Sorry, client confidentiality prevents my disclosing any information but I can say that the work going on here has had the approval of the buildings inspector and as no changes are being made to the external appearance planning permission is not an issue goodbye".

Client confidentiality? Where had this shaved headed ape learned such words? thought Mrs Judd.

"I promise you I'll be keeping an eye on all this. If I see any plastic window frames arriving, a satellite dish going up or the front lawn being turned into parking spaces I'll personally hand you the Stop Notice" and with that Mrs Judd stormed off.

Hilda Judd to her credit had helped Market Repton's central core retain its compact Victorian/Edwardian look. The High Street, Park Square and Station Road area which formed the conservation zone were free of corporate shop frontages, plate glass, neon signs and concrete lamp posts. One national coffee shop chain had set up in the High Street and soon found the absence of their usual garish, ostentatious appearance was no hindrance to trade as people flocked to the pleasant little town.

Outside the conservation zone and especially the west side of town beyond the railway line and the north-south trunk road was a different matter and a lost battle. They were the new areas and Mrs Judd accepted the industrial estate brought jobs to the town and the hundreds of new houses within walking distance brought trade to the High Street. But Hilda Judd was not one for complacency. The likes of Simon King, she thought, wouldn't hesitate in bulldozing a row of fine, Victorian terraced homes (like her own for example) and replacing it with a block of flats. She had to keep on top of the game and to do so needed multiple sources of information. Being on Repton Unitary Authority's Planning Committee she had access to every planning application but sometimes it paid to know about potential problems before they got to Committee stage.

Her main sources of information in this regard were Market Repton Bridge Club and the town's Golf Club. These two organisations were stuffed full of gossips, rumour mongers, busy bodies and nosy parkers. She was of course a member of both. She was poor at bridge and even worse at golf but that wasn't really the point. Add in the information coming from the allotments sub-committee (of which Mr Judd was a member) and Hilda had all bases covered.

Simon King was well aware of planning laws, conservation area rules and building regulations. His livelihood depended on it. He had put most of his workforce onto the flats conversion job at 22 Station Road. He would do the best possible job for his mate Andy.

The work continued throughout that year and well into the next. Apart from creating 2 spacious flats some work was needed in the loft and the cellar. The first floor flat was provided with easy access to the loft through a ceiling hatch from which unfolded a newly installed ladder. A few roof tiles had to be replaced, the inside of the roof lined with insulating material which was then covered in strong, thick, black plastic sheeting. Most of the final roll of the plastic sheeting was unused after the job had been completed. The roofers engaged to do this work put it into the cellar. It wasn't worth taking it to their next job. And it might prove useful to somebody one day.

The cellar held a few surprises. It was totally free of damp and unusually clean and dust free. In the past some effort had clearly been made to keep it so. A radiator had been installed down there connected to the house's central heating system. One of Simon's men mentioned to him that three large, locked chests had been left in the cellar. Simon went down to have a look. He'd tell Andy about it next time they met. The only work needed in the cellar was the installation of new electricity, gas and water meters for the 2 flats. The utility companies took care of this.

In July, twenty months after Andy Edge had inherited the property from his grandmother, the work was completed. Two new flats with top-of-the-range fittings were ready for occupation. Spring & Fall Estate Agents had taken photographs and their advert seeking tenants had gone onto their website. They had also filmed a walk through video and placed that onto the ad on their website. One hot evening in that month Andy rode his Honda 750cc motorcycle the 12 miles north to Market Repton from his home in Repton Magna. He met Simon at 22 Station Road and the 2 men walked slowly together through the entire building. In the cellar Simon pointed out the three locked chests. Before the building work had started Andy had engaged a house clearance firm to remove all his grandmother's furniture. He had kept all the personal papers and all the photographs he could find.

"Got the keys to these chests, Andy?"

"I've got some small keys back home. I´ll check when I get back"

"When we looked around here in....er....February last year I think there were some pictures on the walls and some big ornaments that looked like sculptures. What happened to them, Andy?"

"I suppose the house clearance firm took them, why?"

"Weren't some of them originals? I mean your grandparents were antique dealers weren't they? And were you here when the clearance was done?"

"Oh yeah, I was here. I had to come up with my keys to let them in. I don't remember seeing any pictures or ornaments now you come to mention it. The men spent most of the day taking the furniture. Needed one of their largest vans"

"House clearance firms don't usually take pictures and ornaments do they?"

"Dunno. I've never had to get a job like that sorted before. No, they just took furniture I'm sure"

"So they've gone missing along with your gran's white van. Did anything come of that?"

"Course not - you know what the police are like !"

"Did you take anything for yourself, Andy?"

"Yes I took grandma's antique bureau. The rest of the stuff was too big and heavy for my place. Anyway I've got everything I want. Furniture I mean. The bureau was a nice piece. Only just managed to get it in the car though with the back seats dropped. One of the house clearance men helped me shove it in the back of the car and when I got home the next door neighbour gave me a hand to carry it into the house"

"Fancy a beer back at my place, mate?"

"Yeah, good idea"

"Here - take my keys. I walked here. Get some beers out of the fridge and get the garden chairs out. You know where everything is"

Andy locked up 22 Station Rd, fired up his Honda and rode the short distance to Simon's house which was situated on a small 10 years old development off the B9916 less than a quarter of a mile beyond the small perfectly square park while Simon walked the same route. The walk took him past Hilda Judd's house. Simon's house was just outside the Market Repton Conservation Area so had UPVC sealed windows, a satellite dish and the front garden removed to create parking spaces. He kept at his home one of his works vans, his car and his motorcycle.

The walk took Simon 15 minutes and when he got home Andy had put out into Simon's back garden 2 chairs, a small table, 2 glasses and 2 bottles of beer. The 2 men sat, poured and started their drinks.

"Andy I've got something to tell you. I met the ex 2 days ago on the High Street. She's still living in Birmingham. She's aware of the 2 new flats and may be interested in renting one of them. I think she's getting tired of the daily commute"

"So would I. Well if she's that interested she'll have to go through Spring & Fall. The ad is already up on their website"

But Simon's 'ex' was too late. By the end of July tenants had already been signed up for both flats. Mrs Laura King for the time being would have to continue commuting between Birmingham and Market Repton.

CHAPTER 7

Rent

- "This turn of events is going to change everything"

- "No, this turn of events is going to delay everything"

- "By about 6 months"

- "Not the way we do things"

(laughter)

- "Have you told……?"

- "About the delay yes, I didn't see any need to mention The Send Off"

- "Any response?"

- "That as all this started a long time ago another 6 months won't matter"

- "The Send Off should set the hounds running in the wrong direction"

- "Indeed"

Messrs Spring & Fall Estate Agents had placed onto their website details of just the ground floor flat at 22 Station Road. Carl Ramsey had signed himself up as tenant of the first floor flat. Carl and his friend and business partner Ian Fall had done the required checks on Carl's suitability one Wednesday night in The Golden Lion and laughingly agreed he would be a risk free tenant. He had spoken firstly to Andy Edge about his letting the flat. Andy of course had no problem with this. The two men were now on first name terms. Carl paid the required deposit and the first month's rent and moved into the first floor flat in early August having given the required period of notice to terminate the tenancy of his flat in Repton Magna.

So Carl no longer had to drive 12 miles to work everyday and 12 miles back home in the evening. He could now walk to work. Another bonus was that when the football coaching season resumed he was now much closer to Dainford FC which was sited on the B9916 road in the south east corner of Dainford. And the B9916 heading north out of Market Repton was close to Carl's new flat. Carl did football coaching on two evenings each week Tuesdays and Thursdays starting mid August and continuing until the end of the football season. And he attended most of the Saturday afternoon home games to see how his team were performing and monitor the fitness of the players.

By the end of July the ground floor flat had been let to a returning ex-pat who had been working overseas for many years and who wished to return to England to retire. His name was Selwyn Myles and he had worked as a railway engineer all over the world. He had family ties with Market Repton although his family had originally come from Birmingham. Selwyn hadn't lived in the UK for nearly 30 years but throughout that time had maintained investments and a bank account in the UK. He was now coming home for good. He had done a virtual tour of the flat on the estate agent's website, decided it was exactly what he was after, liked the fact it was close to a railway station and signed the tenancy agreement electronically. His rental payments started arriving in Andy's bank account. He would occupy the flat as soon as he'd finalised his overseas affairs.

Although Andy had devolved all of the lettings administration to Spring & Fall he nevertheless thought it a courtesy to pay a visit to Carl Ramsey as soon as Carl had installed himself into the first floor flat.

"Happy with everything, Carl?"

"Superb place, really happy with everything thanks, Andy. And walking to work is a real bonus"

"Any teething problems with the plumbing or the new boiler?"

"None but of course I won't be bothering you if anything does need looking at. I'm administering the lettings myself so I´d just get Simon King over. I understand the two of you are mates?"

"Yeah. I've known him for years. Over 20 years in fact. When is the other tenant moving into the ground floor flat?"

"Later this month. He's sorting out some issues overseas. Stuff like closing his foreign bank and savings accounts and transferring everything over to the UK. But he started paying the rent last month"

"Yes I'd noticed it had gone into my bank account. Is it normal to start renting a place without actually seeing it ?"

"Normal, no. But it isn't unusual nowadays. As you know we did a walk-through video and put it onto the website. The virtual tour also showed the parking spaces, the street outside and the station nearby. It was just what he was looking for"

"But he hasn't actually signed a tenancy agreement has he?"

"Electronic signature is legally binding, Andy. Don't worry, we've done it loads of times before"

"Is he married?"

"I don't know. If he is he certainly isn't bringing a wife with him. It's just him"

"What happens on the day he arrives. Where does he get the keys?"

"I should be here to meet and greet, give him his keys, show him how the boiler works and where the new meters are in the cellar. But if I'm not available when he arrives I'll put his keys into that new secure key-safe on the wall near the main door and message him the lock combination"

"What about his furniture, clothes and other stuff? He knows it's an unfurnished flat doesn't he?"

"I've never really thought about his furniture and personal effects, Andy. That's his affair. Our ad made it clear it's a brand new fla

"OK. I'll call in one day to introduce myself. When does football coaching start, Carl?"

"The week after next. On Friday this week I'm off on a stag week to Marbella. Dainford FC's captain is getting married later this month. We were hoping most of the lads could go to Spain but some have to work and a few of the wives seemed to object to the idea of their husbands spending a week off the leash so there's just eight of us going. We've rented a villa"

"So a stag week not a stag night?"

"Yeah. Sounds great doesn't it?"

"Rather you than me, Carl. Right then, I may as well call in on Simon and scrounge a cuppa. See you, Carl". Carl escorted Andy from number 22 and waved him off. He still thought he looked like a thug. "Must remember to ask him where he works" Carl thought to himself.

Carl and his pals from Dainford FC departed from Birmingham Airport on a flight to Málaga for their stag week in Marbella on Friday 9 August. A good time was had by all.

Email dated Monday 12 August from mylesaway@xmail.com to springfall@quickpost.com - 'Dear Mr Ramsey - I shall be arriving in England on Tuesday 13 Aug and would like to get the keys to my new flat early next day. My furniture etc is being delivered Wednesday 14 Aug.

What are the arrangements for getting my keys please? Thanks, Selwyn Myles'

Email dated Monday 12 August from   springfall@quickpost.com to mylesaway@xmail.com - 'Hi Mr Myles. Carl Ramsey is on holiday this week. I am Ian Fall his business partner. I'll put the keys to your new flat into the keysafe box which you'll see inside the porch at the front door at 22 Station Rd. The keysafe combination is 4479. Any problem don't hesitate to call me. Or visit our office which is in Market Repton High St just a short walk from your new home. Carl is the tenant of the first floor flat at number 22. You'll probably meet him when he returns from Spain on Friday. Carl is lettings manager for the 2 flats on behalf of the landlord so he's on hand to sort out any issues. Welcome back to UK'

Email dated Monday 12 August from springfall@quickpost.com to carlramsey@postwiz.com - 'Hi mate hope u r sober enough to read this. Selwyn Myles just contacted moves into ground floor flat wednesday'

When Carl got back to his new home on Friday evening 16 August the worse for wear after a week of boozing, shouting and hangovers he noticed plain grey blinds had been fitted at all the windows of the ground floor flat. The blinds were all down. His new neighbour had arrived. He also noticed the new neighbour hadn't placed a vehicle into the parking spaces in what used to be the back garden. Carl was very grateful for the absence of any noise. He was due back at work next morning and he had a headache to nurse.

CHAPTER 8

Tainted Love

The busy railway line running north south through and beyond County Repton joined the dots which formed the pattern of Mrs Laura King's weekly routine. North beyond the county boundary was the town of Westwich where Laura was born and where her brother John still lived. South of the county was Birmingham where Laura continued to live following her two year training contract with a firm of corporate lawyers in that city.

Every work day Laura took the train to and from Market Repton;

Every Monday after work she and Audrey Hinstock took the train south to Repton Magna college where the two women attended an evening class in Advanced Level Spanish. Audrey lived in Repton Magna so walked home after the class while Laura took another train south to her flat in Birmingham;

Every Wednesday after work Laura took the train north to Westwich to have a pub meal and a gossip with her brother John after which she took the train home to Birmingham.

And so it went on. And on and on. Laura was getting tired of it all. It would be better to live in Market Repton and walk to work and after all there was nothing to keep her in Birmingham any more. Laura knew from a chance meeting with her ex husband Simon King that he had been working on a high end conversion job to create two flats from an elegant Victorian house close to Market Repton railway station. She was disappointed to find both flats had been let before she had had the opportunity to register her interest. She was annoyed to find Carl Ramsey had helped himself to a tenancy agreement. She would be having words with him about that.

Laura had had a short, unsuccessful marriage to Simon King. They married 17 years earlier, separated in the following year and were divorced in the next year. They remained on reasonably good terms and both realised they had been too young, naive and silly to make their marriage work. But she liked the name Laura King. It was strong sounding, short, memorable and good for an ambitious lawyer so Laura retained the surname after the divorce. Apart from which after qualifying it was the name under which Laura became one of the 153,000 solicitors listed on the Solicitors Regulation Authority Register For England And Wales.

The lust affair between Laura and Carl Ramsey couldn't last. Laura knew it but Carl didn't. Carl thought as he now had a new home within walking distance of both their offices his affair with Laura might become something with an element of regularity or even permanence. The two of them next met for a quick midweek lunch in a cafe in Market Repton

High Street. They were both dressed to impress their respective clients. Laura brought up the subject of the new flats at 22 Station Road.

"So you helped yourself to the first floor flat without advertising it. No one else had a look-in"

"My client is happy with the arrangement. Ground floor flat went too, within hours of it going up on the website. That's what I call good business. And it was advertised"

"That's what I call unethical, like insider trading"

"Unethical ! I'm an estate agent, you're a lawyer ! It's too late for us to start learning new words. Look I'll make it up to you. Stay over on Friday night, I'll give you a guided tour and save the best bits 'til last".

So Laura did stay over on Friday night and Carl showed her around the property including the clean, dust free cellar where Laura asked to whom the three large chests belonged.

"Dunno. I'll mention it to the landlord"

"I know who your landlord is. He's one of Audrey's clients. Do you know what he does for a living ?"

"No but from the look of him I'd say a cage fighter or a nightclub bouncer but he's pleasant enough. Big mate of Simon King who did the conversion job here"

When they were back in the first floor flat Laura said "The workmanship everywhere is superb. Just what I'd expect from Simon"

"You know Simon then?"

"Er…...yes. Simon King, Laura King we were married"

"Oh….oh right…..oh OK…...I just never…..I didn't…...King is a common name…....sorry I meant widespread surname…...I never associated…."

"It was a long time ago when we were both young and daft"

"Let me show you some more workmanship in the bedroom".

Next morning Carl went to work and Laura went back to her own flat in Birmingham on the train from the railway station less than 3 minutes walk from where she'd just spent the night with Carl. Laura remembered she had been carrying something as Carl had shown her around. Yes, she'd put it down in the cellar and hadn't picked it up again. But it wasn't something she used very often. She'd retrieve it on her next visit.

The following Wednesday two couples met in two pubs in two towns separated by one stretch of railway line. In The Golden Lion in Market Repton Ian Fall and Carl Ramsey were having their weekly management meeting.

"…....and she stayed over on Friday night. Might be the start of a regular affair with the lovely Laura" Carl hoped

"and you say she was interested in renting one of the flats for herself? Why?"

"Why not? She's sick and tired of all the commuting to and from Birmingham"

"Have you met Selwyn Myles yet?"

"No but if he's started as he means to go on he'll be the perfect neighbour. Never heard a sound yet from the ground floor flat. Signs of life though, new blinds gone up"

"Has he got a car?"

"No or if he has it isn't here yet. He's not using any of the parking spaces. Did you meet him when he arrived, that week when I was in Spain?"

"No. Just had an exchange of emails. I put the keys in the keysafe box in the front porch early morning on the day he said he was arriving. He didn't contact me again so I guess everything was OK"

Three train stops from Market Repton and 20 miles north was the town of Westwich in the adjacent county. There was nothing wrong with Westwich but there was nothing right about it either, just a bland town in a bland, flat landscape. Laura and her brother John were having their weekly catch up session.

John was aged 37, four years younger than Laura, tall with black hair and the two bore a striking facial resemblance. Their usual venue was a pub in the J D Wetherspoons chain which had been a bank. It was conveniently close to Westwich railway station. Wetherspoons had done their usual commendable job of retaining as many of the building's architectural highlights as possible. The main bar was fashioned from what had been the banking hall and featured a huge domed ceiling. The former vault had been crafted into a cosy dining booth which was where Laura and John were eating and drinking. Wishing to give the pub a name which reflected its past Wetherspoons had decided to call it 'The Crooked Copper'.

"So why do you want to get rid of the estate agent guy? Sounds like a nice, uncomplicated arrangement"

"I don't want to get rid of him exactly but he doesn't fit in with my idea of the future"

"You're 41 Laura, when does this 'future' happen?"

"Watch this space. How's work by the way?"

"Promising. I feel it's time to take advantage of the permanent state of chaos caused by one reorganisation after another".

CHAPTER 9

Something's Coming

In the south east corner of the beautiful Snowdonia National Park in North Wales lies the remote lake Llyn Brenig, the perfect place to spend a few days hiking or sailing. Mrs Navya Anand lived in the nearest town Llanrwst and owned a cottage on the east side of the lake which boasted its own small boathouse complete with boat and a landing stage giving direct access to the waters of Llyn Brenig. It was available for letting all year round. Peak season was of course Summer but the Snowdonian Autumn held the special charm of the dazzling colours of the leaves as the millions of trees braced themselves for the cold Welsh Winter.

9 Sept from mylesaway@xmail.com to anandlettings@cymmail.com

'I am making an enquiry about the cottage on Llyn Brenig. Is it available for 4 nights Friday November 8, to Monday November 11, inclusive? If so what are the payment arrangements? Thank you Selwyn Myles'

9 Sept from <u>anandlettings@cymmail.com</u> to <u>mylesaway@xmail.com</u>

'Dear Mr Myles thank you for your enquiry. I am pleased to confirm the cottage is available for the 4 nights you ask about. If you wish to go ahead with the booking please pay a deposit of 100 pounds into bank account number 64353 76139 sort code 96 34 00 which will secure the booking. Please then pay the balance at least 24 hours before your arrival.
Thank you'

9 Sept from <u>mylesaway@xmail.com</u> to <u>anandlettings@cymmail.com</u>

'Thank you. I have paid the deposit. I would like your confirmation that the boat mentioned in your ad will be available for the 4 days of my visit many thanks Selwyn Myles'

9 Sept from <u>anandlettings@cymmail.com</u> to <u>mylesaway@xmail.com</u>

'Dear Mr Myles I can confirm the boat will be at your disposal for your visit. Two days before your arrival I will send you an email giving the postcode for Sat Nav purposes (the cottage is quite isolated) and also the combination of the secure key box you will see adjacent to the main door of the cottage. Deposit received thank you. Enjoy your stay, Mrs Navya Anand'.

CHAPTER 10

Elected

The loathe affair between Councillor Mrs Hilda Judd and Max Graden started on 15 November 2012, the date of the first ever elections in England and Wales for the newly created role of Police And Crime Commissioner. The then Prime Minister had announced the creation of the posts in his party's manifesto for the preceding general election. There had been no demand from the public for the creation of the role and the historically low voter turn-out in November 2012 showed there was certainly no interest from the public in this politicisation of the police. The minister in charge was the then Home Secretary who in early 2016 admitted fearing a monster had been created by setting up the Police And Crime Commissioner posts.

Max Graden had been a card carrying member of the Conservative party since his 18th birthday. He was a self employed accountant approaching 50, he was short, bald, overweight and bad tempered. His marriage of 15 years ended when his wife decided she was no longer prepared to put up with his tantrums and left him. Mercifully their union was not blessed with issue. On the plus side Max was a competent accountant. Some years earlier he had attended two months of a three year business management course so felt justified in adding 'Business Advisor' to his stationery. His 'business advice' was always to sack as many people as possible.

He had magnanimously suggested he be the Conservative party Police And Crime Commissioner candidate for the Mid Land police area election of 2012. No other names came forward so his candidature was nodded through. The Mid Land Police Service was created in the 1980s when 4 traditional county constabularies had been merged. Max Graden heartily agreed with this. Four chief constables and their retinues had been replaced by one. County Repton Constabulary was one of those to disappear forever.

Max knew nothing about police officers and police work and did not see this as any impediment to his candidature. He knew that police constables and sergeants did the real police work and couldn't understand why another 7 grades of increasingly overpaid (in his view) officers were piled up on top of them. They called themselves Executive Officers and Max detested the lot of them. All they seemed to do was have meetings with each other and parade around in uniforms covered with shiny badges and strips of coloured ribbon which they liberally awarded to each other. Max enjoyed hearing the rank and file joke

"How can you tell when an executive officer is lying?"

"His lips are moving !"

Once elected the redundancy axe would be swinging long and hard.

On 15 November 2012 a mere 12% of the total electorate resident in the Mid Land Police Service area bothered going out to vote. Out of that total possible electorate 6% voted for Max. It was enough to secure his election. Once in office one of his first triumphs was to remove the word 'Service' from the name. No need to confuse the public unnecessarily. So Mid Land Police Service became just Mid Land Police. Max then set about doing what he believed his party wanted of him. His policy of slash and burn started.

This is what brought him into contact and conflict with the formidable Mrs Hilda Judd. Max had ordered the rationalisation (he called it) of police tasks by insisting on the creation of teams each specialising in one area of work. Many police stations across his region were closed and those which remained each had their allocated team with their allocated task. He tried to sell this idea to the officers by using words like 'centre of excellence' , 'paradigm shift' , 'added value' and anything else he could remember from that part of the business management course he bothered to attend.

One of the police stations to be closed was that at Market Repton. It had stood at the southern end of High Street since 1830. Max wanted to demolish it and sell the land to a property developer. Hilda Judd and her allies had it declared a Grade 2 listed building and Max's plan was thwarted. Hilda also frequently reminded Max of his election pledge to have more 'bobbies on the beat' and more 'boots on the ground'. These were promises Max did not wish to be reminded about. But the closure of the police station was something Hilda couldn't prevent. It remained intact but was converted into flats.

After Max had finished his rationalisation County Repton was left with just two police stations - at Dainford and Repton Magna. Dainford in the north of the county had drawn the short straw. The Missing Persons team for the whole of the Mid Land Police area would be based there. It was the most thankless area of police work. It was either distressing if a child were involved or pointless if an otherwise law abiding adult simply wished to move without bothering to tell anybody.

In addition to the day to day response and patrol duties needed for the big town of Repton Magna the police station there was also made the base for the region's drug crimes team.

The headquarters of the Mid Land Police and the office of the Police And Crime Commissioner were both situated in the region's biggest town Blackbird City. It was far away from Repton Magna and it ensured that the most senior grades of police officers who were all based in Blackbird City were kept well clear of real police work.

Police officers doing whatever tasks their team had been allocated soon learned the best policy was to find out which figures would keep Commissioner Graden quiet each month and then re-imagine their statistics to make sure that's what he saw. After all no-one ever bothered to check.

In May 2016 Max was re-elected for another 4 year term in another poor voter turn-out. Hilda Judd had attempted to challenge Max on his 'boots on the ground' empty promise but few people outside Market Repton had heard of Hilda and most of the electorate of the huge Mid Land police area were outside County Repton.

Some years later after many money saving initiatives and what seemed like endless reorganisations few of the rank and file officers were aware of who their most senior managers were or even where they were geographically located. And they cared even less.

There was widespread confusion about who did what, who needed to see what and where boundaries of responsibility started and ended. Add into the mix the atmosphere of suspicion and mistrust created between the men and women out on the streets and their senior bosses and the result is a policing infrastructure too disparate and remote to tackle efficiently any complex, carefully planned criminal enterprise.

CHAPTER 11

Pandora's Box

Four people worked full time in the offices of Lapley & Hinstock, Solicitors in Market Repton High Street :

Brian Atchley (senior partner)
Audrey Hinstock (partner)
Laura King (partner)
Tina Proudfoot (qualified, diploma holding legal secretary)

Audrey's father Ben Hinstock (also known as Ben Junior) had retired from full time practice ten years earlier when Audrey took his place but Ben Junior was retained as a consultant as and when needed.

Tina Proudfoot in addition to being the practice's legal secretary for 15 years also answered the telephone, kept the computerised appointments diary, did the meet and greet for all visitors and filed all the paperwork. Tina was in her early fifties and lived within walking distance of her office. Only just within walking distance. Tina and her husband Ray lived on the west side of Market Repton beyond the railway line and the trunk road in one of the many houses which had been built over the past 20 years. Every Friday night after work Tina met her husband in The Golden Lion pub in the High Street and after a few drinks they walked home. The walk took 35 minutes.

On a Friday morning in November Tina, Audrey and Laura were having their morning coffee break in the staff room at Lapley & Hinstock.

"Tina, you knew Mrs Edge from Station Road didn't you?" asked Audrey

"Yes I met both Mr and Mrs Edge. At first they were clients of your father when they moved here from Birmingham. That was about thirty years ago I think, long before I joined the practice. They also met your grandfather but he'd retired by then and just acted as consultant like your dad does now. But then if I remember rightly the Edges usually asked to see your grandfather, Ben Senior. So if the Edges booked an appointment your grandfather would always come in to the office to see them".

"And you know Mrs Edge's grandson Andrew?"

"Mmmm"

"What does 'mmmm' mean?" enquired Audrey mischievously. Both Audrey and Tina knew what it meant but Laura had never set eyes on Andrew Edge.

"Do you know what he does for a living?" Audrey continued

"No, it's never cropped up. Why?"

"We just wondered. He's a very rich man now and I've asked him to consider making a will. Has he booked an appointment?"

"No. Do you want me to ring him and remind him?"

"No leave it for the time being" Audrey replied

"It was a pointless exercise putting his name into Google - it got 675 million hits" Laura added

"Spring & Fall might know more about him. Technically he isn't one of our clients but he is one of theirs" Tina said trying to be helpful.

In the offices of Spring & Fall directly across the street Ian Fall was at that very moment wondering why his friend and business partner Carl Ramsey hadn't turned up for work that day. He'd phoned him but Carl's phone had gone straight to voicemail. He'd sent text messages but had not received an answer. At midday Ian decided to walk the short distance to 22 Station Road to investigate. As lettings managers for the property they held duplicate keys to the doors and to the two individual flats so Ian was able to let himself into number 22. He ascended the stairs and knocked on the door of Carl's flat - no reply. Ian made another phone call - no reply. Ian put the key into the door and entered his friend's home - silence. He called out Carl's name - silence. Ian checked each room and noticed an unmade bed and some unwashed dishes in the kitchen sink. Nothing unusual in that but there was no sign of Carl.

Ian knocked on the door of Selwyn Myles's ground floor flat but there was no reply. He exited the house through the back door and noticed Carl's car in its parking space. The engine was cold. At least Carl hadn't been involved in a car crash. He made sure all the doors were locked and walked back to his office.

Ian compiled a list of people to contact who he thought might know Carl's whereabouts -

Dainford FC
Laura King
Carl's parents

No point in calling Dainford FC on a Friday afternoon. It was an amateur club and there wouldn't be anyone there. But the next day Carl was due at the club to watch their Saturday afternoon home game.

Ian knew that Carl was having an affair with Laura but was reluctant to contact her immediately. And he certainly wouldn't be worrying Carl's parents just yet.

Next day, Saturday, Ian repeated his actions of the day before including a visit to number 22. Inside Carl's flat nothing had changed. The same unwashed dishes and the same unmade bed. At 2pm he drove the seven miles north to Dainford FC, parked, entered the clubhouse, had a look around and saw no sign of Carl. He found a club official and asked if he knew where Carl was. The official didn't adding that they were annoyed when Carl hadn't arrived on Thursday night to deliver his coaching session. He mentioned Carl had done Tuesday night's coaching session and being 5th November had then stayed on for the club's annual Guy Fawkes Night bonfire and barbeque leaving it was thought around midnight.

Nothing had been heard from him since. Ian didn't sleep well that weekend.

On the following Monday morning there was still no sign of Carl so Ian decided it was time to speak to Laura King but he didn't want to visit her office. The two businesses kept a stock of each other's business cards and from one of Laura's cards he obtained her mobile number, called and told her of his concern about Carl's apparent disappearance. Laura said she last saw Carl more than two weeks before and he hadn't said anything then about leaving town. The two agreed it was unheard of for Carl to go off somewhere without telling anybody. Carl had now been missing for 3 days.

"What are you thinking of doing next, Ian?" Laura asked

"I haven't contacted his parents yet. I don't want to worry them unnecessarily". Ian was wondering how his next comments should be phrased. Was Laura Carl's girlfriend or just an occasional bedmate? Certainly from what Carl had told him Carl regarded their relationship as something more than just an occasional bonk.

"I was just wondering Laura bearing in mind your friendship with Carl which one of us should take the matter forward and when?"

"Well the problem is I don't have contact details for any of his friends or relatives. You say you've checked his flat and drawn a blank. Odd his car is still there. Suggests he's either gone somewhere on a train or someone picked him up. But he'd never just go off without telling you obviously. I think the next step has got to be to contact his parents".

So Ian rang the home number of Carl's parents who lived in Chester. They were surprised and worried by Ian's information but said they'd contact those of Carl's old friends they knew. They made no progress. Late Monday afternoon Carl's father rang Cheshire police to report his son missing. They took some basic details - full name, date of birth, home address, work address, physical and mental condition and also asked Mr Ramsey Senior to locate his son's National Insurance Number and National Health Service Number. A constable would call at their house to collect these along with an up to date photograph. Two days later this was done. Cheshire Police realising that the alleged missing person was a resident of a different police area referred the matter to Mid Land Police.

The matter of Carl Ramsey's apparent disappearance was in turn referred to the Missing Persons Team at Dainford Police Station - seven days after Carl was first reported missing. The case was picked up by Detective Constable Peter Guild whose only initial actions were to telephone all the hospitals within a 20 miles radius to ask if the missing Carl had been admitted anywhere - no he hadn't. DC Guild also found Carl's Facebook page and saw photographs of a fit, robustly built young man. When prioritising Missing Persons cases 33 year old non-vulnerable single men come low down on the list. DC Guild would visit Market Repton and conduct some routine interviews next week perhaps. Or the week after.

Ian Fall meanwhile had been thinking about informing Andrew Edge of the disappearance of his tenant. This sort of thing had never happened before. He decided to go ahead and put Andrew in the picture.

"Do you know if the police have been informed?" Andy asked Ian

"Yes. Carl's parents live in Chester so his father reported it to Cheshire Police but a couple of days later he told me they'd referred it to Mid Land Police"

"OK thanks for letting me know, Ian".

Andy considered what if anything he should do about this strange development. As owner of the property he had a link to the missing man who had been his tenant since the Summer of that year. He would have to declare the connection to his police bosses. Then Andy remembered the missing white van. It had slipped from his mind given all the work at 22 Station Road. A missing van and a missing man both from the same address, surely there was no possible link?

Andy was working the 8am to 4pm shift this week. He had not mentioned at work his ownership of let property, he was not under any obligation to do so. But since two different incidents had now been reported to the police connected to his property it would be inappropriate not to mention it now. Andy spoke to his sergeant who remembered the missing van conversation.

"Missing person is a different matter, Andy. The van is probably not connected, it went missing before you'd even thought about the flats conversion. You certainly need to have a word with the investigating officer. Let's have a look".

The sergeant logged onto the Mid Land police internal computer system, called up the Missing Persons section and saw that Carl Ramsey was the most recent addition. His Facebook main photograph had been used in the report being more up to date than the one his father had supplied to Cheshire Police.

"A detective constable Guild is the named officer, Andy, at the MissPer team in Dainford but before you give him a call I think you should speak to the duty inspector here and take the fed rep with you"

"Why, sarge?"

"Strange days, Andy. Probably nothing in it but just in case it turns into something else it would be better for you if everything you say officially were to be witnessed. Duty Inspector today is Mrs Prisha Gayan".

So Andy contacted his federation rep Police Constable Chloe Gibbs who was based at his police station and conveniently on duty. He outlined his link to the missing man and also mentioned the missing van. PC Gibbs agreed with the sergeant's suggestion about informing their inspector and also suggested the meeting be recorded. She noticed this had alarmed Andy but told him she'd been involved in many seemingly innocuous cases which had turned into serious investigations where information given at first contact with senior officers had been forgotten about, denied or mysteriously lost.

Chloe Gibbs had seven years experience as a police officer. She held a university degree in industrial relations and was not intimidated by rank no matter how senior. She always remained calm and polite and had acquired an encyclopaedic knowledge of police regulations quoting when needed chapter and paragraph numbers. She arranged a meeting with Inspector Mrs Prisha Gayan. Mrs Gayan was an officer of over 20 years experience. She was regarded by all her staff as reliable, efficient and fair. Mrs Gayan was saddened but not at all surprised that one of her constables who wished to see her was not only bringing his Fed Rep but also having their meeting recorded. She wasn't surprised because she was well aware of the toxic mistrust which existed between rank and file officers and their senior staff caused by the recent years' regime of target chasing, box ticking, buck passing and scape goating.

As their meeting started Inspector Gayan noticed PC Andrew Edge's unease as the digital recording device was placed on the table between them. The unease was mainly down to the fact that Andy liked and trusted Mrs Gayan. PC Chloe Gibbs spoke first and explained that it was beneficial to all concerned to record meetings like this so there could be no room for doubt at a later date about what had been said should the matter turn into something serious.

"PC Edge wishes to declare a connection to a missing persons case recently registered for investigation at Dainford police station" began Chloe "PC Edge , over to you"

Before the meeting had started Chloe had coached Andy to make a statement which amounted to a list a facts :

- I inherited a property from my grandmother
- I had it converted into 2 flats
- I engaged a firm of estate agents to manage the lettings
- One of the estate agents became a tenant
- That tenant was recently reported to be a missing person
- A white van belonging to my late grandmother had previously gone missing from the property and I reported it as stolen

And basically that was what Andy did.

"Did you know Mr Ramsey prior to this, Andy?" Inspector Gayan asked

"No, ma'am. I first met him when I engaged his firm to manage the lettings"

"How long was Mr Ramsey resident in the flat before he disappeared?"

"Just over three months, ma'am"

"Was any more heard of the missing van?"

"No, ma'am"

"Have you spoken to the MissPer team at Dainford yet, Andy?"

"No ma'am. I wanted you to know first"

"Thank you, Andy. Next thing to do is inform Dainford of your link to the case. They'll probably take a statement from you. After that you should not involve yourself in the matter in any way. Your duties here are quite separate so there shouldn't be any conflict of interest"

"Yes, ma'am"

"Thank you for seeing us, ma'am" added PC Chloe Gibbs.

Meeting over Andy telephoned the MissPer team at Dainford and spoke to Detective Constable Peter Guild. The two men had never met. Andy introduced himself as a police constable at Repton Magna and informed DC Guild he owned the property where Carl Ramsey lived. DC Guild asked Andy the same questions which Mrs Gayan had asked him.

"And there's nothing further you can add, mate?" Guild asked

"No. What does your team do when a man like Carl disappears? I mean he isn't a vulnerable person"

"I'll visit Market Repton and speak to his business partner Ian Fall. You say there are two flats in the house. Who lives in the other one?"

"Guy named Selwyn Myles. Haven't seen him yet. He's retired. I don't have any direct involvement with the tenants or the lettings. That's what I pay the estate agents for. They're Spring & Fall by the way in Market Repton High Street"

"Right, I'll speak to Selwyn Myles too. Apart from that we notify the national missing persons register and that's that. In my experience when healthy young professionals disappear it's just a trip they'd already planned and mentioned to somebody who promptly forgets they were told and in a few days he's back and wondering what the fuss was all about"

"I've just had a meeting with my Inspector to mention my connection to this case. Could you make a note on your computer file that we've had this chat"

"Course, mate".

Andy made a note of the date and time of this call. He'd also recorded the conversation.

CHAPTER 12

Welcome To My World

- "Should we be bothered?"

- "It's an unexpected thing but I wouldn't say it's a game changer. No, we'll work around it. Carry on as planned"

- "May have to be a bit more cautious, be careful about overlap"

- "It could work to our advantage, I'm thinking information and misinformation"

- "Misinformation - our specialist subject"

(laughter)

At Dainford police station Detective Constable Guild was slightly annoyed. He hadn't intended doing anything about the Carl Ramsey case until the new year but as a colleague had contacted him it would now be prudent to bring forward his interviews in Market Repton. It seemed PC Edge was anxious to keep himself at arms length from the case but he could at any time check the Mid Land Police internal computer system to see if any progress had been made. So in the first week of December DC Guild drove south to Market Repton. First on his list was the now over-worked estate agent Ian Fall.

"I'm DC Guild from Dainford police MissPer team sorry I mean Missing Persons Team"

"It's a bit of police jargon I know from TV" replied Ian Fall

"I take it you still haven't heard from Mr Ramsey?"

"No, his disappearance is a complete mystery to me and totally out of character. No one has seen him in nearly a month"

"Sorry to ask what may seem like a daft question but in the days running up to his disappearance you're sure he didn't mention going somewhere and it just slipped your memory?"

"Absolutely sure. We don't do business trips, all our work is based locally"

"I'd like to have a look around Mr Ramsey's flat. Is that possible without a forced entry?"

"Yes as it's one of our managed tenancies I have keys to the building and to the two flats. Do you want me to come with you? I've already checked Carl's flat. Unmade bed, unwashed dishes but nothing else out of place as far as I could see"

"No sign of leaving in a hurry or any indication something violent had occurred?"

"Nothing like that at all. It all looked normal"

"OK. No I don't need you to come with me, just lend me the keys please. All I'm going to do is have a quick look around. I'll also have a word with the other tenant while I'm there. Remind me of his name"

"Selwyn Myles, ground floor flat"

"Is there anyone else close to Mr Ramsey I should speak to while I'm here?"

"Well…...er…...yes. Carl is having a bit of a fling with Laura King. She's a solicitor at Lapley & Hinstock just across the street. But I had a word with

Laura a day or so after Carl disappeared. It was news to Laura, she hadn't seen him for a couple of weeks"

"May as well speak to her first then. Have you got her number please?"

Ian handed DC Guild one of Laura King's business cards. He rang her. She could see him right away. Their interview was brief. Laura told DC Guild she had last seen Carl towards the end of October about two weeks before he disappeared. They were not in a steady relationship, they saw each other occasionally when it suited them both. Yes, she had stayed over at Carl's flat a couple of times. No, Carl had never stayed over with her at her flat in Birmingham. She had no idea where Carl had gone or why.

DC Guild drove the short distance to 22 Station Road and let himself into Carl's flat. It was just as Ian Fall had described. Unmade bed, unwashed dishes, no sign of anything suspicious. Peter Guild descended the stairs and knocked on the door of the ground floor flat to speak to Mr Selwyn Myles.

Normally interviews like this lasted three or four minutes and consisted of
- I saw nothing
- I heard nothing
- I know nothing

DC Guild's official police notebook would record that his interview with Mr Myles lasted 1 hour 35 minutes. It was surprising and revealing and it altered both the course and the nature of the police enquiry.

Interview notes (abridged)   Tuesday 3 December

Detective Constable Peter Guild Dainford Police Station Missing Persons Team ;

Mr Selwyn Myles date of birth 25 June 1955 British citizen, retired
Flat 1, 22 Station Rd, Market Repton RE15 8EP

"Mr Myles when did you occupy this flat?"

"It was 14 August this year. I returned to England the day before after working overseas for many years. What's this all about?"

"What was the nature of your work, My Myles?"

"I was a railway engineer. My final job was working on the technical specifications for an extension to the Dubai Metro. Why do you want to know?"

"Sorry it's just to give me a bit of background information. My enquiry concerns your neighbour Carl Ramsey from the flat upstairs. You know Mr Ramsey?"

"Yes I met him a few days after I moved in. He'd already occupied the first floor flat but was on holiday in Spain when I arrived. I met him when he returned. Has something happened to Carl?"

"I hope not but he's been reported as a missing person"

"Missing? I don't understand. Missing in what sense?"

"Missing in that he hasn't been seen since the 7th of November, that was a Thursday. When did you last see Carl?"

"I can't remember but now you mention it I haven't seen him for quite a while. Some weeks I guess but he's so quiet you wouldn't know he were here even when he is. He's the perfect neighbour when you live in flats"

"Do you ever chat with him and can you remember the last time you did so?"

"Yes. We always chat when we meet coming into the building or leaving it. I'm a football fan so I'm interested to hear about his coaching work. You know he's head coach at Dainford FC?"

"Yes. Can you remember what you talked about the last time you saw him?"

"Oh of course yes I do remember because it was Bonfire Night the 5th of November. He was on his way out to do one of his coaching sessions. He told me he'd be back later than usual because of the football club's annual Guy Fawkes Night bonfire and barbeque"

"Did he mention having to leave home for a while?"

"No, nothing like that. I said I'd like to see his team play so he said he'd give me a lift to their next Saturday home game. I haven't got a car yet"

"Does he have any regular visitors?"

"I've noticed a rather attractive blond arriving a couple of times but not what you'd call regularly. I think she stayed overnight so I guess she's his girlfriend"

(note - this would be Mrs Laura King, solicitor at Lapley & Hinstock)

"Did you ever meet or speak to this lady?"

"No"

"Is there anything else you can tell me which might help our enquiry?"

"Well....I don't know what to say....it's probably nothing....it's just that....I'm not sure it's relevant"

"Please continue, Mr Myles. Let me decide if it's relevant"

"Well, when the football season started in early September I became aware Carl had started going out in the early hours of Sunday morning. I think after the match the team make a night of it at the club. Carl tells me you can get a decent cooked meal there. They have a meal then spend the night drinking. Carl comes back here in a taxi around 2am and at 2.15am goes off in a second taxi. I guess he leaves his car at the football club to avoid drinking and driving. Never noticed what time he gets back but it happens regularly.

But he doesn't always leave by taxi. One warm Saturday night in mid September around 2am I heard him running down the stairs, go out through the front door and walk off along Station Road towards the town. I remember he was walking briskly and purposefully as though he had somewhere to get to urgently. I thought to myself at the time 'where can you possibly be going to urgently in Market Repton at 2am on a Sunday morning?'

Anyway on that occasion he got back at 7am so he was gone for 5 hours throughout the early hours.

This pattern of going out around 2am Sunday mornings continued right up til early November when I last saw him"

"Sorry to interrupt, Mr Myles, but how did you become aware of these activities? Are you usually still up and about at 2am?"

"No but around 2am I wake up and have to visit the bathroom. It's what men of my age do. So I notice Carl's comings and goings. Now it's got to the stage where I'm waiting for it to happen. It's always Saturday night, well I mean the early hours of Sunday morning, never any other night. Then I became aware of something else a bit odd. Every Thursday night he gets home from the coaching session at 10pm. He sits in his car and makes a lengthy phone call. Then next morning, Friday, he drives off at 6am and returns here at 8am. Then goes out to work around 9am. He's an estate agent so I can't see this regular trip can be connected with his work"

"This happens every Thursday night?"

"Yes I'd say so, followed by the Friday morning's 2 hour early trip somewhere"

"Have you asked Carl where he's going in the early hours of Sunday mornings and 6am to 8am Fridays?"

"Good Lord no ! We're not on terms that friendly"

"If you had to make a guess what would you say these comings and goings are all about, Mr Myles?"

"Drugs. I'm sorry to say it because he's such a pleasant neighbour but I think it's drugs. I've thought about it many times. I asked myself 'what is he up to at these odd hours?' Then I had this idea - every Saturday he sees the football team and a few hours later it's the early hours of Sunday morning routine. Every Thursday night he sees the football team again, makes a long phone call and then it's the Friday morning 6am to 8am routine.

My thinking is those members of the team who are taking...well, whatever you'd call it nowadays -

chemicals, substances, stimulants give Carl their orders and he contacts a supplier then some hours later goes out to get the order. 6am to 8am would give him time to drive to Birmingham and back every Friday morning. Then next time he sees the team the goodies get distributed.

There's something else. Let me think. Just after the football season started and coaching had become intense I noticed Carl was walking with a limp. It got so bad he could only get up the stairs to his flat by using walking sticks. He told me it was a recurring knee problem. Anyway after a few days he seemed better and told me a member of the team had given him what he called some 'ludicrously strong painkillers'. I think stuff like that is only available on prescription and I'm pretty certain you shouldn't be sharing prescription drugs around !"

"Can you think of anything else, Mr Myles?"

"No, I think that's all I can add"

"This is unexpected information and may need us to rethink where to go next with the enquiry"

"Well if I were a detective with Mid Land Police I'd interview all the members of the Dainford football team and I'd search all their lockers with a sniffer dog"

"Thank you for your assistance, Mr Myles. I may return to speak to you again and we may have to search Mr Ramsey's flat".

End of interview notes.

The mention of the word 'drugs' was all DC Guild needed to hear to close the Missing Persons Enquiry, tick a box and transfer the case to the Mid Land Police Drugs Team at Repton Magna. As far as he was concerned it was case over. As a matter of courtesy he rang PC Andrew Edge at Repton Magna Police Station and told him of this development.

CHAPTER 13

Going Nowhere

At 5pm on a dark, rainy Thursday in the middle of January after Carl Ramsey had been missing for over two months a police people carrier vehicle stopped outside 22 Station Rd Market Repton and from it descended nine characters. Four detectives from Repton Magna Drugs Team, four uniformed constables and a Cocker Spaniel drugs sniffer dog named Molly.

One of the larger uniformed constables was equipped with a hand held door battering ram known to officers as The Big Red Key. He had attended the police MOE (Method Of Entry) training course to learn how to use it and held a certificate to prove it. He was disappointed when the lead detective Meredith Wynne visited Spring & Fall Estate Agents a few minutes earlier and obtained from Ian Fall the keys to the property.

The nine of them entered Carl Ramsey's cold flat and Molly was unleashed to do her stuff. Nothing drugs related was found. They also checked the cellar where Molly sniffed the three large locked trunks. She sniffed nothing of interest so the trunks were left undisturbed. After returning the keys to Ian Fall they headed to Dainford FC. As the players arrived for the regular Thursday evening coaching session each man was searched by one of the uniformed constables, sniffed by Molly and individually interviewed by one of the detectives. All of their lockers were searched and sniffed too.

Again nothing drugs related was found. Each player expressed amazement and disbelief at the idea Carl Ramsey might be involved with drugs. The individual interviews did though identify the player who had supplied Carl with the 'ludicrously powerful painkillers'. He was the centre forward who had suffered a non-football related neck injury and had been prescribed the tablets by his GP. He was advised not to share prescription drugs again. No further action was taken. No one could suggest where Carl might have gone or why he had been going out in the early hours of the morning.

Later that month the Repton Magna Drugs Team closed their enquiry, ticked a box and referred the case back to the Missing Persons Team at Dainford.

The lead detective on the non-productive searches at 22 Station Road and Dainford FC had been Detective Sergeant Meredith Wynne known as Merry. The Welshman had joined the police service in the same intake as

Andy Edge almost twenty years earlier. Merry was Andy's closest pal within the police community and the two men met for a drink and a chat when their shifts allowed. Andy had told Merry about his grandmother's death, the subsequent inheritance and his decision on the flats conversions. Merry had respected Andy's request not to mention any of this at work although since the disappearance of Carl Ramsey and Andy's information about his link to the case it was now widely known at Repton Magna police station.

A couple of days after the fruitless searches the two men were having early evening post-work drinks in a traditional pub near to their police station.

"So we've found nothing to make us think this is drugs related. We've shut our enquiry down and sent it back to Dainford as a Missing Persons case. Ticked a box first of course, another case closed and another statistic for Max Graden. Of course Dainford MissPer team have opened a new file, wiped the slate clean and started afresh. Makes it looks like there's loads of activity when really there isn't"

"So no drugs and no leads about Carl?" Andy asked

"No leads about Carl and the only drugs involved turned out to be prescription painkillers one of the players had given to Carl when he had a bad knee"

"How did that come to light, Merry?"

"During the interview DC Peter Guild had with Selwyn Myles in your ground floor flat in December. Mr Myles had seen Carl limping badly and Carl told him about a recurring knee problem. A few days later though he was OK and he told Mr Myles it was down to some strong painkillers one of his players had given him. We asked each player during the interviews which one of them had supplied Carl with the painkillers. One of them admitted it, he thought it was harmless enough and that he was helping Carl. We just told him not to do it again"

"Did you interview Selwyn Myles when you visited Station Road?"

"No. No need. Of course it was his information to DC Guild that triggered the possible drugs link but we couldn't find any evidence. Carl's disappearance is still a mystery. What are you going to do about Carl's flat, Andy?"

"I don't know. Bit early to do anything yet. I'll have to get legal advice if Carl isn't found. I've no idea what the law says about regaining possession of a let property in circumstances like this. Another pint?"

"You're keeping yourself well clear of the enquiry?" Merry asked as Andy returned from the bar with two fresh pints -

"Yes, I told you I made that statement to my inspector Mrs Gayan about my link to Carl. She said I should have no further involvement"

"Quite right. Keep yourself well out of it. I'll let you know if there are any developments. Whatever you do don't log on to any of our computers to look for yourself"

"What would you do, Merry, about the empty flat I mean?"

"Might seem a bit uncaring to do anything right now but if I were you I'd get some legal advice. No harm doing that now. You know how slow legal procedures take. If you need to get a repossession order it'd probably take months. At least you'd know where you stand. Have you got a solicitor, Andy?"

"Not as such. Those solicitors in Market Repton handled grandma's estate very quickly. Lapley & Hinstock, I dealt with Audrey Hinstock"

"Did you know one of their solicitors Laura King had been having an affair with Carl?"

"No. Who told you that?"

"More information from DC Guild's notes. First Ian Fall told him then Selwyn Myles told him he'd seen her arriving at Carl's flat. So Guild interviewed her but it seems there was less to it than meets the eye. Just the occasional shag-fest when it suited them. She'd no idea where Carl might have gone"

"I think on my next rest day I'll go to Market Repton and speak to Ian Fall, ask him if he's come across this sort of thing before. You know, a tenant disappearing and what to do next. Hope he doesn't think it's insensitive with the tenant being his business partner. Then I'll go and see Audrey Hinstock about the legalities"

"Andy when anybody sees you I don't think 'sensitive' is the impression they'd get"

The two men laughed, finished their drinks and went to their respective homes.

Andy's next rest day was the Wednesday of the following week. He made appointments to see both Ian Fall and Audrey Hinstock. On meeting Ian Fall Andy expressed sympathy on the unexplained disappearance of his business partner and hoped what he'd come to ask wouldn't upset Ian but he was thinking of the future and wondered if Ian had any experience on re-letting of property should a tenant leave and not come back. As they were lettings managers Ian explained it was an issue they had had to handle before. In his experience it took at least six months for the legal system to revoke a tenancy agreement thus allowing the property to be re-let. Either Andy could instigate the process himself or Spring & Fall could do it on his behalf. Andy told Ian he'd prefer it if he did it for him so he could remain detached from the process. They agreed that if nothing were heard from Carl by the end of February, which would be the best part of four months since Carl had disappeared, the legal process would commence through Lapley & Hinstock who handled all Spring & Fall's legal affairs.

Following his meeting with Ian Fall Andy crossed Market Repton High Street for his appointment with Audrey Hinstock.

"There are two issues I want to talk about" Andy started "getting Carl Ramsey's tenancy agreement cancelled so I can re-let the flat and I think it's about time I made a will"

"I was sorry to hear of Carl's disappearance. I understand the police have got nowhere. I can see your dilemma. I'd suggest starting the tenancy termination process now. If Carl returns it's no problem cancelling it. Are you going to be the named applicant or are Spring & Fall doing it on your behalf?"

"Yes Spring & Fall will do it. I've just seen Ian Fall and we agreed to start the process at the end of February"

"Fine but no harm in starting the paperwork now. And on the second matter yes you should make a will especially given you're a high net worth individual. We'll make a further appointment to draft your will. Do you know what you want your will to say, Mr Edge ?"

"Yes I think so. It's going to be straightforward"

"Are your parents still resident in Australia, Mr Edge?"

"Yes they'll be there for good, why?"

"You have to name someone as executor of your will and also think about an LPA, that's a Lasting Power Of Attorney. Remember I mentioned to you a couple of years ago it's what your grandmother had done? That's so someone can handle your affairs should you become unable or incapable of doing so. It would be difficult for your parents to handle either task from Australia. We can do both for you if you wish but you can have a think about that before our next appointment. If you wish to name us as executors of your will, and that would be the normal thing to do, I'd ask you at some point in time to supply us with a list of your banking and savings accounts and any other investments. Do you mind if I ask if you live on your own Mr Edge?"

"Yes I do"

An appointment was made for the preparation of Andy's will. He was now officially a client of Lapley & Hinstock.

Andy had a thought as he left the offices of Lapley & Hinstock and went to see Ian Fall again.

"I just wondered if you'd actually met Selwyn Myles yet" Andy asked

"No I've never seen him. Carl must have seen him many times though"

"I think while I'm in town I'll go to Station Road and introduce myself"

"OK, Mr Edge"

Andy drove the short distance to 22 Station Road and let himself into the building using his key. He knocked on the door of the ground floor flat. There was no reply, Mr Myles was not at home. Finally Andy phoned his pal Simon King to see if he were at home and if so to get the kettle on. No luck there either. Simon was working in Dainford. Andy drove back home to Repton Magna.

CHAPTER 14

Invisible

For three weeks in that February Simon King and his team of builders were busy on a major project inside the detached house next door to 22 Station Road in Market Repton. Simon was aware that the first floor flat at number 22 was empty because of the still unexplained disappearance of Carl Ramsey. His friend Andy Edge had told him that the ground floor flat had been let to a retired man called Selwyn Myles. Simon noticed that at no time during that dark, dreary month did he see any lights go on in the ground floor flat. The place remained in darkness. Nor did he see the elusive Mr Myles either leaving or arriving at the property. He mentioned this curious fact to Andy.

Meanwhile the MissPer team at Dainford Police Station decided to do something about the case of Carl Ramsey. From Ian Fall they obtained details of Carl's bank account and then they got a court order to compel the bank to reveal what transactions had taken place since 5 November. The answer was - nothing. No debit card usage, no credit card purchases, no cash withdrawals, no contact with their call centre. Carl seemed to have disappeared into thin air.

At the end of February Lapley & Hinstock Solicitors informed Spring & Fall Estate Agents that they had started the legal process to revoke the tenancy of the first floor flat and regain vacant possession of the property. If anyone had bothered to check they would have discovered that Lapley & Hinstock had already started the process before the end of the previous year. But rarely did anyone check anything nowadays.

By the end of May the legalities were finalised. Spring & Fall could now re-let the first floor flat. To Ian Fall fell the sad task of contacting Carl Ramsey's parents and asking them to remove Carl's possessions from the flat. He would of course do all he could to help at this distressing time. Carl's replacement had been recruited and now worked for Ian.

The day Lapley & Hinstock received the court paper granting the repossession order Laura King walked across Market Repton High Street with the document in her hand to see Ian Fall.

"Hi, Ian. This arrived today so the first floor flat can be re-let. I'd like to be the new tenant"

"Oh….er….OK….didn't know you were interested, Laura"

"I was interested before the building work was even finished. My ex husband told me about the flats but they were both let before I got my name down"

"So when do you think you'd be wanting to move in ? I presume you'll have to give notice to quit your place in Birmingham"

"Already done. I can pay the deposit and my first months rent now"

As indeed she did.

"Curious how popular these flats have proved to be" thought Ian Fall to himself. He rang Andy Edge and told him the good news. In the first week of June a van arrived from Birmingham containing all Laura's stuff and she became the latest tenant at 22 Station Road Market Repton RE15 8EP.

Also in the first week of June Andy Edge kept an appointment with Audrey Hinstock for the preparation of his will. He had delayed making this appointment, there were things he needed to research, questions he needed to ask his friends.

"Did you think any more about creating a Lasting Power Of Attorney, Mr Edge?" Audrey asked

"Yes, I don't need to do it now though do I?"

"No but it makes sense to get all this sorted now otherwise it might get forgotten. Like I mentioned before we can hold Power Of Attorney for you if you wish"

"No thank you. I have already decided who I want to be as executor of my will and that same person will also hold Power Of Attorney if I go ahead with that"

"So you don't wish Lapley & Hinstock to hold either role?"

"No thank you. We'll just do the will"

"Yes that's fine, Mr Edge" concluded Audrey Hinstock. Was it Andy's imagination or was there a hint of annoyance in Audrey's voice?

The paperwork done Andy walked to 22 Station Road and knocked on the door of the ground floor flat to say hello to his tenant Selwyn Myles whom he still hadn't met. Mr Myles was not at home. The window blinds were all down. For no particular reason Andy descended into the cellar. His grandmother's three large storage trunks were still there. Andy made a mental note to see if any of the keys he'd taken from the house a couple of years ago fitted the trunks.

Andy noticed the new electricity, gas and water meters for the two flats fitted by the utility companies as part of the building work. He walked over to the meters and looked at them. He was momentarily rooted to the spot. He couldn't understand what he was seeing. "But....that's impossible....." he said to himself.

Andy drove southwards back to his home in Repton Magna contemplating what he'd just seen, trying to think of an explanation. He decided to check something else. Next day during his (very late) lunch break he walked the short distance from his police station to Repton Unitary Authority offices and into the Council Tax department. As it was after 2pm the lunchtime rush was over and the office was quiet. He wondered if the enquiry he was about to make would be met with the now frequent response 'I'm sorry but the Data Protection Act means I can't give you this information'. His large frame in his police uniform he approached the clerk and showed his warrant card, he also produced proof he was the owner of 22 Station Road Market Repton and asked the clerk to tell him if the Council Tax payments were up to date on Flat 1, the ground floor flat.

The Data Protection Act didn't seem to be a barrier to this request and the clerk told Andy that the Council Tax payments were fully up to date. The resident, Mr Selwyn Myles, was paying monthly by direct debit.

That same day Andy had an early evening drink with Meredith 'Merry' Wynne. Earlier in the day he'd asked his pal Merry to check the Mid Land Police internal computer system to see if there had been any developments on the Carl Ramsey mystery. Once seated and with pints of their favourite ale in front of them Merry started -

"There's still nothing to report on the Carl Ramsey case. They've checked his bank records, took their time about it mind, and no financial transactions since the day he disappeared"

"I got a repossession order on Carl's flat, Merry. I've already got a new tenant. You won't believe this. It's that solicitor Laura King who you told me was having an affair with Carl"

"I'm amazed you got a repossession order that quickly. I thought it normally took at least six months"

"I'll say this much for Lapley & Hinstock - they don't mess about. They settled grandma's estate within a month. Merry, I'm concerned about something else. My ground floor tenant Selwyn Myles has been there over 10 months now and I haven't set eyes on him yet"

"Why should that be a problem, matey? Is he paying the rent on time?"

"Yes the rent money goes into my bank every month regular as clockwork and I've checked at the council. He's paying the Council Tax every month"

"So what are you worried about?"

"I was at the property yesterday. Just happened to look at the meters in the cellar and in 10 months Mr Myles has used just one unit of electricity and zero units of gas and water. Merry, that's impossible. He's obviously not living there"

"But he's paying the rent so why are you worried?"

"I've got one tenant who's disappeared off the face of the earth, another who seems to be paying rent on a flat he doesn't live in and my grandma's van was stolen from the property. Oh and I've just remembered something else - before my mate Simon started the building work he asked me where my grandmother's works of art were. They seem to have disappeared as well. My grandparents were antique dealers so Simon was probably right when he said the stuff would be valuable. It makes my head spin when I think about it all, mate. Are all these things connected do you think?"

"The van went before you even thought about turning the house into flats so I'd forget that. It's a bit creepy Laura King occupying her missing boyfriend's flat but she is a lawyer remember ! Oh and don't forget Selwyn Myles was at home when DC Guild interviewed him. Perhaps he's gone on a world cruise or something. Know anything about him?"

"Only what the estate agent Ian Fall told me. He's a retired railway engineer. Worked all over the world then came back to England to retire"

"Well there you are then. He's probably gone off to see his mates all over the world"

"And the missing paintings and other stuff?"

"Perhaps your gran had it all put into storage. Have you checked through all her paperwork?"

"There wasn't that much paperwork as I remember. No, there was nothing like an invoice from a storage company"

"Far as I can see we've got one big mystery here - Carl Ramsey's disappearance. He could have contacted someone at any time, his parents at least. I think after seven months we've got to assume Carl is dead. I wouldn't worry too much about the rest. You've got two lots of rent coming in every month to soften the blow. I'll fetch us two more pints"

"Do me a favour, mate, run a check on Selwyn Myles spelt M -Y - L - E - S one day soon. See what our computer says. I don't want to do it myself"

"Sure but I'll need his date of birth"

"The estate agent should have it. I'll let you know".

CHAPTER 15

Lazy Afternoon

The final week of July was forecast to be hot and dry. Andy Edge had booked a week's leave. Andy and his pal Simon the builder had planned a few motorcycle rides and beer nights. On the afternoon of the Sunday which started Andy's period off work he decided to visit 22 Station Road to introduce himself to his new tenant Laura King. He had found some keys in his grandmother's bureau which didn't look like door keys so took them with him to see if they would unlock the three storage trunks in the cellar.

Laura was staring out of one of the windows of her first floor flat thinking about nothing in particular when she noticed a car pull up directly outside number 22. She observed a large, well dressed man get out of the car and approach the house. The visitor was wearing sunglasses, a light blue short sleeved polo top, navy blue knee length tailored shorts and tan deck shoes without socks. This was the first time Laura had seen her landlord Andy Edge.

Andy didn't go straight into the house but walked along the side of the building to what had been the back garden. He was stopped in his tracks at the sight of a white Citroen Berlingo van in one of the parking spaces. Had his grandmother's van mysteriously returned after over two and a half years? But he couldn't recall the registration number so took a couple of photographs with his phone. He entered the house through the back door and descended into the cellar. He put one of the small keys he had brought with him into the lock on the first of the three storage chests but discovered it was unlocked. As were the other two. All three were empty. Andy was certain the chests had been locked when he last saw them. Next he looked at the three utility meters serving the ground floor flat. They still showed :

Electricity 1 unit used
Gas 0 units used
Water 0 units used

So three mysteries in three minutes he thought to himself. What is it about this place?

He left the cellar and emerged into the spacious hallway. It was difficult to know who was more surprised, Laura seeing her landlord exiting the cellar or Andy seeing his tenant standing in the hall.

"Sorry if I startled you. I'm Andrew Edge, you must be Laura?" Andy extended a large, warm hand in greeting and Laura shook it.

"Yes, pleased to meet you at last. I saw you arrive in your car a few minutes ago and wondered where you'd gone. Anything of interest in the cellar?"

"I was just having a look at my late grandmother's storage chests. I'll get them moved if they're in the way"

"They're not a problem to me. I'll get you a drink, what would you like?"

"Nothing for me thanks. I've just come to say hello and welcome to your new home. Any problems with the flat just contact Ian Fall. He handles all the letting issues for me"

"Yes I know. I've known Ian for some years now"

"Have there been any issues? With the flat I mean"

"None whatsoever, it's perfect for me"

"Mind if I ask - is that your white van outside?"

"Yes. No. I've rented it for the weekend to do some fetching and carrying. My flat in Birmingham was a new build so a lot of my stuff didn't go well in this Victorian home with its high ceilings. I've been buying some better quality things. I haven't got a car. Never felt I needed one"

By now Laura had taken in the man's robust build, short neat black hair, the absence of a wedding ring and the aroma of an expensive cologne.

"Have you met your neighbour yet in the ground floor flat?"

"Yes. We've had a couple of chats. Selwyn Myles. He had an interesting career building railways all over the world. I think he mentioned his final job was something to do with the Dubai Metro. He's very quiet, the perfect neighbour. I never hear any music nor the TV. He's returned to England to retire"

"You know more about him than I do. When was the last time you saw him?"

"The day before yesterday I think. Why?"

"Well, he's been my tenant for nearly a year now but he's always out when I call. I only want to introduce myself, say hello like. His tenancy agreement was done by remote control. I'll knock on his door, see if he's in today"

"Remote control?" questioned Laura

"I can't remember the right words. Mr Myles contacted Spring & Fall after seeing the flat on their website. Took the virtual online tour, decided to rent it and paid up. Seems it can all be done with an electronic signature. That's what I mean by remote control"

"Right, I see. On a different matter I understand you're one of our clients now, at Lapley & Hinstock I mean"

"Yes. I've just made my will. Audrey Hinstock dealt with it"

"Her great grandfather was co-founder of the firm way back in 1923 and her father Ben still does the occasional consultancy work for us. Both Ben and his father Ben Senior knew your grandparents"

"It must be handy having everything within walking distance"

"Yes". Their talk was somewhat animated and Laura sensed her landlord was finding this conversation awkward. She wondered why.

"OK then, I'll just see if Mr Myles is in and leave you in peace"

And with that dismissal Laura returned to her flat. Mr Myles was not in. Andy knew there was no point in going to the nearby home of his pal Simon because he was visiting his parents in Dainford so he drove back to Repton Magna. He had arranged to meet his police buddy Meredith Wynne for a late afternoon pub meal. 'Merry' had been on duty all day heading the CID office at Repton Magna police station.

"Fancy eating outside, Merry?" Andy asked as he saw his friend approaching

"Not bloody likely, screaming kids running around all over the place. I get enough of that at home"

"I'm a bit surprised you got permission for a pub meal with a mate on a Sunday"

"I'll tell the wife I got delayed if she asks, which is unlikely. What are you wearing? You smell like Joan Collins' handbag !"

"Something I picked up at Dubai duty free I think. Mate, you smell like someone who's been sat at a desk for 8 hours on a hot day in an office with no air conditioning"

The pleasantries over the two men ordered meals and drinks.

``Listen, matey, while I was sat sweating at that desk I checked the Police National Computer for Selwyn Myles. Nothing. Not even a speeding ticket. But if he's been living and working overseas for decades that's hardly surprising´´

"I visited the house today and said hello to Laura King. Selwyn Myles wasn't in. But Laura said she's met him and chatted with him a couple of times, she described him as the perfect neighbour. Also I checked the meters again. No change, mate. No electricity, gas or water has been used since I last checked"

"I've been thinking about that. The meters might be faulty or wired up incorrectly. It's not unusual. He could be using power and it just isn't getting registered. One day they'll cotton on and he'll get a massive bill"

"Hadn't thought of that"

"You're on leave for a week now aren't you. What are you up to? The forecast says it's going to be the hottest week of the year so far"

"I'm going to spend a couple of hours each morning tidying up the back garden. Then get some biking in in the afternoons and boozing in the evenings"

"How the other half lives. What it must be like to be single and rich. Here come our meals".

CHAPTER 16

Human Nature

- "Phase one completed a bit later than expected"

- "And a lot more profitable than expected. Just under ten million pounds"

- "We could start phase two at the end of the Summer. What do you think?"

- "Or we could wait and start phase two when one of the time bombs gets triggered. It would be riskier but more exciting"

- "As I see it there are three potential time bombs. First Carl Ramsey, second Selwyn Myles and third Andrew Edge"

- "Is Andrew Edge going to die?"

- "He's got a powerful guardian angel"

- "And killing a policeman would have quick and dramatic consequences"

- "Have you considered the aftermath, the repercussions?"

- "Problems that can be solved by having money thrown at them and there's plenty of that sloshing about"

(laughter)

- "How about this - we start phase two in the Spring of next year or when one of the time bombs gets triggered whichever happens first?"

- "Agreed"

The second day of Andy Edge's week of leave from work was hotter than the day before had been. He had arranged a late afternoon motorcycle ride with his pal Simon King who would be working on one of his building projects until 3pm. Andy got up early to get some gardening done before the heat built up. He also rang Ian Fall at Spring & Fall Estate Agents and asked him to contact the water and power companies to send someone to 22 Station Road to check the meters for the ground floor flat which he explained were stuck on 'zero'. Ian did as directed.

Meanwhile across the street in the offices of Lapley & Hinstock Solicitors Audrey Hinstock had something interesting to show to Laura King.

Laura's Irish Catholic ancestry rarely had reason to reveal itself. Laura herself had almost forgotten it was there but at moments of shock or extreme annoyance it would resurface and manifest itself in the form of a colourful phrase or a traditional oath. Such a moment was rapidly approaching.

Audrey bustled into Laura's office brandishing a document she was clearly excited about.

"You've got to see this" began Audrey waving the document around

"Why, what is it?"

"Andrew Edge's last will and testament"

"And?"

"He's left his entire estate to a sole beneficiary"

"So?" sighed Laura becoming a little annoyed at this interruption

"Read this" insisted Audrey handing the document to Laura who sighed again and began reading. She knew which bits to skim through quickly to get to the key details, then came the astonished outburst -

"Jesus, Mary and Joseph ! How could I have been such a feckin blinkered eejit !"

After a light lunch Andy Edge extracted his red Honda 750cc motorcycle from the garage and cleaned it. It was one of those very rare days in England when it was warm enough to enjoy a ride without having to put on layer after layer of clothing. Andy would need to wear only pants and a tee shirt under his red and white one piece biking leathers. After showering, at 2.30pm Andy eased his bulk into his leathers, fired up the powerful bike and headed north to Market Repton. The twelve mile journey would take only a matter of minutes.

Just before 3pm Andy arrived at Simon's home and rode his Honda onto the paved parking area which had once been the front garden. He was expecting to see his pal's green 650cc Kawasaki Ninja motorcycle outside and ready to start their ride so why wasn't it there? Simon had heard Andy arrive and opened the main door of his house. Andy was puzzled and a bit annoyed to see his friend wasn't dressed for biking, he was barely dressed at all, barefooted, bare chested and wearing only a pair of shorts.

With a slight backwards tilt of his head Simon beckoned Andy into his home. Andy entered and stepped from brightness and heat into the cool of the hall. The two men stood wordlessly facing each other hardly eight inches apart, aware of each other's body heat. Simon reached up with his left hand towards Andy's chin, inserted his index finger into the metal ring attached to the fastener on the zip of Andy's biking leathers and slowly pulled it down undoing the full length of the zip to its lower point near Andy's groin. He wrapped his arms around Andy's broad neck and pressed his lips onto the opening mouth of his lover of twenty years.

It was Monday 27 July, Andy Edge's 40th birthday.

CHAPTER 17

Private Investigations

On a Wednesday night in late August Laura and her brother John were having their regular pub meal, gossip and general catch-up. This night out was now a much easier affair for Laura since Westwich was only three train stops north of Market Repton and there was no tedious train trip back to Birmingham. Once installed in their favourite booth in The Crooked Copper pub with meals and drinks before them the gossip started.

"So let me get this straight, sorry wrong choice of words. Your ex husband the beefy builder and your landlord the biking cop have been at it together for years. We've got half The Village People here !"

"Why don't you speak a bit louder there's someone at the far end of the bar might not have heard you"

"Sorry"

"Of course I knew Simon was gay 48 hours into the honeymoon. But there were other…..er…..incompatibilities. He wanted children and I didn't, he wanted a settled English suburban existence and I didn't. Good thing about it was we both learned valuable lessons when we were young. I'm actually glad he's happy. I still like Simon, he's clever I mean in a skillful way. He can create beautiful things, he'd come home with a pile of wood and next there was an item of furniture he'd built with his hands. And you've seen the workmanship in my flat"

"And what about the boyfriend?"

"Not the sharpest knife in the box but otherwise quite presentable. He's one of our clients now, well one of Audrey's. Oh, that reminds me - I saw something odd yesterday. I was arriving home from work and Ian Fall the estate agent was coming out of the cellar at number 22 with a man with a clipboard. They said they were checking the meters"

"What's so odd about that?"

"The man-with-clipboard looked more like an engineer type, you know collection of tools with him, not a meter reader. And I'm not aware of any problem with the meters. I must remember to ask Ian what it was all about and does it affect me. The meters are new and they're smart meters anyway so they don't need reading"

"Are you and Audrey still doing those Spanish classes?"

"Yes but the Summer break has started. We'll be back at Repton Magna college at the end of September"

"Are the classes useful?"

"Yes and will be more so in the future. Are we having a pudding?"

Puddings consumed Laura got the two of them fresh drinks from the bar.

"Is that man in the ground floor flat still being the perfect neighbour?"

"You'd hardly know he were there. Changing the subject, are you going away this year?" Laura asked her brother

"Nothing booked yet, I'll see what develops. How about you?"

"Likewise. We're a bit busy at work surprisingly. If the opportunity arises I'll be off somewhere"

"Somewhere Spanish speaking?"

"Ideally, yes".

1 October from springfall@quickpost.com

To edgybiker@swiftmail.com

Hi Mr Edge just to let you know Ive heard from the water and power companies about the meters at the ground floor flat. no problems reported. meters working readings correct
Ian Fall

"Merry, this is just crazy. I'm going back to 22 Station Road on my next rest day"

"Have you got Selwyn Myles's phone number?"

"Yes"

"Ring him up right now". Andy did so. The call went to voicemail.

"Have you got keys to the property, Andy?"

"Yes. I may own the place but I can't just enter someone's home, I'd have the human rights lot onto me. And wouldn't I be involving myself in the case?"

"But we don't know there is a case yet do we? Besides you can be a property owner and a concerned citizen as well as a cop. Look, when is your next rest day? I'll come with you. Do you have a key to the letterbox as well?"

In the second week of October Andy Edge and his pal Meredith Wynne drove to Market Repton and parked outside 22 Station Road. They noticed all the window blinds were down in the ground floor flat. Andy rang Selwyn Myles's phone, it went to voicemail. Next he opened the letterbox, it was empty. They went into the cellar and Andy pointed out the meters which still read -

Electricity 1 unit used
Gas 0 units used
Water 0 units used

They stood outside the door to the ground floor flat, Andy knocked on the door. There was no answer so Andy knocked again more robustly, still no answer.

"This is it, Merry" Andy said putting the key into the lock. The two men entered the stillness and the silence of the flat's hallway.

"Mr Myles" Andy called out. Nothing. They entered the large kitchen diner which was devoid of table, chairs and white goods - no fridge, no washing machine, no microwave, no food. Andy opened all the cupboards, they were empty. Next they entered the sitting room in the centre of which was an office type grey desk and two office chairs. There was nothing on the desk. To the side of it was a locked steel, grey filing cabinet. There was nothing else in the room. They checked both the bedrooms which were just as empty as when Andy last saw them well over a year ago. The bathroom looked like it had not been used.

"This flat has never been lived in, Merry. I don't understand this, what the hell is going on here?"

"You're sure the rent is still being paid?"

"Yes, I checked my bank statement on-line before I left home"

"Right then, let's go and have a word with Ian Fall. What's his smartphone number?" Andy supplied it and Merry became Detective Sergeant Wynne. "We need to be careful here, Andy. This isn't an official police enquiry or interview. No one has reported Mr Myles missing, there could be an innocent explanation. We're just concerned citizens. I say we but I want you to keep your mouth shut"

"Mr Fall, I'm DS Wynne of Repton Magna CID. I want to speak to you about one of your lettings. I'm on my way to your office now"

Within ten minutes they were sitting opposite Ian Fall in his office. Both Merry and Andy produced their police warrant cards.

"I didn't know you were a policeman, Mr Edge. What's this all about?"

Merry spoke - "We're concerned for the safety of one of your tenants Mr Selwyn Myles. Have you personally ever met Mr Myles, Mr Fall?"

"No, not personally. The tenancy agreement was done electronically which is legally binding but I'm sure Carl Ramsey met him"

"Did Mr Ramsey specifically mention meeting Mr Myles?"

"Well....er....no, actually I don't recall Ian ever saying he'd met him. I'm sorry, I don't understand. What's the problem exactly?"

"We've just visited the ground floor flat and it's unoccupied. No furniture, no food and in over a year there hasn't been any electricity, gas or water used"

"Oh, is that why you asked about the meters, Mr Edge?"

Merry raised a hand in a gesture to stop Andy responding.

"What contact have you had with Mr Myles since the tenancy agreement was entered into?"

"None at all really. Carl was manager of the lettings so Mr Myles would have dealt with him initially. Let me check the file". Ian located the file for the Station Road lettings. "No, there's no record of any contact after the agreement was finalised apart from an exchange of emails I had with Mr Myles just before he moved in. Carl was on holiday in Spain at the time. I left the keys in the secure key safe in the porch and emailed the combination to Mr Myles. We just assumed he'd moved in like he said he was going to. Are you saying he didn't? Why would he be paying the rent every month? Has someone reported him missing? Oh my god this isn't connected to Carl's disappearance is it?"

Merry avoided answering any of Ian's questions and said "At this stage we're just concerned for Mr Myles's safety. We've seen nothing which indicates any unlawful activity.   Do your records show an emergency contact number for Mr Myles, next of kin, anything like that?"

"Well, no. That sort of thing doesn't form part of our paperwork, never has"

"Mr Myles was returning to the UK after working overseas for some years. Do you know which country he was coming here from?"

"Again sorry but no. Not the sort of thing we need to ask"

"But you do have his email address on record?"

"Yes"

"Mr Fall I'd appreciate it if you'd send an email to Mr Myles and ask him whether or not he has actually occupied the ground floor flat yet and if not when he intends to do so"

"I'd need a reason to be asking wouldn't I? After all he is paying the rent every month and on time"

"These are rental properties so the boilers would have to be serviced every year. You could say that when you arranged for the first annual service it was noticed the flat was unoccupied. Have the boilers been serviced yet by the way?"

"Er….well….no….actually they haven't been yet. It would have been Carl's job to sort it. After Carl disappeared I was rushed off my feet, doing everything here myself. I didn't want to recruit a replacement immediately but I have now so I'll get on with it"

"Thank you, Mr Fall. Here is a card with my contact details, please get in touch as soon as Mr Myles replies to your email"

The unofficial interview over Merry and Andy were driving back to Repton Magna and discussing the mystery of the elusive Mr Myles.

"He must have been there at some point. Let's remember Detective Constable Guild from Dainford interviewed him at the flat after Carl Ramsey disappeared" Merry said

"And I know Laura King the solicitor has met him several times. She told me that herself when I went to introduce myself and had a quick chat with her" Andy added

"Did she say if she'd been inside his flat?"

"No I don't think so, they've chatted in the hallway. Merry, you know I'm in a relationship?"

"With Simon the builder, yes I know, you told me that years ago. Don't tell me he's disappeared !"

"No we're sound but a long time ago Simon was married briefly. His ex wife is Laura King who's now the tenant of my first floor flat"

"Jeez whatever next, talk about wheels within wheels. Why didn't you mention this before?"

"It never occurred to me, I never thought it was relevant to anything. As we've said there isn't actually a case yet as far as we know"

"OK, well for now we'll just see what Ian Fall says after he's sent that email. But listen, matey, it's more important than ever now you keep yourself distanced from this. Don't be tempted to look at any police computers unless it's directly linked to your own day to day assignments, goddit?"

"Goddit"

"That letterbox was empty. No junk mail, no takeaway flyers, no local trade mags. I get junk mail every day. Andy, somebody is emptying that letterbox regularly".

CHAPTER 18

All This And More

In mid October Ian Fall received a reply from Selwyn Myles to his tactfully worded email about the occupancy of the ground floor flat in Station Road. In his response Mr Myles explained he had been offered out of the blue very lucrative consultancy work by the Saudi government concerning an extension to their high speed train line. It was a fixed term arrangement and he would be back in Market Repton by Christmas. Ian relayed this information to Detective Sergeant Wynne who relayed it to Andy Edge. Seemingly the mystery was solved.

"But, Merry, it doesn't explain why there's no furniture in the flat or why he isn't using any water or other stuff. He's been my tenant for over a year and I haven't set eyes on him yet. He's never been there when I've visited"

"Andy, we can't start an enquiry just because someone has a small gas bill and works overseas. We've got our answer"

"And I don't suppose anything is being done about Carl Ramsey?"

"You suppose right. You know we spend most of our time nowadays chasing our own arses to meet unmeetable targets so we can tick boxes so our bosses can give Max Graden the stats he wants to see. To get resources committed to anything something crucial would have to happen"

"Carl's been missing for nearly a year, isn't that crucial enough?" Andy reminded his friend

"Look, I led the team which searched his flat remember. We found nothing"

"You were looking for evidence of drugs and didn't find any. His disappearance hasn't been looked at from any other angle has it?"

"Like what?"

"I don't know, Merry. I'm not a detective. Detective Constable Guild from Dainford police station just did a quick walk through of Carl's flat some weeks before you and your team went in and he saw nothing out of place. But he wasn't looking for anything specific. So are you telling me nothing would be done unless he'd seen all the furniture upside down and a pool of blood on the floor?"

"That's policing nowadays, Andy. Maybe one day something will come to light that will start a new line of enquiry. It's just a question of what and when but at the moment Carl Ramsey is registered as a non vulnerable, apparently fit, young adult who's missing possibly of his own accord. In the current climate we're never going to commit resources to that. Laura

King replaced Carl in the first floor flat in June this year so you've got rent coming in from both the flats. Forget it, Andy, relax"

"It started off so well, Merry. After grandma died nearly three years ago the solicitors settled everything quickly. Work started on the building conversion early in the following year, there were no delays thanks to Simon. Both flats were ready for occupation by Summer last year and tenants found straight away. Perfect I thought. But now, I don't know Merry, I find the goings on there a bit unsettling"

"So this Selwyn Myles guy hasn't spent much time in the ground floor flat. It means the wear and tear on the property is virtually nil and he's paying the rent on time every month. Look on the bright side, Andy".

~

In late November Tina Proudfoot was completing her final task of the day in the offices of Lapley & Hinstock Solicitors, putting away the files Laura King had been working on that day. The names on two of the files caught her eye - Mrs Mary Montgomery-Gradbach and Mr Selwyn Myles. The former name was that of Tina's deceased great aunt. Tina wondered what could be happening concerning the affairs of her great aunt so opened the file.

"But that's extraordinary" Tina said to herself "I don't understand this".

Tina called up the computer records for the case and was so shocked at what she saw she was momentarily frozen to the spot, staring open mouthed at the screen. When she regained some of her composure she checked the computer records for Selwyn Myles. Tina remembered why his name seemed vaguely familiar. She had dealt with a letter a few years ago and the name and address on it had stuck in her mind as it was a particularly attractive, unusual street name overseas. Mr Myles's computer records revealed transactions with some similarities to those of her great aunt. Tina decided to speak urgently to her cousin about Mrs Montgomery-Gradbach. She logged off the computer, put her coat on and left the office. Both the computer files recorded that Tina had accessed them giving the date and the time.

Once outside in the street Tina rang her cousin.

"Hilda, hello, are you at home? I could do with seeing you urgently. Can I come now?"

Mrs Hilda Judd was at home and available. Tina walked the short distance to Hilda's home. Once seated with a pot of tea between them Hilda asked -

"What's the matter, Tina?"

"Hilda I've just seen something quite extraordinary in the office. Something that can't be right and it concerns great aunt Mary"

"But she's been dead for years"

"Since 2000. I remember because Aunt Mary always said she wanted to live long enough to see in the new millennium and she did. Hilda I'm in a quandary because I'm bound by our professional rules about client confidentiality and the Data Protection Act so I want you to promise me you'll not mention a word about this to anyone. I could get the sack and face prosecution"

"I promise, Tina. What's got you so worked up?"

"Hilda our files for Aunt Mary are still live, still open. We're running a bank account in her name and there's thousands of pounds going in and out of the account every month. Her Old Age Pension and employment pension are still being paid more than 20 years after she died. And that's just the start. One day there'll be a huge amount of money paid into the account and then transferred out the day after, sometimes five figure sums. Hilda it's crazy, impossible"

"How can her pensions still get paid if she's dead?"

"Well, Lapley & Hinstock were executors of Aunt Mary's will and she also signed a Lasting Power Of Attorney so the firm had control of her finances. If someone neglected to tell the Ministry Of Pensions and her ex employer she'd died they'd just continue making the payments"

"But Aunt Mary would be, let me work it out, well over 100 years old now. Does nobody check these things? What about the bank? Don't they think it's a bit strange?"

"Hilda, nobody checks anything these days. None of Aunt Mary's relatives including us bothered to check that Lapley & Hinstock had told the pension payers that she'd died. Why would we? The payments would just continue forever. And the banks are staffed by kids in call centres who just react to what customers tell them. They're not trained bankers, they don't have to pass any bankers' exams and haven't had to for decades. The old skills are all gone. What am I going to do?"

"So the bank would continue running an account for someone aged say 160 if there were regular activity on the account?"

"I don't know. I don't suppose it's ever been put to the test but I wouldn't be surprised"

"How did you discover this, Tina?"

"I was doing today's filing and amongst them was Aunt Mary's file. Very noticeable name of course. I wondered what could possibly be going on with aunty's affairs after all these years so I had a look"

"Which solicitor is working the case?"

"Laura King"

"Oh I know her. Ex wife of that dreadful Simon King the builder. If he had his way within six months this town would look like a miniature version of Milton Keynes. Did you speak to Mrs King about it?"

"No. Not yet anyway. But if she's handling the case she must be aware the client died over 20 years ago. Suppose it's some sort of fraud?"

"There's no suppose about it. Who is the senior partner at Lapley & Hinstock nowadays?"

"Brian Atchley but he's on holiday for three weeks"

"Late November is a strange time of the year to go on holiday. Where's he gone?"

"The Bahamas"

"The first thing I think of when I hear 'Bahamas' mentioned is offshore accounts, tax dodging and every other kind of financial sleaze imaginable. And that's before we get onto the drugs trade. What was that other name you mentioned, Tina?"

"Selwyn Myles. He's from Market Repton but went to work overseas many years ago. Made his will with us and signed a Lasting Power Of Attorney. He keeps a UK bank account open, a pension arrangement and several savings accounts. I only had a quick glance at his records but I saw a similar pattern to Aunt Mary, money in and out of his account regularly. Have you heard of him?"

"No I don't think so but I know a friend who may. I'm meeting her tomorrow at the golf club, I'll ask her"

"Hilda please don't mention any of this to your friend or to anyone else"

"Of course I won't. Listen, Tina, don't do anything about this until I've spoken to my friend about - what was his name again?"

"Selwyn Myles"

Hilda wrote the name down and Tina pointed out it was Myles with a Y.

"Are you going home now, Tina, or back to work?"

"I've finished for the day. I'm off home now"

"Right, I'll phone you tomorrow night and tell you what I've discovered"

Mrs Boyce-Harmon was in her mid eighties and had lived in Market Repton all her life. She had been a local councillor for over forty years and only discontinued in this role when the local councils were abolished on the formation of Repton Unitary Authority. She knew everything worth knowing about Market Repton. She held the position of Honorary Life President of Market Repton Golf Club. Hilda Judd kept Mrs Boyce-Harmon informed of present day council affairs and MrsBoyce-Harmon provided Hilda with any historical detail most other people had forgotten about or never knew in the first place.

The day following her cousin Tina's visit Hilda met Mrs Boyce-Harmon in the club house of Market Repton Golf Club for one of their regular chinwags. Pleasantries done, gin and tonics served the two women got down to some serious gossip.

"Do you know the name Selwyn Myles, dear?" Hilda asked her friend

"Rings a faint bell, why do you ask?"

"Oh the name cropped up yesterday when I was talking to my cousin, Tina, who thinks Selwyn Myles comes from Market Repton and has been working overseas for many years. The name doesn't mean a thing to me but I thought I'd ask you"

"Let me think. Yes, I knew his father. Clever lot, made a fortune in engineering in Birmingham then moved here. His father joined this golf club, won a trophy if I remember rightly. It was decades ago of course. There should be a picture on the wall. We usually take photographs of all our trophy award ceremonies. Let's see if I can find it"

The two friends got up and walked to the club room's end wall where stood a trophy cabinet. On the wall on either side of the cabinet were symmetrically hung framed photographs of trophy awardees. After a few moments study Mrs Boyce-Harmon found the one she was looking for.

"There. That's me presenting the trophy to Nelson Myles for best newcomer of the year"

Mrs Judd found herself staring into the smiling, black face of Selwyn Myles's father.

"So Selwyn Myles is also bla….Afro-cari….a person of colour whatever we're supposed to say now?"

"Of course" replied Mrs Boyce-Harmon

"Do you know what became of the two of them?"

"If I remember rightly Nelson Myles used to tell us it was his plan to go back to the Caribbean island his grandparents came from and spend a few years playing golf in a decent climate. Used to say he'd made so much money he could probably afford to buy the island"

"And what about his son Selwyn"

"I don't think I ever met him personally but he was just as clever as his father, went into engineering. I believe he went off building railways all over the world. He'd be retired by now or approaching it. Like I said, clever lot".

That evening Hilda telephoned her cousin Tina and passed on what she'd learned about Selwyn Myles. Hilda suggested Tina keep quiet about what she'd seen from the files at work until Brian Atchley returned from holiday and then ask Brian some innocent sounding general questions about activity on elderly clients' accounts.

CHAPTER 19

Chain Reaction

At work the following day in late November Tina Proudfoot tried to exclude from her thoughts what she'd seen in her employer's records for her late Great Aunt Mrs Mary Montgomery-Gradbach. It was going to be a challenging day. In the staff room for their morning coffee break she and Audrey Hinstock and Laura King engaged in assorted chit chat about last night's television, the approaching festive break, where their annual Christmas staff meal should take place and next year's holiday plans.

Mention of holidays was the cue Tina needed.

"Has Brian been to the Bahamas before?" she asked as nonchalantly as she could

"I'm not sure" Audrey started "I know Brian and his wife Betty usually have a holiday in the sun at this time of the year to get away from the gloom and misery here. I'm aware they like Florida and the Canary Islands and they went to Cuba once but the Bahamas may be somewhere new for them"

"Perhaps they're checking potential retirement destinations. Spend a few years in the warm while they're still reasonably fit and active" suggested Laura King

"Has he said anything about moving abroad when he retires?" Tina enquired

"Has he?" Audrey asked Laura

"He might have mentioned it but I can't remember anything specific. Isn't it something we all think about during the Winter months? Anything to distract us from the endless dark and cold of November and December" Laura added

"Well he's back next week so we'll ask him" Tina said. With that they changed the subject.

Morning break over the three returned to their duties. Tina avoided looking again at the computer records for her great aunt aware that each and every access of a computer record is electronically registered. And once such an access is recorded it is impossible to remove it. But Tina did retrieve and open the paper file for Selwyn Myles. She went back through a few years of documentation until she found the letter she'd dealt with some years earlier, the letter from the pretty sounding overseas address. Tina re-read the letter.

~

A full meeting of Repton Unitary Authority took place on the final Thursday of each month, excluding December. Councillor Mrs Hilda Judd always took the train from Market Repton to Repton Magna to attend these meetings. The council chamber was within walking distance of Repton Magna railway station. Just after midday Hilda was walking the short distance from her home to Market Repton railway station when she spotted one of Simon King's vans parked outside number 22 Station Road. Simon King himself was standing outside the property motionless and staring at the house.

Hilda had learned through the town's gossip grapevine that the solicitor Laura King was now occupying the first floor flat having moved from Birmingham. The rumour mongers had also observed that it was the flat formerly occupied by the disappeared Carl Ramsey with whom, it was thought, Mrs King had been having 'an affair'. But as yet Hilda and her cronies had failed to identify the occupant of the ground floor flat. Hilda decided to seize the moment and be as pleasant as she could with Simon King.

"Hello, Mr King, I'm on my way to the monthly council meeting at Repton Magna. From all accounts you did an excellent job of converting Mrs Edge's house into two flats". This was a total lie. There had been no 'accounts' excellent or otherwise but it was a polite starter.

"Thank you, Mrs Judd. Yes, the work went well"

"And we hear your ex wife is now in residence in the first floor flat. Are the two of you heading for a reconciliation?"

Simon almost laughed out loud. Clearly the gossip grapevine had some serious shortcomings.

"That's not very likely. We divorced nearly twenty years ago. No, we're not reconciling although we get on well"

"That's always a good thing. I was just wondering - who lives in the ground floor flat? I'm not asking you to betray any confidences because it's public information from the register of voters". But Simon knew his pal Andy Edge was concerned about the apparent absence of his ground floor tenant and also realised how useful Mrs Judd could be as a source of information. He decided it couldn't do any harm to answer Hilda's question.

"A man named Selwyn Myles is the tenant". He wasn't expecting the reaction he witnessed, Mrs Judd's jaw dropped, she seemed to go pale and for what Simon thought must be the first time in her adult life was rendered speechless. "Whatever is the matter, Mrs Judd? Looks like you've seen a ghost"

"I….no….it's just that….er…..must rush for my train"

Simon wondered why Mrs Judd had been so shaken at the mention of the name Selwyn Myles. Hilda, once installed on her train, wondered why Mr King had been staring at 22 Station Road.

~

Late in the afternoon of that same November day Tina Proudfoot finished her day's work, said goodbye to her colleagues, put her coat on and started her 35 minutes walk home. It had already gone dark. Immediately her thoughts turned to the letter in Selwyn Myles's file. The information in that letter could mean only one thing - major financial irregularities. And as Laura King was working the case she had to be involved.

Tina was approaching the dual carriageway to the west of Market Repton town centre. The road was at its busiest as the evening rush hour was well underway and she should have been concentrating on crossing the road safely but her mind was in a state of turmoil about her discoveries and what she should do next. Her cousin Hilda had suggested Tina wait until Brian Atchley returned to the office and then seek his advice. Could there be an innocent explanation? Surely not given what she'd read in the letter in Selwyn Myles's file.

Tina reached the main road with its four crowded lanes of traffic - buses and cars taking people home, Royal Mail vans heading back to their depot on the nearby industrial estate and huge heavy goods vehicles thundering past as fast as the traffic flow would allow. But Tina barely noticed it today, her thoughts were racing through her head as she tried to make sense of what she'd uncovered.

Tina pressed the button to activate the pedestrian crossing signals and then stepped into the road without looking or even thinking about the traffic. The blaring horn of a lorry had Tina jumping back onto the pavement. The lights changed, the traffic stopped and Tina made it safely to the other side of the road. Now it was a short walk along a connecting road then Tina turned into the quiet lane which led to her house. No traffic to think about now, just a few hundred yards to go and she'd be home.

Tina became distracted from her thoughts by the sound of a vehicle engine revving loudly behind her. 'Some silly boy racer' she thought. She turned around to discover the source of the noise but was dazzled by the vehicle's headlights which were switched to full beam. The white van mounted the pavement, hurtled towards Tina then struck her forcefully flinging her through the air. Her head hit a tree. She was dead before she hit the ground.

PC Andy Edge was working the late turn 4pm until 12am at Repton Magna police station. His boss Inspector Prisha Gayan had recently given Andy a task, something he'd done many times before and really enjoyed - mentoring a new recruit. In police jargon it was known as puppy walking. The youngster, Mike Perez, had completed basic training and was now to be let loose upon the Great British Public. His shifts had been rostered to coincide with Andy's so he could accompany Andy on his call-outs and learn the day to day practicalities of police work.

Just after 6pm the emergency call handlers took details from a concerned citizen about a vehicle blaze she'd just seen. Something was on fire on one of the streets on the small business park behind Repton Magna railway station. Andy and his new charge Mike were dispatched to the incident. Everything was a new adventure to Mike who even thought that working until midnight was exciting.

"So what'll we be doing first, Andy?" Mike asked as they ran towards their police car

"Look to see if anyone needs medical attention, make sure the road is clear so the fire service get a clear run, it's a narrow road so we'll have to close it to all other traffic"

They arrived at the scene within 5 minutes and saw a fireball lighting up the now quiet street. Fortunately it was a cul de sac road with several small business units all of which had already closed for the day. There was nobody in sight.

"Sometimes, Mike, we can have a go at a small blaze with the fire extinguisher in the car but it won't have any effect on a blaze as fierce as this"

"And if there's anybody inside that car or whatever it is they'll be burned to ashes by now, Andy"

"So you won't get to practise your first aid skills tonight"

The fire engine arrived, the crew descended from it and soon extinguished the blaze leaving a blackened metallic shell from which poured thick black smoke. It was impossible to identify the make of the vehicle but from its shape it appeared to be a small van.

"What now, Andy?" the enthusiastic youngster asked

"When it's cooled down we'll get it shifted back to the police yard and try to identify it. Numbers plates have melted so we'll try and identify it from its VIN. Remember what that is, Mike?"

"Vehicle Identification Number"

"Correct. And if we manage to retrieve the VIN we can trace the vehicle's latest registered keeper".

- "What?"

- "Is it done?"

- " 'course"

- "Where's the van?"

- "Torched it behind Repton Magna railway station then got a train back home to Birmingham".

CHAPTER 20

Wow

Birmingham - many years ago

George and Marjorie Edge's careers of deception began with a house clearance enquiry. Their antiques business was then in its infancy and their small shop was stocked mainly with items acquired from the homes of their own relatives, friends and neighbours - small items of furniture, second rate framed prints, third rate framed original paintings, Staffordshire figures, the family silver, costume jewellery.

There were also items regularly brought to them by a young man who seemed to have an endless collection of what he called aunts and grandparents who were anxious to get rid of their possessions. The Edges would pay him a few pounds for a bag full of, for example, hallmarked silver and sell it on for a few hundred. Then the young man would disappear for a few months and when they next saw him he'd have a paler complexion and another amateur tattoo clearly done by a cellmate. Fortunately the young man's seemingly inexhaustible collection of elderly relatives all appeared to reside across the other side of Birmingham, far from the Edges' shop. But for a few years until he disappeared permanently he had been a regular source of quite decent stolen goods.

Then one day when George Edge was in the shop on his own a man in his early forties entered in a hurry and asked George :

"Do you do house clearances?"

"Oh yes we do those" replied George although they had never actually done one and he wasn't entirely certain what the term even meant

"Right. My father died last month, the estate's been finalised and now I just want the house emptying as quickly as possible. I live in Canada and for business reasons can't remain in this country much longer. How much do you charge?"

How much do we CHARGE? thought George, surely he means 'how much will you give me for the house contents?'

"Well of course it depends on how large the house is and how many items you'd like us to remove" George bluffed

"It's a four bedroomed detached house in Mulberry Avenue and I want every room emptying so I can sell the place. My father was a widower. My mother died five years ago. I have to get back to Canada for my work"

"I see. Give me the full address please Mr ….?"

"Cork, Adrian Cork". Mr Cork supplied the full address adding "It's a short walk from here. Can you have a look through the entire house within the next day or two and let me know as soon as possible how much you'd charge for clearing the place. Here's my card with my local phone number. Let me know when you can visit and I'll meet you there to let you in. We can proceed from there"

"Would tomorrow afternoon be convenient?"

"Yes fine I'll meet you at the house at 3pm tomorrow" and with that the busy Mr Cork rushed out of the shop. At 6pm George closed the shop, walked home and reported this conversation to Marjorie.

"Mulberry Avenue you say, some decent properties along there and usually well furnished. You're sure he's paying us not the other way around?"

"No, Marjorie. He said to me twice he wants to know how much we'd charge him for emptying the place"

"Did he appear to be sane?"

"Yes, just in some great rush to get back to Canada. I'm meeting him at the house at 3pm tomorrow"

"We'll both meet him at 3pm tomorrow"

By 4pm next day they'd agreed to empty the house of all its contents for £400. To sound professional and to convince Mr Cork they knew what they were talking about they said they'd do so by the end of the week although they had no idea at first how this could be achieved. Once returned home they discussed the logistics of the task, decided upon renting a large van and moving as much of the small stuff as possible into the shop and storing the rest of it temporarily in their own home which was a smallish three bedroomed semi detached house even if it might mean filling every square inch of every room they had. This proved to be the case.

At the end of the week Mr Cork declared himself satisfied, gave Marjorie £400 in cash, engaged a firm of estate agents to sell his late father's house and booked the next available flight back to Canada.

Over the following days George and Marjorie conducted an inventory of what they now had on their hands. They took the beds and soft furnishings to the local council tip. Everything else they deemed sellable. It seemed too good to be true, it was mostly decent stuff which would keep the shop stocked for months. Some of the pictures they'd removed were re-hung onto the walls of the shop and it was while doing this task they made a startling discovery.

They had made enquiries of their local friends and acquaintances about the Cork family and learned that Adrian Cork's wealthy maternal grandparents had fled eastern Europe in 1938 bringing with them everything they could carry. They headed west and ended up in Birmingham, England.

They made the sensible decision to leave furniture and clothing behind and carry with them small valuable items. They took from their walls their most treasured pictures, removed them from their frames and packed into their cases as many of them as possible. Once established in England they re-framed the pictures and hung them on their walls. And there many of them remained until George and Marjorie Edge arrived with their rented van.

Initially all the stock was taken to the Edges' home which by now looked like a fully stocked warehouse from where they selected items to take to their shop for sale. One day George Edge was at the top of the stairs carrying more stuff than he could safely manage when he dropped a framed picture. It bounced all the way down the stairs and by the time it came to rest on the tiled hall floor the frame had split.

"Shame, but it wasn't a very attractive frame anyway. We'll get it re-framed" Marjorie said

"The old frame is coming off in chunks and it doesn't seem to have been attached properly to the backing board. Hello, what's this? Look here, Marjorie, there are two canvases here one on top of the other. The original picture has been covered over"

"Perhaps they liked the top one better. I can't imagine why, it's just a dull rural scene. Get it off and let's see what's underneath"

They noticed the second picture had been folded over the original and attached to the four edges of the backing board with small tacks.

"I can't get these tacks out, Marjorie. Looks like they were hammered in about a hundred years ago"

"Somebody seems to have gone to a lot of trouble. We'll have to cut it off. Hand me a sharp knife"

Marjorie slowly and carefully cut around the edges of the second picture and peeled it back to reveal what it was concealing. A portrait of an elegant woman was gradually exposed done in oils in art nouveau style with the image created using a multi-layered, mosaic effect. The predominant colour was gold. Both George and Marjorie recognised the artist's groundbreaking style immediately.

"It can't be" whispered George

"Why would anyone go to so much trouble to hide a fake?" questioned Marjorie.

In the bottom left corner the artist had written his name in capital letters, first name above the surname the way he usually did :

GUSTAV
KLIMT

"George, if this is a genuine Klimt it'll be worth millions. First step is to get it authenticated and valued"

"First step is to check all these other framed pictures to see what else we have here" George suggested. And so they did. And they discovered a concealed pencil sketch of a bird and a bull signed 'Pablo Picasso'.

"Neither of us is an expert, Marjorie, could be some sort of hoax. I still can't believe it"

"So we show them to an expert" Marjorie replied

"They'll want to know where we got them from, provenance"

"We are bona fide antique dealers, George. All we need to say is that a client who wishes to remain anonymous has asked us to get these two pictures authenticated and valued for insurance purposes"

So they contacted the Birmingham representative of Sothebys who arranged for an expert from their London based authentication unit to visit the Edges. Within a few days she was looking at the two pictures in the Edges' cluttered home.

"My first task is to decide on the likelihood of their being genuine and then if it's worthwhile to recommend you go to the next stage which would involve both pictures going to London for a while. In my opinion there is a chance the Picasso may be genuine. It's simplicity is the key here. Nobody knows for sure how many works Picasso and Klimt actually did, their catalogues list everything we know about but who knows what else is out there? I'd recommend you allow me to take both of them to London".

Two months later the Edges learned that Sotheby's London authentication unit had declared both of the works genuine. An advisor returned them to the Edges.

"The sketch has been analysed by our Picasso experts and the painting likewise by our Klimt specialist. They're genuine. The Picasso is dated 1895 and he was only 14 years old then. It's little more than a doodle but it would fetch upwards of a million pounds if we put it into an auction. The Klimt is from the start of his gold period in the early 1900s. It's probably one of his private commissions as most of his work was at that time. His work is much rarer. A lot of it was destroyed by the Nazis. So it's potentially much more valuable than the Picasso. It's estimated the Klimt would fetch about six million pounds at auction. What do you intend to do with them?"

"That would not be our decision to make" Marjorie lied "our clients have asked us to get the two items authenticated and valued for insurance purposes. It's up to them to decide but I understand there was no intention of selling. Of course with figures like this they may change their mind"

"If your clients wish for Sotheby's or anyone else to sell the pictures their provenance and ownership would have to be thoroughly investigated first. We'd be happy to do that for them"

"Thank you for all you've done. We'll relay this information to our clients and they'll have to think about what to do next. I would guess the costs of insuring these pictures would be huge?"

"Enormous. Here are the certificates of authenticity for the two items and here's our invoice for the work we've done so far"

After the Sotheby's advisor had departed George and Marjorie Edge sat in stunned silence for several moments. George spoke first -

"Of course there's the moral dimension to consider, Marjorie"

"What do you mean, George?"

"Adrian Cork has mistakenly given us pictures worth millions"

"And how do we know the Cork family didn't acquire them in exactly the same way? Obviously Adrian Cork was unaware of the concealed pictures but if his parents or grandparents had been aware surely they would have made their family aware, at least their next of kin"

"Something else has occurred to me, Marjorie. We can't possibly go into ownership and provenance without contacting the Cork family. And we don't know where they are"

"So we'll keep the pictures and sell them privately" Marjorie replied definitively

"Let's sell one for now and keep the other. See if there are any unsavoury repercussions" George suggested

"We'll have a go at selling the Picasso. He has much more uncatalogued work than Klimt"

"How do we know that if it's uncatalogued?"

"We've visited the Picasso museum in Málaga, George. They scoured the world for every doodle and scribble on the back of a fag packet they could get, framed it all and stuck it on the walls but the only significant collection of Klimt pictures is held by the Austrian government and they got them illegally via Nazi seizures"

"So we sell the Picasso. But how? We can't put it through an auction house. It would have to be a private sale, a collector perhaps who isn't going to lie awake at night worrying about its provenance"

"And where in the world is the best market for private art collectors, George?"

"USA. California and Florida"

"Precisely. I shall take the Picasso to Florida with its certificate of authenticity, visit some of the prominent galleries in Miami, find out who the most discerning local collectors are and take it from there"

"Do you want me to come with you, dear?"

"No, George. Stay here and keep the shop ticking over".

Within a week Marjorie was in Miami putting the plan into action. She had the names of two potential buyers and had chosen which gallery she would prefer to handle the viewings. Both buyers were invited to view. One expressed interest in buying. He brought with him his personal Picasso expert who declared himself satisfied with the drawing's authenticity. A price of $1,100,000 was agreed and transferred to the Edges UK bank account. Marjorie was back in Birmingham less than four weeks after she'd left.

They used the money to buy and stock bigger premises in the middle of the main street of their increasingly affluent area of Birmingham. They decided the painting by Gustav Klimt would be kept as their pension fund.

Their business went from strength to strength and became the essential go-to place for the discerning buyer of quality antiques. They realised and took advantage of the fact that the country was awash with all manner of items whose owners had little concept of their value. Another house clearance produced a collection of ceramics, jewellery and miniature sculptures by the Belgian artist Pierre Caille. A six figure profit was realised. It was time for the Edges to retire. They sold their business premises and their house in Birmingham and kept for themselves a fine collection of the best items from their large stock including the still unnamed and uncatalogued painting by Gustav Klimt. They bought and moved into number 22 Station Road, Market Repton.

In 2004 the United States Supreme Court made their ruling in the case of the Republic of Austria v Altmann at the centre of which was the ownership of the painting 'Portrait Of Adele Bloch Bauer I' (also known as The Lady In Gold) by Gustav Klimt. The artist and his works became more famous than ever. The Edges realised the Klimt painting still in their possession would now be worth at least $40,000,000.

Selling the Klimt would not be such an insurmountable problem. They would take it to Miami or Los Angeles and find a private collector. The problem was the money transfer arrangements. By now money laundering rules imposed upon the reluctant banks by the European Union, the British Government and the Bank Of England meant it would be impossible to move from the USA into Europe the amount of money they expected to raise for the Klimt without arousing attention and questions. The Edges had no idea how to overcome this problem. The solution was to be found just a short walk from 22 Station Road, Market Repton

CHAPTER 21

Design For Life

Market Repton - many years ago

When the Edges retired and moved from Birmingham to Market Repton they engaged Lapley & Hinstock to do all their legal work. So far that had amounted only to the conveyancing procedures for the purchase of 22 Station Road. Soon after their move had been accomplished and they had settled into their new home they each prepared a new will. At that time the firm's two partners were Ben Hinstock (Audrey's father, also known as Ben Junior) and Brian Atchley, a nephew of the last of the Lapleys.

Ben's father Ben Senior was then aged 67 and had retired from full time practice but acted as their consultant as and when required. Ben Junior was on holiday when Mr and Mrs Edge made the arrangements for the preparation of their new wills so Ben Senior arrived at the firm's office to meet the Edges and complete the legalities. Ben Senior looked like a small town lawyer should look - tall, grey haired, clean shaven, charcoal grey three piece suit, white shirt, grey tie, grey eyes, glasses with black frames and very shiny lenses.

The wills were simple affairs. Each spouse left everything to the other with the stipulation that should the spouse pre-decease them then everything would go to their only child - their son Greg.

Business completed Ben Senior seemed happy to chat with these two new clients for a while, he had nothing else to do that day.

"I understand you ran an antiques business in Birmingham for many years"

"Yes" George Edge replied "we started the business over twenty years ago when our son Greg was ten years old

"What was the business called?"

"We did consider calling it 'Cutting Edge Antiques' until we realised it is a contradiction in terms so we went with simply 'Edge Antiques'"

"And has Greg now taken over the business?"

"No, Greg has no interest in antiques, he did an engineering degree course at university"

"Just as well really" Marjorie added "because we've sold the business and all the stock except for a few favourite things we've kept for ourselves"

"I've no doubt 22 Station Road is exquisitely furnished" Ben Senior offered

"We like to think so" said Marjorie. "We had the business for around twenty years which is really a very short period of time in the antiques business but we had one or two lucky breaks didn't we, George ?"

"Quite extraordinary really although being in a well heeled area of Birmingham helped a lot" George replied with a knowing sideways glance at his wife

"Have you completely retired from business now? You're both still quite young to be retiring if you don't mind my saying, only in your early fifties"

"No we don't mind your saying that at all. Like we said we got lucky, right place at the right time. We still keep our eyes open for anything of interest. This town for example, Market Repton, like our suburb of Birmingham has a fine stock of Victorian and Edwardian homes and I'd guess most of them contain valuable furniture and family heirlooms and most people don't realise the true value of what they've got" Marjorie suggested

"I wonder if I may ask you something?" Ben Senior enquired. He chose his next words carefully then continued "I have access to a collection of items, jewellery mainly, which I am considering selling but I need advice on how to go about it, which collectors may be interested and how to proceed to contact potential buyers without having to advertise. I would prefer to avoid going through an auction room. This is a bit awkward really but some of the items don't seem to have a satisfactory traceable ownership history"

The thought went through Marjorie's head "Is this man asking us to fence some stolen goods? And I wonder what 'I have access to' actually means?". Marjorie said "We still have several contacts. We'll be happy to help in any way we can. Now may I ask you something?"

"Please do, Mrs Edge"

"What's the maximum amount of money we could transfer out of the UK without triggering money laundering alarm bells?"

Ben Senior should have been taken aback by this question but he wasn't. He sensed a coded conversation had been underway between the three of them so replied -

"What sort of figure would we be looking at, Mrs Edge, for the sake of discussion?"

"For the sake of discussion let's say £30,000,000"

Ben Senior was now thoroughly taken aback but managed to continue "Obviously a figure like that would produce questions from local banks but talking hypothetically if I were moving that sort of money around I wouldn't move that sort of money around. I'd break it down into smaller amounts and I wouldn't use local banks. The sudden arrival of a large amount of money would be unusual in most bank accounts so would draw attention but some special accounts have a history of handling large sums regularly almost to the point where it becomes normal"

"Talking hypothetically how would one access such an account?" Marjorie asked as innocently as possible

"By becoming a client of a firm which ran a number of such accounts. Changing the subject completely have the two of you ever considered a Lasting Power Of Attorney arrangement? We often recommend clients think about this at the time a will is prepared". Ben Senior explained the options offered by his firm in this area. George and Marjorie became very interested in what they were learning.

"Let me put a scenario to you" George suggested "let's say a client....er....realised an asset in for example the USA and that a large sum of money were involved which the client wished to transfer out of the USA but not to the UK not even to Europe but that client didn't have access to the USA banking system. How would that client get that sum of money to where they wanted it?"

('Well done, George' Marjorie thought)

Ben Senior replied "I don't suppose you've ever noticed the small print at the foot of each letter page on our business stationery. I'd be very surprised if you had. It says amongst other things 'Associates in most major cities in Australia, New Zealand, Canada and USA'. This isn't some form of idle boasting intended to impress our clients, like I said hardly anybody ever reads this footnote. There are legal firms in those countries with whom we are associated. It started many decades ago and is a consequence of so many British people having relatives in those countries. Normally these link ups are used in day to day matters of civil law where for example the terms of a will originally drawn up in the UK are executed in say Australia. One of our associated law firms in Australia would oversee matters on our behalf.

It's quite normal to have these overseas associates, most firms of solicitors in this country, even the smallest ones, would have and nowadays with so many British people retiring to countries around the Mediterranean link ups with Spanish, Greek, Italian etc law firms are increasingly commonplace.

But here at Lapley & Hinstock we specialise in facilitating legal and financial arrangements for British citizens who need to handle some issue in one of the countries I mentioned - Australia, New Zealand, Canada, USA.

So to answer your question, Mr Edge, if a British citizen who was one of our clients realised an asset in the USA we would contact our nearest American associated law firm who would open a client account for them into which the money realised could be placed. Then when the client decided their chosen destination for that money our associate would handle the money transfer.

If we were to hold a Lasting Power Of Attorney for that client the transactions could be completed by ourselves with minimum contact with the client"

"This is all very interesting information, Mr Hinstock" Marjorie continued after a moments silence during which they absorbed what Ben Senior had said "and presumably these overseas associates have associates of their own in other countries which the client could make use of?"

"Yes that would be the case, Mrs Edge"

"Do you have associates in Miami and Los Angeles?" George asked

"Yes"

Later that day back at 22 Station Road George and Marjorie Edge discussed a plan.

CHAPTER 22

Us And Them

At 9am on a Friday in late November Hilda Judd received a telephone call from Ray Proudfoot, the husband of her cousin Tina. The distraught Ray had telephoned to inform Hilda of the tragic events of the previous night. His wife's broken body had been discovered by a dog walker in the lane leading to their house. Tina had it seemed been the victim of a hit and run. The vehicle and its driver had not yet been traced.

"Ray that's terrible news, I don't know what to say. Tina came to see me earlier this week. Where are you now?"

"I'm at home"

"Is there anyone with you?"

"Yes, my sister came over last night and stayed here with me. She's going to stay for a few days"

"Right. You shouldn't be on your own at this time. Ray did Tina say anything to you about something that was worrying her at work?"

"Yes, she mentioned something was playing on her mind but didn't go into details. Why?"

"Oh it's probably nothing, Ray. Forget it. Listen, Ray, if there's anything I can do don't hesitate to call me. I can be over in a few minutes"

And with that their conversation ended. Hilda had deliberately dismissed the issue as 'probably nothing' to avoid causing Ray any more distress. Hilda didn't really think it was 'probably nothing'. Quite the reverse. Hilda thought her cousin Tina had discovered serious financial malpractice at her place of work and now Tina was dead.

A few minutes walk from Hilda's house Simon King had been having his breakfast and considering a course of action. He had one or two small jobs to attend to for regular customers while his men were working on a large property extension at the edge of town. But Simon decided that before he started work he would visit Hilda Judd and speak to her about Selwyn Myles.

A few minutes after her distressing conversation with Ray Proudfoot Hilda's doorbell rang and she was surprised to see Simon King standing at her door. Simon noticed that for the second time in two days Mrs Judd looked like she'd just seen a ghost.

"Mr King, what can I do for you?"

"Mrs Judd are you alright?"

"No, not really, I've just had some very distressing news"

"I'll come back another time. It's probably not important"

"No come in, Mr King". Hilda escorted Simon King into the sitting room overlooking the perfectly square park opposite the front of her house.

"Sit down, Mr King. What's on your mind?"

"Thank you. I just wondered if there's anything you can tell me about Selwyn Myles. When I mentioned him to you yesterday I got the impression you'd come across the name before"

Selwyn Myles - one of the names her cousin Tina had mentioned shortly before being killed. She needed to know why Simon King was interested.

"Firstly could you tell me why you're asking, Mr King?"

"Yes alright. The new owner of 22 Station Road is my friend Andrew Edge and he is the grandson of the late Mrs Marjorie Edge. He inherited the property from his grandmother. My pal Andy engaged my company to do the building work at number 22. Almost immediately after the flats were completed a man named Selwyn Myles entered into a tenancy agreement for the ground floor flat. He hadn't seen the flat. It was all done through the internet, he was working overseas. He started paying the rent and still is paying it but as far as we can tell he hasn't spent any time at the flat yet. There's no furniture in the flat and Andy Edge has noticed that in the 15 months since the letting started no electricity, gas or water has been used. But Mr Myles continues to pay the rent. And Andy has discovered from Repton Magna council offices that he's paying the council tax too. It seems very odd to us and Andy is a bit concerned about it. Then I noticed your reaction to the name yesterday. I just wondered if there's anything you can tell me about Selwyn Myles that I can relay to Andy, you know, to put his mind at rest"

Hilda didn't know what to say. Should she confide in this man? Something was clearly going on at Lapley & Hinstock concerning Selwyn Myles and now her cousin was dead. Was this a coincidence?

"Mr King, Simon, I don't know Selwyn Myles and hadn't heard the name before until a few days ago when my cousin Tina Proudfoot mentioned it. Tina was killed last night in an apparent hit and run incident near her home"

"I'm so sorry to hear that. Is this conversation making matters worse?"

"No, it couldn't get any worse. But it's suggesting something very strange is going on. I think I need to speak to the police"

Simon wasn't expecting this reaction so asked "About your cousin?" Hilda didn't answer Simon's question but instead asked -

"Do you or your friend Andy know the nature of Mr Myles's work overseas?"

"Yes, he's a railway engineer recently retired and he wanted to return here to live back in England"

So this information at least matched what Hilda had learned from her friend Mrs Boyce-Harmon. Simon continued "What is going on that you think is strange? Is it in connection with your cousin or this Selwyn Myles?"

"Maybe both. My cousin Tina had come across something very odd at work concerning both Selwyn Myles and also a long deceased relative of ours"

"Where did your cousin work, Mrs Judd?"

"Please call me Hilda. She was the legal secretary at Lapley & Hinstock in the High Street, had been for many years. She told me she'd seen something odd concerning Selwyn Myles and our great aunt and now she's dead"

Both Hilda and Simon were trying to connect a different line of dots. Hilda was thinking Selwyn Myles - Great Aunt Mary - fraud - Lapley & Hinstock - Tina dead.
Simon was thinking Selwyn Myles - Lapley & Hinstock - Laura King - Carl Ramsey missing.

"Mrs Judd, Hilda, you don't think your cousin's death is anything other than an accident do you?"

"I don't know what to think right now, Simon. But there's something going on here and I think the police need to be told what we've both found out. Problem is the police under that clown Max Graden have had their resources slashed and their ability to undertake costly and time consuming enquiries damaged.

Everything we're both talking about is linked to 22 Station Road and Lapley & Hinstock. Has everybody forgotten that estate agent man Carl Ramsey disappeared not long after moving to Station Road? I don't suppose the police are doing anything about that. Then his girlfriend Laura King moves into his flat. Sorry I know she's your ex wife but doesn't that seem a bit odd to you?   And that's before we get onto the mystery of Selwyn Myles"

"Oh, I've just remembered something else, Hilda. Just before I started work on 22 Station Road Andy told me that after his grandmother had died her white van had been stolen from her driveway and some of her antiques and paintings had also disappeared. Of course it might be nothing to do with what we've just been talking about"

"So more weird goings-on at 22 Station Road. Did your friend report the thefts to the police?"

"He reported the van as stolen but mainly for insurance purposes. He didn't mention the missing items from the house. He couldn't be certain what had gone missing, wouldn't be able to give any descriptions. He'd just noticed blank walls where pictures used to hang and empty shelves where small statues and ornaments used to be displayed. But there's something else - Andy is a police constable and has been advised by his bosses not to involve himself with the enquiries"

"But it sounds like there aren't any enquiries underway. I see another hurdle here. Unless the police are pointed in the right direction they're never going to connect all these things"

"So what do we do, Hilda?"

"I now have a personal involvement, my cousin was killed last night. I'm going to insist I speak with a senior detective. Of course we used to have a police station here until that Graden creature closed it down. A town this size with an increasing population needs a permanent police presence but.......oh I'm sorry, Simon, I've gone into a party political rant...... the nearest police station now is at Dainford but their CID set up is small. And if some sort of fraud is at the bottom of this it'd be beyond them anyway. I think I'll go to Repton Magna police station. I'm going to make a few notes, let's recap what we've said so far"

So they did and Hilda wrote down the main points. Simon decided his next move would be to inform his mate Andy Edge of this turn of events.

"Once I start on something, Simon, I don't give up. I'm not going to allow the police to treat Tina's death as a random hit and run incident. It happened in the quiet lane leading to Tina's house. It's a dead end for cars, the lane peters out into a footpath. The idea of an accidental hit and run on a road like that is nonsense. After I've spoken to one of the detectives at Repton Magna is there any way your pal Andy can keep an eye on the case?"

"Andy has been told by his sergeant and his inspector to have no involvement with the case even if it isn't a case yet. If he looks at any of their computers it leaves some sort of permanent electronic trail. But I know one of Andy's closest mates in the police is a detective sergeant at Repton Magna. Andy can tell him off the record everything we've been talking about"

"And you tell me your pal Andy has never seen Selwyn Myles. Has anybody seen him since he left the country years ago?"

"I know the estate agents haven't. All their contact with him was on the internet. Me and Andy guess Carl Ramsey must have seen him because they were neighbours and when Andy went to 22 Station Road to say hello to Laura after she'd taken over the tenancy of the first floor flat she told Andy that she'd spoken to him. That's how she knew he's a retired railway engineer"

"Did Laura King give Andy a physical description of Selwyn Myles?"

"She just said he was a recently retired man so we're assuming he's in his sixties"

"Nothing else?"

"No. I don't suppose Andy thought to ask her what he looked like, why do you ask, Hilda?"

"My friend Mrs Boyce-Harmon knew the family when they lived here decades ago. Selwyn's father Nelson was a member of Market Repton Golf Club. They were a wealthy, talented family. Nelson Myles decided to spend some years towards the end of his life living on the Caribbean island of his grandparents. Both Nelson and Selwyn are of Afro-Caribbean descent"

"Right, interesting. Of course everyone has assumed Selwyn Myles is white"

"Of course they have. Understandable in a way. Market Repton is one of the least ethnically diverse towns in the British Isles"

"I'm seeing Andy for a drink tomorrow. If it's OK with you Hilda I'll tell him about everything we've been saying"

"Of course you must. Let's see, it's Friday today, I'll try to get to Repton Magna police station this afternoon. Simon, how about we keep in touch about all this? We could have a regular meeting and discuss any developments. Could you possibly ask your pal Andy to find out from his friend in the police what's happening with their enquiries into Tina's death?"

"Yes of course. In that case I'll phone Andy this afternoon instead of waiting until tomorrow night to tell him all this" and with that the two parted company. Hilda phoned Repton Magna police station and asked to speak to a detective inspector in the CID office. An appointment was made for her to speak to DI Ruby Scott later that day. Hilda now had an ally with direct contact into Mid Land Police. She regretted previously thinking of her new friend as a shaved headed ape.

CHAPTER 23

Suspicious Minds

In the Criminal Investigation Department at Repton Magna police station a meeting was underway the main subject of which was the fatal hit and run traffic incident in Market Repton the previous evening. It was late morning on Friday 27 November and Detective Inspector Ruby Scott was addressing her officers amongst whom was Detective Sergeant Meredith Wynne.

"The Scene Of Crime Officers have finished their initial survey of the road where it happened. Odd thing is it's not where we'd usually expect a hit and run. A cul de sac lane with just a few houses, the driver would have to turn the vehicle around and leave the same way he entered. I've never come across anything like it before"

"What do we know about the victim ma'am?" a young detective constable asked

"Name Tina Proudfoot, early fifties, walking home from work in fact she'd nearly arrived at home when the incident happened, she'd worked for many years as legal secretary at the solicitors Lapley & Hinstock in Market Repton High Street" DI Scott replied

Meredith Wynne absorbed this information in stunned silence. Lapley & Hinstock again, for the moment he would just listen and learn.

"Any info on the vehicle involved ma'am?" another detective asked

"Nothing yet. But less than an hour after we think the hit and run happened one of our units attended a vehicle blaze behind Repton Magna railway station. No sign of the driver but the fire was so intense some of the firefighters have said unofficially it looks like an accelerant was used. The vehicle's now in our yard and first signs are it's what's left of a Citroen Berlingo van and it seems someone had filed off the VIN so identifying it is going to be impossible now. Of course we don't know if it was the vehicle involved in the death of Tina Proudfoot, it may be unconnected. Forensics are still examining paint fragments removed from Tina's clothing and we should know for certain tomorrow the make of the vehicle involved"

The words 'Citroen Berlingo van' sent another shock wave through Meredith Wynne. DI Scott was continuing -

"I've got someone from Market Repton coming to see me this afternoon about this case. Says she's a local councillor and the deceased is her cousin. Claims to have some information. But right now I want all the CCTV footage from the railway station checked for the 2 hour period 6pm to 8pm last night. Let's see if any known faces appear. Do it now please and let me know the results by 5pm. By then I'll know what this councillor woman has to say"

At 1pm when he knew his pal Andy Edge would be taking his midday break Simon King phoned Andy and told him about his meeting with Hilda Judd that morning, about the death of Tina Proudfoot, about Tina finding something worrying at Lapley & Hinstock and about the ethnic background of Selwyn Myles. Andy exchanged text messages with Meredith Wynne and they agreed to meet in the pub near to the police station at 6pm.

Between 2pm and 4pm DI Scott listened to what Councillor Mrs Hilda Judd had to say - allegations of financial irregularities at Lapley & Hinstock, her recent conversation with her troubled cousin the now deceased Tina Proudfoot, the unresolved case of Carl Ramsey who disappeared a year ago, the apparent theft of a Citroen Berlingo van from 22 Station Road the same address where Carl Ramsey had lived, the mystery of the seemingly invisible Selwyn Myles a customer of Lapley & Hinstock. And what did DI Scott intend doing about it all?

By 4pm DI Scott's head was spinning. She spoke by telephone several times a week with her boss Detective Chief Inspector Graham Radway who was based at Mid Land Police HQ in far away Blackbird City.

Ruby Scott was in her late forties, single, tending to overweight, drank just a little too much but it definitely wasn't a problem and at 5' 9" tall and of robust build she could certainly handle it. She had short, curly, prematurely greying hair. DCI Graham Radway was one of her oldest friends and allies within the police. They both understood what real policing should mean and loathed the current box ticking, target chasing madness they had to manage. And that was the crux of the issue. Their work now prioritised management over policing and they both hated it.

Graham Radway usually telephoned Ruby Scott at 5pm on Fridays for the final update of the week, to be kept abreast of developments on anything he needed to know, anything potentially going pear shaped, anything in the pipeline that could use up money or manpower, what to tell Max Graden to keep him quiet or as quiet as possible. Graham was in his early fifties and most of his fair hair had gone about ten years earlier as had his wife.

At 4.30pm Ruby Scott telephoned Graham. This was unusual and Graham knew it meant something serious had happened. After pleasantries had been exchanged Ruby began -

"Graham, have you ever heard the name Hilda Judd?"

"Oh Jeeez no ! I thought we'd heard the last of her"

"Er......am I missing something here?"

"She was one of the last members of the old Police Authority. From the way she went on at the meetings you'd think Market Repton was the crime hotspot of Western Europe. Always going on about wanting boots on the ground and bobbies on the beat and keeping the police station there open 24 hours a day. Then we got Police And Crime Commissioners and Max Graden, the Police Authority ceased to exist and Market Repton police station was closed down. Although compared to what we have to put up with now I'd have Hilda and her cronies on the Police Authority back in a trice even if it was like Jurassic Park with tea and macaroons. So what's happened that involves Hilda Judd?"

"Phew ! Quite a rant, Graham. Well she came to see me today about a fatal hit and run in Market Repton yesterday. Brace yourself, seems she could be right. Market Repton may be a crime hotspot after all"

And Ruby repeated to her boss the complex tale of intrigue she'd spent two hours listening to that afternoon.

"So the thing is, Graham, Hilda Judd maintains her cousin was killed because of what she discovered at work. Claims the solicitors Lapley &

Hinstock are running vast amounts of money through the bank accounts of dead or missing people but it's unclear why"

"But she doesn't have any proof does she?"

"One of the accounts they're allegedly using belongs to some elderly relative of both Hilda Judd and Tina Proudfoot who died yesterday in what now seems like a highly suspicious hit and run. This relative of theirs died over 20 years ago but Mrs Judd said she's going to start digging around. Graham I got the impression she's the sort of person who once they get the bit between their teeth never lets go"

"That's very true annoyingly. I'm going to have to refer this upstairs. An allegation as serious as this about a firm of solicitors is something the Chief Constable will need to know about even though we've got a long way to go before we even pay them a visit. We'll have a daily phone call at 5pm from now on. Tell me everything that happens"

"OK, Graham. My team are reporting back to me at 5pm on some tasks I've set them. I'll be off to the pub later".

Ruby was already sipping a pint of Guinness in a quiet corner of the pub near to Repton Magna police station when she spotted one of her sergeants Meredith Wynne walk in with PC Andrew Edge. Ruby decided to leave them in peace for a while. She'd join them later for her second pint.

Both Andy and his mate Merry knew that the early doors 'swift pint' they'd agreed upon wouldn't involve literally just one pint. Their first drinks served they chose a table.

"I hear you're puppy walking again. How's the new charge getting on, mate?"

"Doing well, at that stage where he's interested in everything. It's quite tiring at times dealing with enthusiasm but I learned today he speaks fluent Spanish"

"Well with a name like Perez he should do"

"Your name's Meredith Wynne and I've never heard you speak a word of Welsh"

"I'm from bloody Wrexham. Nobody speaks Welsh in Wrexham"

"Anyway Mike tells me his dad is Spanish from Algeciras in Andalucia. Dad worked as a traditional British bobby in Gibraltar, seems most of them are actually Spanish men posing as British coppers. He met Mike's mum there when she was in the RAF. Mike was born in the hospital at Algeciras and was brought up on both languages. Then they moved to this country about ten years ago. His dad is now one of the airport policemen at Birmingham.

Young Mike earned some Brownie points today sorting out a problem at the front desk. Unbelievably some people from Honduras turned up in a state about something and they had little command of English. Mike to the rescue. They couldn't believe it when a British copper started talking to them in their own lingo. I can't believe people from Honduras turned up at our nick, that must be a first"

"What and where is Honduras?"

"Country in central America I think"

"So are you and the lad working over the weekend?"

"Tomorrow 8am til 4pm then I'm off to Market Repton for a takeaway and pub crawl with Simon. Got Sunday off"

"Same here except for the takeaway and the pub crawl. So what is it you wanted to tell me, pal?" Merry asked

"You're going to thump me for this" Andy said

"I never hit people who are bigger than me"

"Simon phoned me earlier today. He'd been to see some local councillor woman Hilda Judd mainly to ask her about my tenant Selwyn Myles. Apparently this woman is a right busybody, wants to know everything about everybody. Anyway this is what Simon discovered..........."

And so Andy brought his mate Merry up to date ending with ".....and this Hilda Judd was supposed to be coming in today for an interview with your Inspector Scott....."

So engrossed in their conversation were the two men they hadn't noticed Ruby Scott with a fresh pint of Guinness in her hand approaching their table.

"Hello, boys. Mind if I join you? Just heard you mention Hilda Judd and my name in the same sentence. What have you got to tell me?"

"......er.....well......ma'am it's......." Andy began

"Stop ! We're off duty drinking in a pub. Call me ma'am again in here and I'll smack you one"

"Don't start a fight with her, Andy, she'll win !" Merry said and the three of them roared with laughter. Then for the second time that day Ruby Scott heard about the catalogue of incidents which had occurred in Market Repton since Andy had inherited 22 Station Road from his grandmother.

"Did you know Tina Proudfoot, Andy?" Ruby asked

"I didn't know her name until today but I have met her a couple of times when I've visited Lapley & Hinstock. She's the receptionist, answers the phone, books the appointments, does the meet and greet and stuff. Pleasant middle aged woman"

"Why were you visiting Lapley & Hinstock, Andy?" Ruby again wondered

"They were my grandmother's solicitors. Grandma died in November three years ago and they were the executors of her will. They sorted everything out very quickly. Seems grandma had signed a Lasting Power Of Attorney with them so they could finalise all her financial affairs without troubling anyone else. I hadn't known anything about that and neither had my mum and dad, they live in Perth, Western Australia.

Then they advised me I should make a will as I'd inherited grandma's house and a fortune in cash. The house is 22 Station Road Market Repton. Audrey Hinstock dealt with me. She told me she's the great granddaughter of the man who started the firm nearly a hundred years ago. Anyway when we were doing the will Audrey Hinstock suggested I make Lapley & Hinstock executors of my will and also to think about signing a Lasting Power Of Attorney with them. But I'd already decided who I wanted to be the executor of my will. I said I'd think about the Power Of Attorney thing but that if I went ahead with it I'd nominate my executor. I got the impression Audrey Hinstock was a bit miffed when I said that"

Andy noticed his mate Merry and Merry's boss Ruby were staring at each other in open mouthed silence. Ruby eventually spoke -

"I bet she was miffed"

"….…..er…….why?" a baffled Andy asked

"Andy, mate, don't you see? If you were to go under a bus either literally or metaphorically speaking Lapley & Hinstock would have total control over all your finances. That's how they were able to sort out your gran's affairs so quickly. No need to consult with anyone"

"So? Isn't that a good thing? I was surprised when I heard about it because grandma was sharp and on top of everything but it meant they sorted everything out quickly"

"Andy" Ruby Scott continued "this Hilda Judd woman I saw this afternoon believes her cousin Tina Proudfoot was killed because she accidentally uncovered financial malpractices at Lapley & Hinstock. If you've got total control over someone's bank accounts and you're a crook - well, just think about it !"

The pub was getting busier. It was early Friday evening and workers from nearby offices and shops were pouring in and occupying nearby tables.

"Look, this isn't the place to be discussing this" Ruby said "but there is just one more thing I'll ask you Andy - do you know who your grandma banked with?"

"Not off hand but at home I've got all grandma's personal papers at least all of them I could find in her house. There might be a bank statement amongst them"

"Right. Have a look when you get home please, Andy. If you find anything with a bank name, account number and sort code on it please bring it to me tomorrow" Ruby asked.

"Anyone for any more?" Meredith Wynne asked but as all three of them were back on duty at 8am next morning they finished their drinks and parted company.

Meanwhile in Market Repton Hilda Judd was on the phone. She was speaking in turn to every one of her relatives on the same side of the family as her late great aunt Mrs Mary Montgomery-Gradbach. Hers was a generation which never threw away anything. Someone, somewhere must have kept the documents of her great aunt. Approaching 9pm she was speaking to her elderly uncle Charles the son of her great aunt who thought that most of his late mother's documents were stored somewhere in his house, either the attic or the cellar. Hilda made arrangements to visit him the next day.

CHAPTER 24

Banging On The Door

The final weekend of that November was cold, dark and very wet. It rained non stop for 48 hours. Not such bad news for police officers as incident rates reduced dramatically in bad weather except for road accidents.

When Andy Edge began his shift at 8am on Saturday morning the first thing he did was enter the CID room to tell Meredith Wynne that he had checked all his grandmother's documents and there were no bank papers amongst them. No statements, no cheque books, no correspondence, absolutely nothing connected to his grandmother's banking affairs.

"Doesn't that seem a bit odd to you, Andy?" his friend Merry had asked

"Compared to everything else that's going on I'd say no, not particularly"

"Was your gran internet savvy?"

"Yes. She was on to it straightaway, more so than me" Andy replied

"So she may have done internet banking?"

"Might have. She never mentioned it though, but it wasn't the sort of thing we ever talked about. I only bother with it when I have to. Don't do Facebook, Twitter or any of that social media rubbish. See you later in the canteen" and with that Andy returned to his own department. Meredith Wynne mentioned to his boss DI Ruby Scott that no banking papers had been found for the late Mrs Marjorie Edge.

In the north of County Repton Hilda Judd was having better luck. She arrived at the large home of her Uncle Charles just outside the town of Dainford at midday as arranged the night before. Hilda had used her car and the driving rain had made the seven mile journey slow and unpleasant even though she had taken the usually quiet B9916 back road. Her uncle was in his early eighties and lived alone. He was fit enough to keep his house and garden well maintained.

Ray Proudfoot had telephoned Charles the day before to tell him the sad news about the death of his niece Tina. Now his other niece Hilda was visiting to look for Charles's late mother's banking papers. Charles wondered what Hilda could possibly find of interest in documents at least twenty years old. Charles thought Hilda's only interest was going to council meetings to shout at the other councillors. But Charles had remembered where all of his late mother's papers were stored. They were in boxes in his attic. They hadn't been touched since they were put up there.

Charles explained all this to Hilda after they had had cups of tea, a catch up chat and enquired of each other's health.

"Why on earth do you want to see mother's old papers, Hilda?"

"All I want to find out is which bank aunty used and to make a note of the account number and sort code"

"I can tell you which bank it was. It was Barclays, mother used the same bank all her life. Why do you want the account number, Hilda? The account was closed when mother died"

"Yes you'd expect that wouldn't you but Tina told me just before she died that she'd discovered the account was still open, she didn't understand why. So I'm going to check with the bank if that's alright with you, Uncle Charles"

"Go ahead. Seems a bit strange to me. I can't tell you which boxes in the attic contain the papers you're after. You'll just have to go up there and rummage about"

"I've come prepared in my gardening gear. Is there a light in the attic?"

"Should be. It was working last time I was up there although that'd be about ten years ago".

Like many of the large, old houses in her uncle's road the attic had a staircase leading up into it. Hilda started her search. After less than an hour Hilda was successful. She found a bank statement dated shortly before her great aunt Mary had died in the year 2000 but there were no bank papers from after the date of her death. Hilda withdrew from the dusty box the latest document showing the reference numbers she was looking for and left the attic.

"Did you find anything useful, Hilda?" Charles asked

"Success !" Hilda declared and showed Charles the Barclays Bank statement which of course had the account number and sort code

"What are you going to do with it now you've got it?"

"On Monday I'll contact Barclays and tell them I have reason to believe the account may not have been properly closed and would they please check. I know exactly what they'll say 'can't tell you anything because of the Data Protection Act' or it'll be 'sorry our records don't go back that far'. I'll cross that bridge when I come to it"

"I've prepared us a light lunch, Hilda. Let's eat and chat". So the two of them chatted for a couple of hours about friends and family. Hilda avoided worrying her elderly uncle about the real reasons she was seeking the banking details. When Hilda drove back home to Market Repton late in the afternoon it was still raining.

Hilda got home at about the same time Andy Edge was finishing his shift. Andy walked the short distance to his house, showered, changed, packed an overnight bag and drove in his car the twelve miles north to Market Repton. He stopped at the excellent Chinese takeaway behind Market Repton High Street, collected a banquet for two and proceeded to Simon's house. Simon had already warmed some plates, set the table and was pouring large glasses of water when Andy arrived.

As they started eating Simon asked "Andy, have you ever googled Selwyn Myles?"

"No, never thought about it. Please, Simon, can we avoid all talk of the goings on at Station Road this weekend? I want to try and put it out of my mind for a while"

"Sure, mate. So to change the subject completely have you thought any more about what I asked you?"

"Yes and the answer's yes but not immediately. I just want all this stuff to be over, you know clean break" Andy replied

"OK that's understandable one step at a time then. It's still raining. Have you brought a coat with you?"

"No. When we go out we'll have to run from pub to pub"

So after their meal they did their pub crawl visiting all five of the pubs in Market Repton's central area All proper real ale venues with welcoming open fires blazing away although the rain had kept some of the regular Saturday night drinkers at home. No need for Andy to worry about drink driving, he spent the night with Simon.

Next morning they woke up to another dark sky and more tippling rain. Over breakfast Simon explained his plans for his back garden. Fewer plants, a reduced lawn, better sitting out areas "just in case it ever stops raining".

During the remaining daylight hours Andy helped his mate do some DIY tasks about the house and then drove back to his home in Repton Magna late on Sunday afternoon.

When he was alone and remembering what he'd asked Andy earlier Simon switched on his computer and put 'Selwyn Myles' into google. Too many hits appeared so Simon added 'railway engineer' to the search term. As the google system presented the results of the search Simon wondered why he hadn't thought to do this before. Simon started to scroll through the information. Almost immediately the newspaper article appeared. It bore a date from four years earlier. Simon read the article and it felt like fingers made of ice were stroking his spine.

Durban Daily News
Monday 10 October

FATAL ACCIDENT VICTIM NAMED

The man killed in a traffic accident in Durban city centre on Friday 7 October has been named as Mr Selwyn Myles the renowned railway engineer.

Mr Myles died after the driver of a bus suffered a heart attack. The bus mounted the pavement hitting Mr Myles who was pronounced dead at the scene.

The incident happened at the junction of West Street and Joe Slovo Street. The bus driver was taken to the nearby Durdoc Hospital where his condition is said to be serious but stable.

Mr Myles was born in England on 25 June 1955 and read mechanical engineering at the University of Manchester. He later specialised in railway construction. He worked all over the world and gave technical advice on the strengthening of the Kaaimans River railway viaduct in the Western Cape.

He lived with his wife Emily in Silver Willow Road, Morningside Village in the north of Durban.

Simon decided to respect his friend's wishes, he wouldn't contact Andy with this perplexing information immediately. What would be the point on a Sunday night? But tomorrow morning he would inform his new ally Hilda Judd of what he had discovered.

CHAPTER 25

Train Of Thought

The next day, Monday 30 November, Hilda Judd got up at 8am with her plan for the day in place. An hour later Hilda was looking through her bedroom window south across the perfectly square park with its now leafless trees. It had at last stopped raining and the morning was almost bright. Then she observed a van marked 'Simon King Builders' stop outside her gate, Hilda watched as Simon King approached her door clutching a folder of papers. 'He's found something out' Hilda thought as she ran down the stairs to her front door to admit Simon to her home. They went into the sitting room and Simon showed Hilda a screen print of the newspaper article about the death of Selwyn Myles.

"Oh my god, Simon ! You know what this means don't you? My cousin Tina was right. Lapley & Hinstock are running bank accounts for dead people. Look at this beautiful address - Silver Willow Road, Morningside Village. Tina said she remembered dealing with a letter on the Selwyn Myles file because of the attractive address in another country. I wonder if the letter was from the widow advising Lapley & Hinstock of the death of her husband and asking them to finalise his UK affairs?"

"That's a big leap, Hilda. I think we should keep this information to ourselves for the moment"

"The speculation yes I agree. But we can't conceal this information. Have you told your friend Andrew Edge about this? A man who died four years ago entered into a tenancy agreement to rent Mr Edge's ground floor flat in the Summer of last year !"

"No, I haven't told Andy yet. I only found this newspaper article on the internet last night. Andy's already stressed enough about it but I'll have to tell him. The letting of the ground floor flat in Station Road started after Selwyn Myles died. So who took out the tenancy and why and why use a dead man's name, and who is paying the rent?"
"Is the rent being paid?''

"Yes, Andy checks it regularly. The rent is paid on time every month"

"Why didn't Spring & Fall check this? Isn't that what they're paid to do as letting agents? Unless of course Carl Ramsey was in on this from the start. But then your question arises again - why? But there's something else, Simon. Over the weekend I found a bank statement relating to my great aunt Mary's account. She died well over twenty years ago but Tina believed Lapley & Hinstock are still running her bank account and passing huge sums of money through it"

"Right. I understand what you're saying but I don't know where this takes us. We can't march into Lapley & Hinstock's office, wave these papers around and accuse them of fraud"

"No of course we can't. But today I'm going to contact Barclays Bank and ask them about great aunt Mary's account, ask them if it's normal for large sums of money to be passing through the account of a dead person"

"Are you going to phone Barclays, Hilda?"

"There's no point in trying to phone them. Even if I got through I'd end up speaking to some kid at their call centre in New Delhi. I'm going to Repton Magna now and I'm going to visit them in person. They've still got a branch open in the High Street. And I won't be fobbed off by some chit of a girl with a clipboard. I shall ask to speak to their most senior person about a possible serious fraud. And then I shall visit Repton Magna police station and ask to see Detective Inspector Ruby Scott again. Have I your permission to tell her what you've discovered about Selwyn Myles?"

"Yes of course. The information is there on the internet for all the world to see"

"Simon do you have an extra print of that newspaper article I can take?"

"Yes I printed ten of them. Here, take two in case the police want to keep one and here is one of my business cards. Call me tonight and tell me how you got on".

And with that they parted company. Simon went to work, Hilda put on her winter coat, walked along Station Road and paused outside number 22 on her way to the railway station. She stared at the property for a moment and observed that as usual the blinds were down at all the windows on the ground floor. No lights were on anywhere in the building. Laura King would of course be at work and the ground floor flat had apparently been rented by a dead man in South Africa.

Hilda took one of the regular trains to Repton Magna and once there walked directly to Barclays Bank in the High Street where she was greeted by a young woman carrying a clipboard and wearing a badge saying 'Here To Help'. Hilda produced her Repton Unitary Authority Councillor photo identity card and her passport and asked to speak to someone about what she believed to be the misuse of the account of a deceased relative. The young woman spoke with her line manager who spoke with her line manager who agreed it was serious enough to hear what the caller had to say. Hilda was shown into the office of the branch manager. Initial greetings out of the way and Hilda keeping as calm as she could began -

"I know what you're probably going to say about the Data Protection Act and client confidentiality but the client in this case is my late great aunt Mrs Mary Montgomery-Gradbach who died in the year 2000. I have here the latest bank statement I have been able to locate for my late aunt and also a photocopy of her death certificate which you may keep. All I am asking you to do is check your records to see if this account is still open and if so if the activity on the account is what you'd expect to see for someone who has been dead for well over twenty years"

"I can certainly check our computer system as you have provided me with the account number but as you rightly said the Data Protection Act does prevent my discussing the matter with you"

"I understand that but it is only fair that I tell you that after I leave here I am going straight to Repton Magna police station to see Detective Inspector Scott about this matter"

The manager had been tapping away at his computer during this exchange and had accessed the account. He saw that the account was still live and showed a credit balance of over £80,000. There were frequent transactions showing on the account many of them involving five figure amounts, money going in one day and out the next was the usual pattern.

"I am able to confirm we are still running an account for Mrs Mary Montgomery-Gradbach but I'm afraid I cannot tell you anything more"

"Thank you. That's all I wanted to know. May I have your name please as the police may want to speak to you about this"

The manager handed Hilda one of his business cards. As Hilda left his office he dialled his bank's fraud division. Later that day a 'block' was put on the account suspending any further transactions.

Hilda walked the short distance to Repton Magna police station, spoke to the civilian employee at the front desk and asked to speak to DI Ruby Scott. DI Scott would see Hilda immediately. Hilda told DI Scott about her visit to Barclays Bank, handed over the manager's business card and also a copy of the newspaper article about the death four years ago of Selwyn Myles in South Africa. Hilda added she believed the death of her cousin Tina Proudfoot in Market Repton last week was connected to Tina's having discovered that Lapley & Hinstock were passing large sums of money through the bank accounts of these two deceased individuals. And she further believed the unsolved disappearance of the estate agent Carl Ramsey was somehow connected to these financial irregularities pointing that Carl Ramsey lived in the same building as someone calling himself Selwyn Myles and that Carl Ramsey's girlfriend had been Laura King, a solicitor at Lapley & Hinstock.

Ruby Scott decided these allegations were serious enough to take a formal signed statement from Mrs Hilda Judd after which Hilda said -

"And if there are resources problems with that fool Max Graden please let me know immediately. I'll report him to the Home Secretary. The last thing I want to see is that jumped up bean counter appearing in the New Year honours list". Ruby escorted Hilda from the building trying not to laugh out loud.

Then Ruby phoned her boss Detective Chief Inspector Graham Radway and told him of these developments. Graham told Ruby that Mid Land Police senior officers would need to discuss the implications of involving a firm of local solicitors in a possible fraud enquiry and the staffing resources and costs of such action. He would get the issue added to the agenda for the final meeting of the year of the senior officers due to take place the following week at police headquarters in Blackbird City. Then Ruby told Graham that Mrs Hilda Judd had referred to their not so esteemed Police And Crime Commissioner as a 'jumped up bean counter'. Their conversation had to end as Graham couldn't stop laughing.

After lunch Ruby Scott spoke to her team and told them of the unexpected development in the Tina Proudfoot case, that they may possibly be looking at not just a tragic hit and run incident and that the disappearance of Carl Ramsey over a year ago (currently going nowhere at the Dainford Missing Persons Unit) may be linked in somehow.

The latest and youngest addition to DI Scott's team was a detective constable named Jason who had only recently completed the detectives basic training course. He spoke for the first time at one of these meetings saying he had an idea. This provoked a good humoured cheer from his colleagues.

"I've remembered something from my training course" was followed by another cheer. Jason continued undaunted "we did this exercise where we were given a list of apparently unrelated events, the lecturer told us that during the lunch break we were each to come up with one question to ask about these events. The suggestion was we all think outside the box and think of a question that's a bit quirky - see if it takes the case somewhere we weren't expecting. Why don't we do that and see if anything comes of it?".

Ruby Scott was never one to quell anybody's enthusiasm so went along with Jason's suggestion. Later that day they'd reconvene and see if any off-tangent questions seemed interesting enough to pursue.

After the team meeting had finished Detective Sergeant Meredith Wynne put a suggestion to his boss -

"We know of two people who've seen Selwyn Myles, sorry I mean whoever is calling himself Selwyn Myles. Those two people are Laura King who's his neighbour and Detective Constable Peter Guild from Dainford who interviewed him about the missing Carl Ramsey. How about we speak to both of them, say we're looking into the possible disappearance of Selwyn Myles and ask each of them to give a physical description of the man they thought was Selwyn Myles. From the descriptions they give we can prepare an e-fit composite likeness.

We'd be speaking to Laura King as the neighbour and not in connection with anything going on at Lapley & Hinstock"

Ruby Scott liked the idea saying "Good thinking, Merry, get onto it. And speak to Laura King at home not at work, then she shouldn't associate what seems to be a routine matter with anything which may be going on at her office".

Det Sgt Wynne returned to his desk and telephoned Det Con Guild at Dainford.

"Hi, mate. This is detective sergeant Wynne at Repton Magna. Anything happened on the disappearance of that estate agent Carl Ramsey from Market Repton?"

"Hello, sergeant. No, nothing at all. No reports, no sightings and no activity on his bank account in over a year. It's like he's just walked off the face of the earth"

"OK. Listen, do me a favour Peter. You interviewed Carl's neighbour in the ground floor flat, Selwyn Myles, on the 3rd of December last year a few weeks after Carl had disappeared. I want you to send me a copy of your interview notes and also add a physical description, as detailed as you can please. Then I want you to get an e-fit likeness prepared and send me that as well. Can you do that asap?"

"Yeah sure but why?"

"Just tying up a few loose ends"

"OK. I can send you a copy of the notes now. The e-fit will probably be tomorrow, hope that's alright with you"

"Sure, thanks, mate"

E-fit (Electronic Facial Identification Technique) is the computer based method of creating a facial likeness of a person of interest to the police from witness descriptions. It runs from a basic laptop computer but needs specialist training to enable the operator to create the facial image from a witness description.

Meanwhile Ruby Scott was speaking to a detective sergeant at Durban's main police station in South Africa. Ruby explained she was phoning in connection with the death of the British citizen Selwyn Myles who had been killed in a road accident in Durban city centre on 7 October four years ago. Could an officer please be sent to interview his widow Emily?

Ruby outlined the information she would like. Her South African counterpart said it would be done without delay.

Then Ruby's team of detectives reassembled to present the questions they'd each thought of. Ruby decided they'd follow up on these :
-   which solicitor at Lapley & Hinstock prepared the will of the real Selwyn Myles and is he/she still alive?

-   where does Ray Proudfoot work, what is his financial standing and was Tina's life insured?

-   was Carl Ramsey's passport amongst the stuff his parents had taken back to their home in Chester last year following his disappearance?

The detective making each suggestion was tasked with pursuing it and reporting back with the answer.

At 7pm that same day as Laura King was finishing her evening meal in the first floor flat at 22 Station Road, Market Repton her doorbell rang. She looked at the video entry screen in her hall and it showed two people standing outside at the building's main door - a large, slightly rotund, white man and a tall, slim, dark skinned young woman with a large shoulder bag.

"We're sorry to trouble you at home, Mrs King. I'm Detective Sergeant Wynne from Repton Magna police station and this is my colleague Kyra Sharma. May we come in?"

Laura pressed the button on her screen to unlock the main door and greeted her visitors at her door.

"Has there been an emergency?" Laura asked

"No but we'd like your assistance in a matter which is taking on an unexpected degree of urgency. If you're free for a few minutes we'd like your help in creating an e-fit composite of your downstairs neighbour Mr Selwyn Myles". Meredith started to explain to Laura what that meant but she stopped him saying she already knew about the process.

"But what's the issue about my neighbour, Sergeant?" Laura asked

"We're concerned for his safety. When was the last time you saw him?"

"I can't recall exactly. Strange you should ask but now I come to think about it I haven't seen him for a few weeks. He is very quiet, I never hear a radio or TV or music. Very much the perfect neighbour. It's impossible to tell if he's in or out"

"So is it OK to proceed, Mrs King?"

Laura King was very cooperative giving a physical description of Mr Myles and then helping Kyra Sharma create a facial image on the laptop computer she had brought in her shoulder bag. Sgt Wynne again apologised for troubling Mrs King at home, thanked her for her assistance and then he and his colleague departed.

Just a short walk away Hilda Judd was telephoning to Simon King to tell him what had happened earlier when she visited the bank and the police in Repton Magna. Simon then telephoned Andy Edge and brought his mate up to date although Meredith Wynne had already told Andy of everything which had transpired at the CID meetings that day.

CHAPTER 26

Family Snapshot

Next day in Repton Magna police station CID office Detective Inspector Ruby Scott and her team studied the physical descriptions and the e-fits provided by both Laura King and Detective Constable Peter Guild. They were reassuringly similar and revealed the man they both separately knew as Selwyn Myles to be in his mid sixties, tall and slim with neat short grey hair, clean shaven and wearing expensive looking rimless glasses. And white Anglo Saxon.

Two days later Ruby Scott received a telephone call from the officer she had spoken to in Durban police station. One of their staff had been to see Mrs Emily Myles and had obtained the information requested by the British police :

- Selwyn Myles had never expressed any wish to return to the UK to retire

- Selwyn Myles had definitely not entered into a property letting arrangement

- She and her late husband had intended spending their remaining years together in Durban

- Her late husband's UK lawyers had been Lapley & Hinstock

- Emily Myles had written to Lapley & Hinstock a couple of weeks after her husband had died in October four years ago, enclosed a copy of his death certificate and asked them to finalise his UK affairs. A few weeks later (much sooner than Mrs Myles had anticipated) the sum realised from Mr Myles's UK savings and pension plan had been paid into her South African bank account.

Ruby had also requested a copy be sent to her of the most recent photograph taken of Selwyn Myles before he died. It did not match the descriptions provided by Mrs Laura King and Detective Constable Peter Guild in any way.

A further item of information then arrived and no-one was sure if it was significant or not - the forensics experts had identified the paint fragments found on Tina Proudfoot's clothing. They were from a white Citroen Berlingo van.

Ruby's team of detectives had also found answers to their out-of-the-box-thinking questions.

- The late Ben Hinstock Senior had prepared the will of the real Selwyn Myles more than thirty years ago just before he left the UK. Lapley & Hinstock were named as executors of the will and the client had been convinced of the advantages of also signing a

Lasting Power Of Attorney in favour of Lapley & Hinstock. At that time Mr Myles had intended returning to the UK should his work bring him back and eventually to retire there. His work never did bring him back. Ben Hinstock Senior had subsequently died aged 85. The only current employee at the firm of solicitors contemporaneous to when the will was prepared was Brian Atchley who had never actually met Mr Myles. Nobody presently at Lapley & Hinstock had ever seen or been given a physical description of Selwyn Myles. There was no business reason to do so.

- Ray Proudfoot was self employed and with his brother Craig owned a business manufacturing made to measure double glazed windows and doors. The business was doing very well, Ray had no financial issues and Tina did not have a life insurance policy. In the unlikely event of Ray having anything to do with his wife's death his motive certainly wasn't financial.

- Carl Ramsey's parents had confirmed their son's passport was amongst the personal effects they had removed from the first floor flat at 22 Station Road. Carl would therefore still be in the UK either dead or alive.

"So where do we go next with this?" a detective constable asked

"We need to find out who is masquerading as Selwyn Myles and why" said Det Sgt Meredith Wynne "obviously no attempt was made to look like the real Mr Myles. In a place like Market Repton that's an odd thing to do. It's a slightly unusual name and given the average age there is around 65 someone would remember him from when he and his family lived there even though it was decades ago. There's that friend of Hilda Judd for a start and there must be other members of that golf club who'd remember the family.

He'd run the risk of his identity being questioned every time he gave his name to anybody locally and it's obvious whoever it is just lazily assumed that Selwyn Myles was a white man"

"Like everybody else then" Ruby Scott added "and we're still no nearer to answering the question 'why?'. What is the point of it all? Right - decision time, I'm going to ask DCI Radway for funding to do a DNA and fingerprint sweep of that ground floor flat. I want you as a team to identify everybody who has visited that ground floor flat over the last 15 months so all the legitimate names can be eliminated. Draw up a list now please. I'm going to speak to Graham Radway"

So Ruby telephoned DCI Radway who agreed with Ruby's DNA and fingerprint sweep plan and promised to request funding when he attended the senior officers' meeting within the next few days. By the end of the day and after consulting Ian Fall the estate agent and PC Andy Edge Ruby's team had compiled a list of individuals from whom DNA samples and fingerprints would be needed to eliminate them from police enquiries :

Simon King and all his men who worked on the flats conversions ;
Ian Fall and Carl Ramsey who visited to prepare their letting ad ;
DC Peter Guild who visited to interview 'Mr Myles' about Carl Ramsey ;
Meredith Wynne and Andy Edge who visited when Andy became concerned about the apparently missing Selwyn Myles ;
The people who fitted the window blinds.

To avoid distressing Carl Ramsey's parents by turning up at their home in Chester to obtain a sample of their son's DNA it was decided it would be better to visit Dainford FC and get the sample from Carl's locker which had remained undisturbed since his disappearance. Carl's fingerprints were obtained from the inside of the door of his locker.

The final senior officers' meeting of the year took place at the end of the second week of December in what they called 'The Board Room' at Mid Land Police HQ in Blackbird City. It was attended by DCI Graham Radway and his equal and senior ranked colleagues, the Chief Constable and The Police And Crime Commissioner Max Graden.

The developments in Market Repton had the potential to become the single biggest resources challenge the force was currently facing not to mention the controversial matter of possibly having to interview formally and under caution everybody working at Lapley & Hinstock - one of the area's oldest and most well respected firms of solicitors. The meeting attendees agreed this would be unprecedented in their collective experience.

Funding was released for the DNA and fingerprints sweep of the ground floor flat which would be done in the first half of January in the new year. By then DNA samples and fingerprints should be obtained from all the people on the elimination list.

It proved to be a quick, simple job to ascertain who had fitted all the window blinds in the ground floor flat. A detective on Ruby's team started telephoning all curtain and blinds companies closest to Station Road, Market Repton and on the second phone call 'Repton Blinds' on the town's industrial estate revealed they'd done the work. The detective also had the presence of mind to ask who had engaged them and how the work was paid for. She learned that a Mr Selwyn Myles had commissioned the job, it was carried out by two of their employees and it was paid for by an internet banking transaction from the current account of Mr Selwyn Myles. The two employees remembered the flat was empty both when they went to take measurements and later when they visited again to install the blinds. They'd been instructed to visit Mr Ian Fall the estate agent to obtain a spare key. It had been an internet order. The customer had chosen the design from the company's website. Nobody from 'Repton Blinds' had set eyes on Mr Selwyn Myles.

All of this information reached Andy Edge through his pal Meredith Wynne. As usual Andy was rostered to work nearly every day throughout the Christmas and New Year holiday period. Simon King was not pleased about this. At this time of the year his building company always closed down for a ten day period so his married employees most of whom had young children could spend the festive season with their families. Simon was an only child as was Andy. Simon didn't fancy again spending Christmas with his parents falling asleep in front of a television screen.

"Why is it always you, Andy? Wouldn't it be fairer to take it in turns on the Christmas shifts?"

"You know why I do it, Simon. It's so I can call in favours later. It's how I get to take four weeks leave to visit mum and dad in Perth. Next time I go to Australia I want you to come with me. Anyway what have you got against falling asleep in front of the telly? It's what the rest of the country will be doing". So that was that.

In Chester Mr and Mrs Ramsey were preparing to spend their second Christmas with no knowledge of where their son was or if they would ever see him again. In Market Repton Ray Proudfoot would spend his first Christmas without Tina for over 25 years.

CHAPTER 27

How To Be A Millionaire

George and Marjorie Edge had followed the story of the court battle surrounding the ownership of the Gustav Klimt painting 'Portrait Of Adele Bloch Bauer I' with immense interest. The outcome of the court case was not the real point as far as the Edges were concerned. The publicity the case generated was making the artist a household name. The value of his paintings was increasing astronomically. When the United States Supreme Court ruled that the painting be restored to its owner and she announced she would be relocating the masterpiece from Austria to the USA the Edges decided it was time to make their move.

In anticipation of this they had requested Audrey Hinstock contact the law firm in Miami Florida with whom Lapley & Hinstock had an 'associate' arrangement and ask that a client account be opened for them. Ben Hinstock Senior was then aged 84 and in failing health so it was Audrey they approached to make the arrangements. The Miami law firm was briefed to expect a large sum of money to be deposited in the client account following the sale of an asset in the USA. At some future date they would be asked to transfer the funds to a nominated bank account.

George Edge had been born in Birmingham. At 5 foot 7 inches he was one inch shorter than his wife but had surprisingly wide shoulders. He had blue eyes and a good head of wavy grey hair and had always been clean shaven. He was a fussy dresser, the possessor of 14 three piece suits all in different subdued shades of blue or grey. He wore unpatterned shirts and never went out without wearing one of his 40 + silk ties. Here George allowed himself to be a little less conservative. Some of his silk ties were patterned and colourful.

Marjorie was also born in Birmingham, a year after the birth of George. She was only 20 years of age when she married George and 21 when their only child Greg was born. Although just one inch taller than her husband when out together George's wide shoulders and Marjorie's life long penchant for heels made it appear she were towering over him. Marjorie had been slim all her life. Her hair and clothes looked, but only looked, simple. She liked to have her straight hair sculptured to the shape of her head and kept not too long. She never wore jewellery, not even a wedding ring. When Marjorie marked her 65th birthday she looked no older than a woman in her early fifties. She had a startling visual attribute caused by the Heterochromia with which she had been born - eyes of different colours. Her left eye was grey, her right eye was blue.

George and Marjorie discussed in their elegant sitting room at 22 Station Road the logistics of their forthcoming Florida trip. They decided to contact the same gallery in Miami which had handled the sale of the Picasso drawing over thirty years earlier, back when they were living in Birmingham. Marjorie took digital photographs of their Klimt painting and from the internet discovered the website and email address of the Miami gallery. She sent a message outlining the task she wanted the gallery to do and attached copies of the photographs she had taken and also a copy of the Sotheby's certificate of authenticity.

Not unexpectedly since Klimt was the main topic of conversation in the art world at that time Marjorie received a very rapid email response from the gallery. An appointment was arranged for Mr and Mrs Edge to visit the gallery two weeks later. They booked their first class flights from Manchester to Miami and a suite for four weeks at the Ritz Carlton Hotel, Bal Harbour, Miami Beach. If necessary their stay could be extended.

"Now we've got to think about how we physically get the painting to Miami, George"

"Without causing it any damage of course. Well we've kept it in its cheap frame for the best part of thirty years. So we'll remove it, pack it between sheets of hardboard and put it at the bottom of our largest suitcase. I've already checked the measurements, it'll fit. And then hope it isn't seized by US Customs on arrival" George added warily

"On what grounds could they seize it, George? It's nothing illegal, it isn't on any missing art list and there isn't a sniffer dog alive that can detect a one hundred year old masterpiece. Arriving in the USA nowadays people of our age have become invisible I'm glad to say. They'll probably be more concerned about the possibility of our bringing illegal fruit into the country" Marjorie said remembering the occasion she'd had a banana confiscated on arriving in the USA

"I'm more concerned about what we say to the gallery" Marjorie continued "because we certainly don't want the painting putting into an auction, we want the gallery to find a private buyer"

"We could say we're concerned about the security implications we'd have to face. The publicity and attention an auction would generate could present us with a threat to our personal safety, especially after all the publicity the court case generated" George suggested

"Yes indeed, George. And of course it's our painting and our decision, the gallery will get its ten per cent regardless"

"We'll go ahead on that basis. If they ask us any awkward questions we'll say we need time to discuss them privately but I think it's unlikely. They'll earn millions of dollars in commission from us so I don't imagine they'll go looking for problems. But now I'm thinking about what happens next. The money from the sale will go into the client account opened for us by the Miami lawyers. Then what do we do with it, Marjorie?"

"We're in our late sixties. It'll be more money than we can possibly squander but we'll give it a shot ! Spend November to April every year away from the British Winter travelling in five star luxury. Buy a place in a decent climate. There's no end to what we can do. We can just make it up as we go along"

"I meant what do we do with the money immediately after it's arrived into the account of the Miami lawyers. We can't transfer it to England or even to Europe without having to answer challenging questions of provenance"

"There'll be no rush. The money can stay in the client account while we decide. We could transfer it to a country where such questions don't usually get asked. A country where the US dollar is the official or semi official currency. A country with a decent climate and good travel links"

"And which doesn't have an extradition treaty with the UK" George added dryly.

"I believe we know just the people to ask" Marjorie replied and they both laughed.

At the time of these discussions and plans their son Greg and daughter-in-law Vanessa had been living in Australia for three years so in the final week of that November their grandson Andrew drove George and Marjorie to Manchester Airport for their flight to Miami. Andrew of course was completely unaware of the real reason for his grandparents' trip to Florida thinking it was going to be just a break in the sunshine for them, getting away from the bleak English Winter weather.

Two days later the gallery owner visited George and Marjorie at their hotel suite bringing with her their Klimt consultant. His initial verdict was that the painting was probably genuine. He was not swayed by the Sotheby's certificate of authenticity which the Edges produced saying

"......obviously the Sotheby's opinion on the painting is interesting and influential but it was decades ago. Validity processes have moved on since then. May I take it to my premises? You are welcome to come too".

So the four of them transferred to the art historian's offices where he explained how what he had called the 'validity processes' would be carried out. The only question the Edges asked was

"How long will it take?"

"Less than 48 hours" was the response of the expert. They left the painting with him having seen the vault in which it would be stored and the other security measures in place. There was also in place an insurance bond valued at 50 million US dollars.

While the painting was being authenticated the gallery owner contacted the potential buyers she had previously identified and advised about the forthcoming sale. They were all serious private connoisseurs who each already had art collections worth hundreds of millions of dollars. Each was advised the painting had a price tag of 75 million US dollars. Each had also engaged the services of their own Klimt expert.

The painting was declared to be a genuine uncatalogued portrait from around 1904. Only one of the would be buyers was prepared to pay 75 million dollars for the painting. But one was all it needed. The money was in the Miami lawyer's client account less than an hour after the sale was agreed. The gallery owner's commission was 7.5 million dollars. Everybody was very happy.

George and Marjorie enjoyed the rest of their holiday, visited the lawyers who now held the proceeds of the sale in their client account and advised them that in due course they would be informing them of the destination of the money. The lawyers were able to add their views on which banks and countries were most 'convenient' for the receipt of such a large sum of money. Their suggestions were all in the Caribbean, Central and South America. Interestingly one of their suggestions matched the advice the Edges had already been given in far away Market Repton.

George and Marjorie next visited the Cartier store in Miami's Design District where George treated himself to a pair of diamond cufflinks and a wristwatch. The total cost was $208,000. Marjorie decided to remain unadorned.

A few days before Christmas the couple left the sun and dazzling colour of Miami and arrived into the monochrome landscape of the Manchester Winter from where their reliable grandson Andrew drove them home.

"Did you have a nice holiday, grandma, grandad?" young Andrew innocently asked

"Yes very nice thank you, dear".

On his drive northwards to Manchester Airport earlier that day Andrew had stopped at his grandparents' house, switched on the central heating and brought a supply of breakfast comestibles. The Edges arrived back into a warm home a couple of hours later. Sitting around the kitchen table enjoying tea and toast George said

"What hours are you working today, Andrew?"

"2pm til 10pm today and nearly every day over the Christmas and New Year period"

"I thought the late shift was 4pm til 12am"

"It is but it gets altered over the festive season so there isn't a shift change during pub chucking out time. We'll have processed the last of the shoplifters and the early evening drunk drivers by ten o'clock. Some of the regular 'customers' as we now have to call them are whole families who are in competition with each other to see which household can steal most stuff from the shops between now and the January sales. Of course they don't really need any of the stuff they nick, it's mostly cheap rubbish anyway made by kids in sweatshops in the far east"

Both George and Marjorie were silently contemplating the totally different world they were now learning about as compared to the world they'd left 12 hours earlier. Marjorie was next to speak

"Andrew, we've decided to pay some money into your bank account this year as a Christmas gift. Then you can buy yourself whatever you want whenever you want"

"Perfect. Thanks a lot, grandma"

"Before you go write down your bank account number and sort code and we'll do it for you".

Andrew had his bank debit card with him so was able to supply his grandparents with the account details. He expected perhaps £200 to £250. When he made a routine on-line check of his bank account in early January he was astonished to find his Christmas present from his grandparents was £10,000.

After the Christmas and New Year holiday period George and Marjorie Edge left England again. This time they were visiting their son Greg and daughter-in-law Vanessa in Perth, Australia. They flew around the world first class taking just one flight each day at the end of which they stayed in the best hotel whichever airport they'd landed at had to offer. They travelled out via North America with stopovers at Toronto and Los Angeles. Then they stayed in Perth for two months and returned to England via Singapore (where they stayed at Raffles Hotel and drank their way through The Long Bar cocktails menu) and Dubai. The cost barely scratched the surface of the interest their money was earning.

In the following year they were out of England for the five months covering January to May. They sailed by luxury liner from Southampton to Perth through the Panama canal occupying the best suite money could buy. They returned from Perth to Southampton via the Indian Ocean, the Gulf and the Mediterranean.

And so this lifestyle continued until one September evening when shortly after supper at 22 Station Road, Market Repton George Edge in his 80th year suffered a fatal heart attack.

CHAPTER 28

Confusion

The DNA and fingerprint sweep of the ground floor flat at 22 Station Road Market Repton was delayed until the final week of January much to the annoyance of Detective Inspector Ruby Scott. Staff shortages and officers who had worked over Christmas and the New Year taking leave in January were the reasons although work had already started to get DNA samples and fingerprints from the individuals known to have visited the flat to eliminate them from the enquiry.

The team of six forensics officers and Detective Sergeant Meredith Wynne arrived at the property by unmarked personnel carrier at 8.30am on the last Wednesday of the month. DS Wynne admitted the team to the house using a key supplied to him by Andy Edge. The forensics officers had put on their white hair coverings, overalls and overshoes before entering. Mrs Laura King had been about to open the main door from within on her way to work when much to her surprise the door swung open to reveal the strange sight of six identically clad figures and a large slightly rotund man with a Welsh accent who looked vaguely familiar.

"Sorry if we startled you, it's Mrs King isn't it?"

"Who are you and what are you doing here?"

"I'm detective sergeant Wynne from Repton Magna" replied Meredith showing his police identity card "we've met before and these people are experts from our forensics department who are here to do a job in the ground floor flat. We have keys from the landlord"

"Of course we met last November when you came about the e-fit. Sorry I didn't recognise you straight away. I just wasn't expecting to see anybody at the door. What's the problem in the ground floor flat?"

"We're concerned for the safety of Mr Selwyn Myles" replied Meredith being careful to disclose only the minimum amount of information in his response "when was the last time you saw your neighbour, Mrs King?"

"Let me think. Many weeks ago, certainly before Christmas"

"Have you ever been inside the ground floor flat?" Meredith asked

"No. I have chatted with Selwyn several times usually in this hall or at his door but I've never entered his flat" Laura replied

"And have you ever been down into the cellar?"

"Oh yes many times. I'm storing some odds and ends down there while I decide what to do with them. And all the meters are in the cellar and when I was thinking about changing power suppliers I was taking readings to work out my annual usage. Why are you asking about the cellar?"

"We're just trying to form a picture of the domestic set up here" Meredith lied "could I have your contact details please, Mrs King, should we need your assistance later?"

Laura opened her handbag and handed Meredith one of her business cards which showed her office phone number, her personal smartphone number and of course the fact she was a solicitor at Lapley & Hinstock.

"Has Selwyn disappeared?" Laura asked

"It's too early to come to any conclusions. Thank you, Mrs King. Sorry to have delayed you" and with that Laura departed on the short walk to her office. Meredith asked one of the forensics officers to take fingerprint samples from Laura's door on the first floor and also from the main door into the house.

The team worked in the ground floor flat for the whole of Wednesday and Thursday and most of Friday. By 2pm on Friday afternoon they had completed their work. Their task had been helped by the fact that the flat had clearly never been lived in. A layer of dust covered every surface, nothing had been disturbed. The only furniture was the office desk, two office type chairs and the filing cabinet which Meredith had seen on his visit to the flat with Andy Edge in the previous October. The filing cabinet was still locked. Fingerprints were obtained from it.

At 3pm on that last Friday in January in the CID office back at Repton Magna police station Ruby Scott and Meredith were discussing the case.

"We won't be able to make any sense of this until all the individuals on our list have provided fingerprints and DNA samples" DS Wynne was saying "and here we have a slight problem. One of the fitters from the blinds firm has taken his family to Disney World or Disney Universe or Disney Nightmare whatever it's called in Florida, two of Simon King's builders are in the Canary Islands and Detective Constable Guild is out of the country visiting his grandparents"

"Do we know when they'll be back?" Ruby asked

"The blinds fitter and the builders are back this weekend. Don't know about DC Guild. I'll phone Dainford nick and ask". Meredith later reported that he'd learned from Dainford CID that one of DC Guild's grandparents had been taken into hospital and Peter Guild was now on compassionate leave to support the other grandparent.

"Where abouts in the world are they" Ruby asked Meredith

"Dunno, boss. Didn't ask. They just said he'd gone overseas"

By the middle of February the fingerprints and DNA samples from the returned workers had been taken and matched with the samples extracted from the flat. DC Peter Guild had still not returned to work so his fingerprints and DNA were taken from his locker, telephone and desk at Dainford police station. After studying the forensics report Ruby asked Meredith to come into her office and close the door to give them some privacy.

"We can match and therefore eliminate from our enquiries Simon King, all his builders, the two blinds fitters, Carl Ramsey and Ian Fall and you and Andy Edge" Ruby began

"And what about Peter Guild and whoever it was he interviewed there who was pretending to be Selwyn Myles?" Meredith asked

"There are just three further DNA samples to be considered and this is where things start to get really interesting. Two of them reveal a Mitochondrial link. Remember what that is, Merry?"

"Yes. We've all attended the training sessions. It's DNA inherited from the same mother. So probably two of Simon King's builders are brothers" suggested Merry

"One of the samples matches DC Peter Guild's DNA and the other two samples are both female DNA" Ruby revealed

"If I'm understanding this correctly, boss, are you telling me the Mitochondrial linked DNA samples belong to DC Peter Guild and his sister?"

"There's a 99.9% certainty. So why would DC Guild be in that flat with his sister, who is this sister and where is she? And that also means there's no DNA left which could belong to whoever was pretending to be Selwyn Myles. So just who did Guild interview? And who does the other female DNA sample relate to?"

"Jeeeeeeez, this is turning into the most complicated case I've ever been involved in, boss. We're going to have to get Guild back from wherever he is the world and ask him what the hell is going on"

"There's more. Two different sets of fingerprints were taken from that filing cabinet in the flat. One set matches the fingerprint samples the team took from Laura King's door. So she's been in that flat although she told you she hadn't. Although that's assuming the prints taken from her door were actually hers. The other prints on the cabinet don't match anybody we've taken samples from so far"

"So some other as yet unidentified female has been in that flat" Meredith said adding "we're going to have to interview Mrs Laura King, boss"

"And what crime are we going to interview her about, Merry? As far as we know what crime has been committed at 22 Station Road? Someone is renting the flat using the name Selwyn Myles. The rent is still being paid on time isn't it?"

"Last time I asked Andy, yes. I'll ask him again when I see him"

"So far as I can see there's no crime here. If someone chooses to rent a flat they can do so using whatever name they want. No one has reported anybody missing from the ground floor flat. There was no evidence an act of violence had taken place there. It's not illegal to have no furniture, well not yet anyway. So just what are we chasing here, Merry? We've spent a small fortune on a forensic sweep of the place. The top brass and Max Graden will do their collective nuts over this"

"We've still got Carl Ramsey's unexplained disappearance, boss"

"And there's nothing to link that to the ground floor flat. You've said yourself it's obvious nobody has ever lived in the ground floor flat and there's no sign any crime has ever been committed there"

"So what's in that locked cabinet with Laura King's fingerprint on it?"

"Somebody's fingerprints, Merry. We've no proof those prints are Laura King's"

"So let's force open that filing cabinet, boss, and see what's inside. That won't cost very much and all we'll need is Andy's permission to enter his property again. Laura King says she's never entered the flat so she's no grounds to complain"

"Agreed, Merry. Get on with it"

"And what do we do about the alleged financial malpractices at Lapley & Hinstock, boss?"

"Not our problem, Merry. We'll refer the matter to our fraud unit, such as it is. I suspect it's just a tired old detective up a corner somewhere approaching retirement. But they can decide if they want to refer it to Action Fraud or as I suspect it should be called 'Inaction Fraud' "

"We still have the death of Tina Proudfoot unresolved, boss"

"And no proof to link it to whatever was going on at Lapley & Hinstock. But when I pass this to the fraud unit I'll make a point of drawing their attention to the possible link. Meanwhile we continue to investigate Tina's death as a separate matter"

"And then there's the issue of Peter Guild. Who's going to tackle him, boss?"

"When he's back from wherever he is he can be interviewed by the Detective Inspector at Dainford. What happens next depends on what he has to say for himself. Go and speak to Andy Edge now please, Merry. Ask him about the rent and to give his permission to enter the flat again".

Less than an hour later Meredith Wynne reported back to his boss that the rent was still being paid on time every month into Andy Edge's bank account and Andy's permission had been given to enter the ground floor flat again.

"Seems Andy was right, boss"

"In what respect, Merry?"

"He's been saying all along his ground floor flat had never been lived in"

"But someone continues to pay the rent. Merry, does Andy know where the money actually comes from?"

"Yes it comes from Spring & Fall Estate Agents in Market Repton. It's paid into their client account, they deduct their fee and pay the balance into Andy's bank account"

"Right another job for you, Merry. Contact Ian Fall and ask him if he knows where the monthly payments are coming from. If necessary ask him to contact his bank. The bank should know the source of the money".

CHAPTER 29

Family Man

After nearly three months of inactivity the Barclays Bank account of the late Mrs Mary Montgomery-Gradbach was accessed through the internet. The operator attempted to transfer £15,000 from the account to an overseas account. When the transfer request was refused the operator tried again and was refused again. Putting it down to an internet problem the operator made a third attempt two hours later. The third attempt was declined. A fourth and final attempt 24 hours later was also declined. Alarm bells started to sound within the operator's mind.

These four attempts were monitored by Barclays Bank fraud division which had purposefully left the account open but blocked transactions and put a signal onto the account to draw their attention to any attempted activity. They established that the intended recipient of the £15,000 was a bank in Nassau, Bahamas. Their IT specialists set to work to establish the location of the computer which had attempted the money transfer.

Within 48 hours Barclays had the location of the computer terminal involved - 27 High Street, Market Repton RE15 8AH. Google street view showed this to be the premises of Lapley & Hinstock, Solicitors.

If anyone wishes to take fraud seriously in the UK the suspected fraud must firstly be reported to an office called 'Action Fraud'. Most of the fraud cases reported to 'Action Fraud' are not investigated but merely added to the National Fraud Intelligence Bureau (NFIB) database. Both 'Action Fraud' and NFIB are parts of The City Of London Police. This does not guarantee anything will actually be done. Usually 'you're on your own out there'. Occasionally a BBC consumer affairs programme will build up a collection of reports from viewers and listeners suggesting repeated and serious fraud by an identifiable company or individual and put the City Of London Police into a position where they agree something should be done.

The matter would then be referred to the police force covering the area where the alleged fraudster appears to be located. However where solicitors, accountants, financial advisors and other professionals who should know better are suspected to be the perpetrators (even if the BBC have not had to point this out) the NFIB will refer it straightaway to the local police force who may allocate resources to the matter if local priorities allow. So Barclays Bank made their report and the NFIB passed it on to Mid Land Police who put the matter on the agenda for discussion at the next meeting of their senior staff due to take place near the end of February. A copy of the agenda was sent to Max Graden and when he saw the complainant was Barclays Bank he realised something would have to be done. He was yet to learn that all of this had been triggered by Councillor Mrs Hilda Judd's visit to the bank.

Before that meeting Detective Chief Inspector Graham Radway had spoken many times with DI Ruby Scott about the case informing her of the Barclays Bank report. The expensive forensics sweep of the ground floor flat had not revealed any criminal activity just a DNA mystery. And if there were any link between the disappearance of Carl Ramsey, the non-appearance of Selwyn Myles and the alleged fraud at Lapley & Hinstock it was not yet apparent what that link was. DCI Radway and DI Scott agreed that an interview should take place with Mrs Laura King and that the two of them should conduct it. The location of that interview would be either at the offices of Lapley & Hinstock or at Repton Magna police station. Before making this decision they would await the outcome of the senior officers' meeting which Graham Radway would be attending.

The Market Repton matter was the main item on the agenda at the February meeting at police HQ in Blackbird City. It was discussed during the morning session immediately before the lunch break. Predictably Max Graden was mainly concerned about the costs so waded in with

"We've already wasted thousands on a futile search of some house in Market Repton. What exactly are you asking me to agree to now?"

"With respect, Commissioner, the search was not futile. The issue is that at the present time we don't know if what was discovered is linked to the alleged fraud at the solicitors' office or not. An interview with one of the solicitors, who also happens to live in the same building as the flat in which the search took place, may help us establish a link" replied Graham Radway "additionally we have reason to believe she was the lover of the estate agent Carl Ramsey who disappeared from that same property. There's too much going on there for all this to be just random unconnected activity"

"Barclays Bank are not going to let this matter drop" the Chief Constable added "their press office and publicity machine are much more powerful and effective than ours, they'll be watching our every move. This woman must be interviewed at the earliest possible date"

"Thank you, Chief. And may I remind the meeting Barclays IT people have pinpointed the computer which attempted fraudulent activity on one of their accounts to be located inside the offices of Lapley & Hinstock. Barclays can go no further. They can't go into the solicitors' office, we can and our IT people are going to have to interrogate their computers to identify which terminal and which user attempted the fraud" Graham Radway continued "and the Chief Constable is right about the pressure we'll all face from Barclays if they perceive we're dragging our feet"

"How is the enquiry proceeding into the suspicious death of one of the employees of the solicitors?" the Chief Constable asked

"Dead end so far, sir. Her cousin is adamant she was killed after discovering financial wrong doing at Lapley & Hinstock. This cousin is a local councillor at Market Repton who's also likely to be chasing the matter up" DCI Radway replied.

Mention of 'local councillor at Market Repton' sharpened Max Graden's attention who asked "Do you know the name of this councillor?"

"Yes, Commissioner, it's a Mrs Hilda Judd"

Max groaned saying "That bloody woman ! I thought I'd seen the last of her. Local trouble maker and busybody. The thought of her and Barclays Bank on the warpath is enough to make all our lives a misery. Get on with it, Chief Constable, top priority".

Lunch was then served by the caterers engaged for the occasion and the delegates as they liked to call themselves enjoyed seared smoked salmon with quail egg and sourdough croutons and crispy fried chicken strips with gherkins and chipotle cream. Vegetarian and vegan alternatives were of course available with a choice of still or sparkling mineral water and elderflower pressé.

Later that same day Det Sgt Wynne and PC Edge were in the canteen at Repton Magna police station having a late lunch comprising sausage, egg and chips and huge mugs of tea. Merry brought Andy up to date on the DNA and fingerprints discoveries and why they wanted to return to Andy's ground floor flat.

"Remember, Andy, all this is confidential"

"Yeah of course I know that, Merry"

"Top brass are having a meeting today at HQ. They're going to decide if Laura King can be interviewed. Does she know you're a copper by the way?"

"I've never told her and my job never cropped up when I went to their offices to make my will"

"…....oh…....I've just thought of something, do you know Laura King's maiden name, matey?"

"No but I can find out easily enough. I'll send a text message to Simon". Andy did so and a few minutes later his smartphone pinged as Simon's reply arrived. Andy showed the message to Merry. Simon was clearly puzzled as to why Andy was asking this question about his ex wife because his reply started with three question marks followed by the words 'maiden name was Guild'. Meredith Wynne rushed from the canteen and into the office of his boss DI Ruby Scott leaving a bewildered Andy saying to himself 'what the freaking hell is happening now'.

"Right, Merry, get off to the flat in Market Repton now and open that filing cabinet. Take a detective constable and a crowbar with you. I'm expecting DCI Radway to call me as soon as their meeting finishes. I'll tell him we now know who DC Guild's sister is".

Two hours later Graham Radway phoned Ruby Scott and informed her that the Chief Constable had given the go-ahead for the interview of Laura King and the interrogation of the computers from her offices. Ruby then told Graham they now believed DC Peter Guild and Laura King were brother and sister.

"Christ Almighty !" Graham shouted down the phone "you know what this could mean. There's a possibility if the two of them are up to something together he's been feeding her every bit of information about police activity on the case he can access through our computer logs. No wonder they gave us identical descriptions of Selwyn Myles and near carbon copy facial e-fit composites"

"Yes of course but the problem is, Graham, we still don't know what the something they may be up to actually is nor do we know who is pretending to be Selwyn Myles and why. I've sent my DS to the flat in Market Repton. He's going to force open that filing cabinet and bring back here anything he finds. Do you want me to call you back with the results, Graham?"

"Please, Ruby"

Ruby's call back to Graham was less than ten minutes later. Meredith had phoned Ruby to inform her all they'd found in the filing cabinet was a laptop computer which they were bringing back with them. A note had been left in the cabinet saying 'Contents taken by Repton Magna police CID'.

"OK, Ruby. Get someone to bring it over to HQ first thing tomorrow morning so our IT team can see what's on it. I've just been speaking to

Detective Inspector Alan Church at Dainford nick. I've told him to cancel DC Guild's computer access. At least Laura King won't learn any more from him. Guild is still on compassionate leave unless that's a load of lies"

"Will do, Graham. But can I just say it isn't a crime being the brother of a solicitor. He may or may not be up to something but at the moment he isn't guilty of anything. He may not have told Laura King anything about our investigations"

"Yes I know. But it's odd no-one knows where he is or when he'll be back. I've authorised a trace to find the current location of his smartphone. That's all we can do today, Ruby. Are you knocking off now?"

"Yes, I'm having a one to one with Arthur Guinness".

On the following day work started by Mid Land Police IT team on the laptop computer removed from the ground floor flat at 22 Station Road. It was password protected but a police software program was running to crack the password. Next task would then be an interrogation of the hard drive to reveal the laptop's activities and hopefully its user identities.

It was decided by the Chief Constable and his senior staff and agreed by the Police And Crime Commissioner Max Graden that at 9am on Monday 1 March a team of detectives would be sent to the offices of Lapley & Hinstock, all the computers accessed and seized if necessary and the staff individually interviewed. Mrs Laura King would be interviewed under caution at Repton Magna police station.

On Sunday 28 February the trace on DC Peter Guild's smartphone had revealed it to be in Dublin Airport at 4pm, Manchester Airport at 6pm and at DC Guild's home in Westwich at 7pm. Calls and messages sent to the smartphone remained unanswered. At 8am on Monday 1 March two uniformed constables from Dainford were dispatched to bring DC Guild back to Dainford police station. Here he was interviewed by Det Insp Alan Church of Dainford CID and Det Sgt Meredith Wynne. Wynne was meeting DC Guild in person for the first time and noticed the facial resemblance to Laura King.

"DC Guild where have you been for the past 4 weeks and when did you intend returning to work?" his boss DI Church began

"I've been in Dublin staying with my grandparents. I'm back on duty here today as I've already informed my line manager Sgt Blake". This was a bad start, Alan Church had not checked with DC Guild's manager because Sgt Blake was on a rest day.

"When did you inform Sgt Blake of your intended return?" Church continued

"I spoke to him yesterday by phone. I've been on annual leave for two weeks then on approved compassionate leave for the other two weeks. I've just been brought here from my home by two of our uniformed constables, can I ask what the problem is, sir?"

"Sorry about the drama, Peter, but something urgent has cropped up" DI Church said introducing a conciliatory tone "but we thought you were abroad meaning overseas. We don't usually refer to Dublin as abroad do we?"

Peter Guild stared at his boss open mouthed wondering if DI Church had gone mad and eventually said "It's across the Irish Sea but I assume we're not here to talk about geography, sir. I'm becoming concerned about this, sir, can you tell me what this is all about please?"

"Yes of course, Peter. But are things now sorted out with your grandparents? What happened?"

"Two weeks ago today my grandfather fell down a flight of stairs in the Jervis Shopping Centre in Abbey Street in Dublin city centre, banged his head and suffered a concussion and also broke a bone in his arm. I called the emergency services and grandad was taken to hospital. In view of his age he was kept in the hospital for nearly two weeks as he was showing symptoms of a mild stroke so I remained to support my grandmother. Grandad is OK now, turns out he hadn't suffered a stroke, he was released from hospital on Friday night and I flew back to Manchester airport yesterday"

"Would these be your paternal grandparents, Peter?"

"Yes"

"We were concerned that calls and messages to your smartphone weren't being answered"

``Oh right sorry about that but when I'm on leave in Ireland I don't always keep my UK smartphone switched on. I think it was switched on in the airports but I don't always hear the messages pinging through with all the airport noise. When I got back to Manchester I did notice some missed calls but as I was returning to duty this morning I didn't think it was necessary to return the calls. I have a separate pay as you go phone that I use in Ireland"

"Well I'm glad things got sorted. We'd like to ask you about an interview you did around fifteen months ago in early December in Market Repton with a Mr Selwyn Myles. Do you remember that interview, Peter, or would you like to refer to your notes"

"I'll fetch my notes if you don't mind, sir" and DC Guild left the room to retrieve his notebook. While he was gone DI Church phoned his detective sergeant and asked him to check with Dublin police about the alleged incident in the Jervis Shopping Centre. DC Guild returned to the room with his notes.

"Peter, Sergeant Wynne here from Repton Magna would like to ask you a few questions about your interview with Selwyn Myles"

"Fine, sir. Sgt Wynne and I have spoken on the phone about Mr Myles. I presume there's no problem with my recording this conversation" DC Guild said getting out his smartphone, switching on its recording app and placing it onto the table between them

"This is not an interview under caution, Peter" DI Church said

"I understand, sir. But it's obviously a serious matter to have me brought from home and I think it's best if we have an indisputable record kept"

"Any reason why, Peter?"

"Any reason why not, sir? If there's a problem with it I think I'd like to speak to my fed rep before we go any further"

"No it's not a problem, Peter. Record the meeting if you wish. You interviewed Mr Myles about the disappearance of his neighbour the estate agent Carl Ramsey. Do you remember?" Meredith Wynne had now taken over the questioning.

"Yes. He thought Ramsey was dealing drugs"

"So you closed your Miss Per case and referred the matter to Repton Magna drugs team"

"Of course, sergeant. I think we'd have all done the same thing"

"Yes I agree. Peter describe for us as best you can the physical appearance of the man you interviewed". DC Guild described a tall, slim, white man in his mid sixties.

"And what about the room where the interview took place, Peter?"

"Sorry, sergeant, what do you mean exactly?"

"How was it furnished, was it cosy, homely?"

"I don't think there was much furniture in it. I didn't pay that much attention, didn't think it was relevant"

"You see, Peter, we have a big problem here. Turns out neither Mr Myles nor anybody else has ever lived in that flat. We did a forensics sweep of the flat recently, identified the DNA of all the people who've ever been in the place including yours but there's neither DNA nor fingerprints for Mr Myles. Don't you think that's odd, Peter?"

"I'm not qualified to answer that, sergeant. I don't think about it at all. I interviewed a man I believed to be Mr Myles, made my notes, referred the case on. I still don't understand the problem here"

"The problem, Peter, is that the real Selwyn Myles died in a traffic accident in South Africa over four years ago so we're trying to establish just who you were interviewing in Market Repton three years later. It appears no one else has set eyes upon the man you interviewed"

"I interviewed three people that day in Market Repton. First the other estate agent Ian Fall, then the solicitor and then the man I believed to be Selwyn Myles. I was interviewing Mr Myles as a neighbour and potential witness. It isn't our normal procedure to ask these interviewees to prove their identity. Perhaps someone with the same name died in South Africa"

"And you didn't have any cause to re-interview Mr Myles?"

"No, sergeant. The case was as we've already said referred to the drugs team, they found no drug link so referred it back here as a Miss Per. The case we were working involved Carl Ramsey not Selwyn Myles. Nothing was uncovered as to the whereabouts of Mr Ramsey, his disappearance remains unresolved"

"Who was the solicitor you saw that day?"

"Mrs Laura King"

"Your sister?"

After a still, silent moment DC Guild replied "Yes, my sister"

"You didn't think to mention this relationship?"

"I didn't think it was relevant, sergeant"

"She was Carl Ramsey's lover wasn't she, the Miss Per you were investigating?"

"Laura told me it was more a case of occasionally spending some time together when their diaries mutually allowed"

"Have you been talking to your sister about this case?"

"This case being Carl Ramsey's disappearance? Well we have a pub meal and drink together most weeks in Westwich where I live and she asked a couple of times soon after it happened if there was any news on Mr Ramsey's disappearance. But there never was, then she stopped asking. The only other police matter I've ever mentioned to Laura is about her landlord. I told her the owner of 22 Station Road is a uniformed constable in Repton Magna, PC Andrew Edge. I learned that when he phoned me to advise me of his personal connection to the Miss Per case being Mr Ramsey's landlord. I'm certain telling my sister that isn't a breach of any police protocol".

DI Church now intervened realising that the interview had gone as far as it could bearing in mind DC Guild hadn't been arrested, wasn't being interviewed under caution and that there wasn't any evidence linking him to any wrong-doing.

"Thank you for your assistance, Peter. Please don't discuss with your sister anything we've covered here today"

"No, sir, of course I won't" and DC Guild and his smartphone which had recorded their every word left the room. DI Church's sergeant entered and informed him that Dublin police had just confirmed one of their officers was on duty at the Jervis Shopping Centre when an elderly man called Mr Guild fell and injured himself. An ambulance had been summoned and the elderly gentleman had been taken to hospital. DC Guild appeared to be telling the truth, at least about that incident.

"So what did you make of that, Meredith?" DI Church asked when they were alone

"If nothing else it served a purpose. It made communication impossible between Guild and his sister at this crucial hour. Our lot are currently raiding the offices of Lapley & Hinstock"

"It doesn't seem to have served any other purpose. Are we barking up the wrong tree here, Meredith?"

"We'll know that sooner or later, sir. Meanwhile it's an interview we had to have. How would it look if we hadn't interviewed him? But the question of who he was speaking to in that flat in Market Repton fifteen months ago is unresolved. He's sticking to his story. He maintains he interviewed a man he believes was Selwyn Myles. There was no DNA found in that flat which could relate to Mr Myles. That doesn't mean Guild is lying, there's no evidence someone wasn't there. We can't ask Guild to prove a negative. Are you going to restore Guild's access to our computer systems, sir?"

"I've no grounds not to, he won't get much work done without it".

CHAPTER 30

Games Without Frontiers

Also on Monday 1 March seven miles south of Dainford just before 9am a marked police van pulled up in Market Repton High Street outside the offices of Lapley & Hinstock. The van carried six officers who were primed to storm the building, Detective Chief Inspector Graham Radway, Detective Inspector Ruby Scott, two uniformed constables (in case anyone tried to resist arrest) and two IT experts from Mid Land Police HQ.

But the storming had to wait as when they got there the office hadn't been opened so they all had to sit in the van until someone arrived with a key. At 9.10am the firm's senior partner Brian Atchley, who lived within walking distance, sauntered toward his office, saw the police vehicle parked outside and assumed there had been a burglary over the weekend which puzzled him because there was nothing in the office of any great material worth.

As Brian put his key into the lock the six officers jumped from their van and surrounded him. DCI Radway informed him he had reason to believe financial crime had been committed and he had a warrant to search the building, interrogate all their computers and interview all the staff. The bewildered Brian had by now opened the door which triggered the countdown for the alarm which their insurers had insisted they get installed.

The trauma Brian experienced on hearing what the policeman was saying rendered him momentarily speechless and motionless. He heard no longer the bleeping of the alarm counting down and even if his legs had started working again he had forgotten the code he was supposed to tap in to stop the alarm going off. So the alarm went off with its deafening noise and the blue light fitted to the building's facade started flashing.

"Can you turn the alarm off please, sir" DCI Radway shouted but Brian still couldn't move. He had entered a state of mild shock and couldn't react or speak. Audrey Hinstock meanwhile had arrived in her car and was parking in one of the spaces at the back of the building when she heard the commotion.

"Brian, what's going on?" Audrey screeched as she arrived at the main door but Brian didn't reply

"Do you know the code to silence the alarm, madam?" DCI Radway shouted

Audrey did, tapped in the code and the alarm's ringing stopped although continued for a few seconds longer in everybody's ears. DCI Radway repeated his message about who they were and why they were there. Audrey looked as bewildered as Brian had been. They all entered the front office.

Ian Fall in his office across the road had witnessed this performance and the noisy alarm had brought out into the High Street all the other shop and cafe owners and their early customers one of whom was Hilda Judd's next door neighbour who immediately phoned Hilda to inform her a police raid was underway at the offices of Lapley & Hinstock. In turn Hilda sent a text message to Simon King to report this development.

Once Brian had regained his composure DCI Radway addressed him and Audrey Hinstock about the purpose of their visit. He explained he needed access to their individual offices as their desk computers were going to be interrogated by the police IT experts so would they please reveal their log-in passwords. Unsurprisingly Brian Atchley's computer was not password protected. Audrey asked to see the warrant and once satisfied of its validity disclosed her desktop computer's password.

"Where is Mrs Laura King?" Inspector Ruby Scott asked

"She'll be here any minute, she lives a short walk away" Audrey replied then continued "I have absolutely no idea what it is you're looking for. This is outrageous, we're highly respected solicitors and have never been involved in any kind of financial irregularity. Where has your clearly false information come from, Inspector?"

"I'm not at liberty to say anything more at this time, Miss Hinstock"

The two IT experts found nothing remotely suspicious on the desktop computers of Audrey and Brian. Just day to day, routine, small town lawyer activity, lists of clients, appointments etc. By 10am Laura King had still not arrived at the office. Neither Audrey nor Brian knew Laura's computer password. A call to her smartphone went unanswered. The two uniformed constables were dispatched to 22 Station Road to bring her in but got no reply when they rang the doorbell. A call was put through to PC Andy Edge to drive without delay to Market Repton and bring his keys but Andy pointed out that Ian Fall just across the road also had keys to both the main door at 22 Station Road and Laura King's flat. The keys were obtained from Mr Fall and entry gained. There was no sign of Laura King.

DI Ruby Scott entered Laura's first floor flat and walked through every room. No unmade bed and no dirty dishes but the bathroom revealed the absence of the usual range of daily toiletries. Also Ruby was unable to locate any travel cases or a laptop computer. Mrs King appeared to have gone on a trip. Back at the office neither Audrey nor Brian could shed any light on Laura's non-arrival. She had been due in at work that day as normal.

The IT experts set to work on Laura's desktop computer attaching password cracking software designed at GCHQ Cheltenham. In less than an hour the password was revealed and access gained. Soon after that another call was put through to PC Andy Edge. He was instructed to drive immediately to Market Repton and to make sure Probationary Constable Mike Perez was with him.

Laura's computer revealed separate files for 8 named clients each with online banking access codes. Brian Atchley was summoned, shown a list of the names involved and asked if any of them were familiar to him.

"Yes I recognise three or four of these names. That first one is a former client Miss Nika Anrepiy. She died in a care home at least thirty years ago. I also remember Mrs Mary Montgomery-Gradbach, she died many years ago too"

"Is there any reason why Mrs King would need to have current computer files for them?" asked DCI Radway

"Only if their estates were particularly complicated with trusts all over the place or overseas accounts which often take years to finalise. But I'm pretty certain the two I've mentioned although very wealthy ladies had straightforward estates and wills".

DCI Radway asked one of the IT staff to attempt to access one of the online bank accounts using the access codes stored on Laura's computer. It was the HSBC account for the late Miss Anrepiy. It was a live account, made no mention of the fact that Miss Anrepiy was dead and showed regular transactions mostly involving thousands of pounds. The final transaction dated 26 February of the present year revealed that the total credit balance on the account amounting to over £80,000 had been removed and transferred to a different account the number and sort code of which were shown.

DCI Radway asked Brian if paper files were held for the 8 people for whom Laura King appeared to be running accounts. Brian confirmed there should be paper files and was tasked with gathering all the files as the police would be taking them away for further enquiries.

At midday a police car driven by Andy Edge arrived with Mike Perez in the passenger seat. Both were intrigued as to why senior officers wanted to see the trainee PC Perez as a matter of urgency. DI Ruby Scott went out to the car and warned PC Edge not to enter the offices of Lapley & Hinstock. She was anxious to keep Andy distanced from the case given his personal connection. She asked PC Perez to accompany her back into the office of Mrs Laura King. A computer file had been opened the text of which was in Spanish.

"What's this all about, Mike?" she asked the youngster and after reading the screen for a moment Mike said

"They're travel arrangements, ma'am. Someone called Laura Guild has made a flight booking to go from Madrid to Mexico City"

"Can you tell if it's a return booking or one way?"

"It's a one way booking. There is no return flight mentioned"

"What's the date of the intended flight, Mike?"

"Sunday 28 February, ma'am, yesterday, she'll be there now".

DCI Radway interviewed Audrey Hinstock while DI Scott interviewed Brian Atchley in their respective offices. Their computers had revealed nothing suspect. They both expressed shock and disbelief at the existence of bank accounts with recent transactions for deceased clients. They both confirmed that they themselves had no dealings with these clients. The three of them each had their own portfolio of clients and rarely had any need to access the records for a colleague's case. The two senior detectives could see no grounds to place under arrest either Brian Atchley or Audrey Hinstock. The 8 paper files and Laura King's desktop computer were taken to Mid Land Police HQ in Blackbird City.

PCs Andy Edge and Mike Perez were driving southwards back to Repton Magna when Andy asked

"What was all that about, Mike?"

"Something about financial irregularities. They had gained access to a computer, opened one of the files but it was all in Spanish so asked me to translate it"

"And was it any use to their enquiry?"

"Well if it was they weren't very happy about it. It was travel arrangements. Some woman called Laura Guild had booked a flight from Madrid to Mexico City but if they're after her they're too late because the flight was yesterday".

Andy Edge had another of his increasingly frequent 'what the hell is happening now' moments. He was beginning to wish he'd never inherited 22 Station Road, it seemed to incite one drama after another. Police rules on confidentiality prevented his talking to Simon King about this latest development. He would continue following his bosses' advice and keep himself well clear of the case. His young charge Mike Perez was still speaking

".......so they're taking this Guild woman's computer back to police HQ so the IT lot can find out what she was up to".

Andy Edge wondered if she'd still be paying the rent.

Mrs Laura King had two passports, two identities and two names and all quite legally. Any British citizen with an Irish grandparent can apply for and get an Irish passport even if they have never set foot in the Irish Republic. Laura and her brother Peter John Guild had paternal Irish grandparents and visited them in Dublin most years. They both held British and Irish passports.

Laura's British passport was in the name Mrs Laura King and had a photograph of a woman with shoulder length blond hair. Her Irish passport showed the name Miss Laura Guild and its photograph was of a woman with short, black, slightly wavy hair.

One of the time bombs Laura had discussed some time ago with her accomplice had been triggered, it was time to go. On the Friday of the past week Laura had finished work at 4pm and walked the short distance to 22 Station Road. She picked up the travel case she'd packed the previous night which contained the personal documents she needed, a laptop computer and a change of clothing. She left her flat and dropped the keys into her letterbox. She would never be returning to the flat nor to Market Repton. Laura walked to the railway station and, changing at Crewe, travelled to Holyhead by two trains. At Holyhead she bought a foot passenger one way ticket on the evening ferry to Dun Laoghaire, Dublin's ferry port, paying in cash.

At embarkation she was asked to produce her ticket, nothing else. No-one was interested in her identity and no-one asked to see her passport - not unusual for sea travel between the UK and the Irish Republic. Had she been asked Laura would have shown her British passport. On arrival at Dun Laoghaire her British passport was given the most cursory of glances. Laura travelled from Dun Laoghaire to her grandparents' home in north Dublin by DART Dublin Area Rapid Transit light rail. She stayed overnight at her grandparents' home and was pleased to see her grandfather had recovered from his recent accident.

Next day, Saturday, after a leisurely breakfast Laura walked the short distance to a hairdresser to keep her pre booked appointment. When Laura made the booking she had explained she wanted a complete change of hair style. She wanted her shoulder length dyed blond hair removing and the shortened hair dyed black and given a slightly wavy look. Laura showed the stylist the photograph in her Irish passport - that was the look she was after and that was exactly what she got.

Some hours later and not in any rush Laura bade goodbye to her grandparents and headed north to Dublin airport again using public transport and paying in cash. On her way Laura used her smartphone to book a seat on the early afternoon Ryanair flight from Dublin to Madrid in the name Miss Laura Guild. She was in Madrid late afternoon and took a taxi the short distance to the Madrid Airport Marriott Hotel. After checking in and freshening up Laura took a taxi into central Madrid and bought a new outfit from El Corte Inglés department store, then she returned to her hotel.

The next day, Sunday, Laura took the Iberia Airlines afternoon flight from Madrid direct to Mexico City travelling business class although Mexico was not her ultimate destination. Laura was not in any hurry, she would spend a day or two sightseeing in Mexico City from where she booked a final one way ticket to complete her journey. She was now using a US dollar credit card for all her purchases and hotel stays.

CHAPTER 31

How Long Has This Been Going On?

The IT experts at Mid Land Police HQ in Blackbird City had completed their interrogation of Laura King/Guild's computer. They discovered Laura had been running the bank accounts of 8 people, most of them dead, through Lasting Powers Of Attorney which the 8 individuals had signed in favour of Lapley & Hinstock. The few still alive were either British citizens living and working overseas or British residents with physical or mental conditions which prevented their being able to run their own affairs. But one thing which all 8 had in common was that they were all high net worth individuals which is financial speak for very, very rich.

The LPA arrangements had mostly been signed by the individuals concerned over a 40 year period ending two years ago and all of them were set up through three generations of the Hinstock family - Ben Hinstock Senior then his son Ben Hinstock Junior then his granddaughter Audrey Hinstock.

The police staff were unable to ascertain when the misuse of the accounts started and who started it but it had clearly been going on before Audrey Hinstock and Laura King had joined the firm twelve years ago. The police knew from the evidence of Hilda Judd that her great aunt Mrs Mary Montgomery-Gradbach had died in the year 2000 which implicated

Audrey's father Ben Hinstock Junior. The problem for the police was that all the evidence of financial malpractice was held solely on Laura King's computer and that evidence covered only the last 7 years. The 8 paper files each contained a signed individual Lasting Power Of Attorney document but no clue on how the bank accounts were being manipulated or, originally, by whom. It would need the cooperation of the banks to learn the full extent of the fraud from their current and archived computer records.

The only thing the detectives were able to do right away was to advise the banks that the accounts were being misused and to ask that all further activity on the accounts be suspended. This was done but was of limited worth because in the two weeks leading up to her flight Laura had emptied all the accounts and transferred the credit balances to a variety of different accounts in different banks in different countries. The police IT experts couldn't ascertain to where in the world all the money had gone. This was something else the banks would need to do.

Meanwhile the team of detectives reading through the paper files for the 8 individuals including Selwyn Myles and Mrs Mary Montgomery-Gradbach had seen letters from next of kin advising Lapley & Hinstock of the demise of their relative and asking that their affairs be finalised. One such letter was from the memorably attractive address of Selwyn Myles's widow. It was this address Tina Proudfoot had remembered prompting her to re-read the letter a few days before she was killed.

The affairs of the deceased were then finalised up to a point. Laura had prepared convincing final statements for each next of kin setting out sums realised from the apparent closure of bank accounts and savings plans, expenses incurred, fees charged by Lapley & Hinstock leaving the net balance available for distribution in accordance with the terms of the individuals' wills. Of course no-one thought to contact the bank of their dear departed to make sure the account had been closed. Why should they? It had all been handled for them by that efficient solicitor in Market Repton. The savings accounts had indeed all been closed but the bank current accounts had been deliberately left open. Pension payers were not told of the deaths of the individuals so pension payments continued to be made into their bank accounts. The computer systems of the pension payers and the banks are not programmed to question whether payments should continue just because the pensioners are getting older and older.

None of the detectives had seen anything like it before. All of the people/victims of this fraud had been wealthy and the sums distributed to their legatees on apparent finalisation and closure were sufficient enough to avoid questions or suspicions arising. Several of the biggest accounts had unexplained large sums paid in which clearly weren't pension payments. They were usually five or six figure sums. Then a few days later the money would disappear, transferred out to another account. The detectives were unable to find or guess what these payments were for or where they were coming from.

The scope of the investigation would be daunting and far beyond the resources of Mid Land Police. They would have to consider referring the matter to the national Serious Fraud Office. The banks' records would later reveal the initial destinations of the monies transferred from the accounts over many years were to bank accounts in the Isle of Man, the Channel Islands, Gibraltar, The Bahamas, The Cayman Islands, North Cyprus and Singapore. Ascertaining to where the deposits went next would need the cooperation of the banks in those territories. In the case of The Bahamas, North Cyprus and Singapore no cooperation was expected. Even the banks in the British territories would have to have the information reluctantly dragged out of them and that would be after months of bureaucracy.

Audrey Hinstock and Brian Atchley were arrested and interviewed under caution at Mid Land Police HQ. Their personal computers were seized and the hard drives interrogated but just like their office computers nothing suspicious was revealed. Court orders were granted to access their bank and savings accounts. They denied any knowledge or involvement in the manipulation of clients' bank accounts. Neither of them appeared to be living beyond their means. Neither was living an extravagant lifestyle, quite the reverse. No charges were brought against them. They returned to work.

After Laura's disappearance her fingerprints and DNA samples were obtained from her flat. Police IT experts had also gained access to the laptop computer discovered in the locked filing cabinet in 'Selwyn Myles's' flat. They learned the laptop had been handled by Laura King and no-one else. The information extracted from the laptop was in turn both astounding and perplexing.

In the CID office at Repton Magna police station three detectives were meeting to discuss the implications. DI Church from Dainford Police was present along with DI Ruby Scott and Det Sgt Meredith Wynne.

The laptop revealed that two years earlier Laura had contacted the estate agents Spring & Fall using the name Selwyn Myles and expressed an interest in renting the ground floor flat at 22 Station Road Market Repton. 'He' had taken the virtual online tour of the flat. The tenancy agreement had been signed electronically and rental payments started. Laura had invented and registered the email address mylesaway@xmail.com

A short while later in that same year Laura writing as Selwyn Myles had engaged a firm called Repton Blinds through their website to fit identical blinds at all the windows on the ground floor flat at 22 Station Road.

Then in the Autumn of that year Laura again posing as Selwyn Myles had booked a holiday cottage in Snowdonia, North Wales, for the four nights Friday 8 November to Monday 11 November inclusive in an exchange of emails with a Mrs Navya Anand.

Finally Laura had replied to an email from Ian Fall about the occupancy of the ground floor flat and writing as Selwyn Myles from mylesaway@xmail.com had told the fictitious tale about working in Saudi Arabia and being back in Market Repton in time for Christmas.

Det Sgt Meredith Wynne was talking……"so nobody has ever lived in that ground floor flat. A fake tenancy was created by Laura King using the identity of one of her dead account holders. Of course she, just like everyone else, assumed that Selwyn Myles was a white man. Lapley & Hinstock's records for the real man didn't mention his ethnic background. Why should they?"

"But why create the fake tenancy?" DI Church asked

"Let's take this a step at a time" Ruby Scott suggested "there was no Selwyn Myles at that property so DC Guild's so called interview is now highly suspect. DI Alan Church here is going to have to decide where to go next with Peter Guild. Let's remember both Guild and Laura gave near identical descriptions of a person who didn't exist. It must be collusion"

"This property is owned by one of your uniformed constables I understand?" DI Church enquired

"Yes, PC Andy Edge who's a close personal friend of mine. Andy has maintained all along there was no-one living in that flat. The weird thing is though the rent continues to be paid and has been ever since July two years ago" Merry answered

"I think, Alan, you're at least going to have to suspend DC Guild from duty, cancel his computer access again and consider if he should be arrested as an accomplice to fraud" Ruby Scott said adding "and I wonder if he's aware of Laura's disappearance and where she is now?"

"Agreed. First thing I'll do is have him arrested then seize his smartphone, see if there's been any contact with Laura King" Alan Church responded continuing with "now why would she rent a remote cottage in North Wales for four days in that November?"

Meredith added "I wonder if we're barking up the wrong tree here? I wonder if her accomplice was loverboy Carl Ramsey? Perhaps their relationship wasn't the occasional off/on affair we've been led to believe. He's on hand at the estate agent's office to make sure the fake tenancy goes through smoothly. It can't be a coincidence that he then starts to rent the first floor flat himself"

"But we keep coming back to the same question, Merry. Why? There must be something else going on here we're not seeing. All this bank account fraud could have been done on any computer from anywhere in the world. And we know it would be impossible for Carl Ramsey to have left this country because his parents took his passport from his flat" Ruby Scott said adding "but the first thing I'm going to do is ask North Wales Police to speak to Mrs Navya Anand the owner of the cottage, ask her what she remembers about the 4 day rental in November two years ago"

"I wonder why Laura King was so interested in Mrs Anand's boat? Look at these emails. She specifically asked about it" DI Alan Church pointed out

"I don't know but I'm getting a bad feeling about this" Ruby said

"So am I" said Meredith checking through his notes "if I remember rightly Carl Ramsey disappeared on Thursday 7 November, the day before this cottage rental period started".

DCI Alan Church phoned his Detective Sergeant at Dainford police station, told him to place DC Peter Guild under arrest, read him his rights, seize his smartphone and tell him that the initial charges against him would be :

Misfeasance In A Public Office
Misconduct In A Public Office
Fraud
Assisting A Felon

As DC Guild was on duty at Dainford these orders were complied with immediately. His smartphone was seized and was found to contain just one short, simple text message from his sister. It read 'Phase 2 completed'. Upon being asked what this meant DC Guild replied "No comment". He was taken to Mid Land Police HQ in Blackbird City where he was interviewed by DCI Graham Radway and the Detective Chief Superintendent in charge of the force's Criminal Investigation Department. It was a one-way interview. DC Guild replied "No comment" to their every question. The only time he spoke more than these two words was to say he would not be taking part in any further interviews unless his solicitor were present.

CHAPTER 32

Memory

DI Ruby Scott contacted a colleague in North Wales police and asked that Mrs Navya Anand be interviewed on her behalf. Ruby mentioned all the points she wanted covering. Mrs Anand lived within walking distance of Llanrwst police station from where a police constable was dispatched to her home. This is what Mrs Anand had to say -

"I do remember the booking for the 4 days in the first half of November the year before last. Yes, I remember the name Mr Selwyn Myles. Most of my lettings for the cottage are from regulars, you know people who visit regularly usually around the same time of the year. But I'd not had a previous booking from Mr Myles, it was his first visit.

When you contacted me to say you were coming, officer, by the way would you like a cup of tea? (yes the officer would) , I re-read the email correspondence I had with him. He didn't say anything about anybody coming with him, he just said 'I'. Coming to a remote cottage alone would be unusual. But he certainly did bring somebody because both bedrooms were used. I didn't meet him. Usually I go to the cottage to meet and greet my guests, explain how the boiler works, that sort of thing, but when Mr Myles came I was visiting my sister in Liverpool. Would you like a biscuit with your tea, officer? (yes the officer would).

Mr Myles paid the deposit on the same day he made his enquiry in the September of that year then paid the balance into my bank account as I'd asked 2 days before his arrival. I then sent him an email with the postcode and grid reference of the cottage and my phone number in case of any problems. Sometimes the problem with first time visitors is finding the place, it's quite remote on the east bank of Llyn Brenig, lovely sunsets. I left the keys to both the cottage and the boathouse in the secure key box inside the porch and I mentioned in my email the combination to open the box. Mr Myles didn't phone me so I guess he had no problems.

He had asked specifically about the boat and I know he used it because after he'd left when I went to the cottage to clean it and get it ready for the next guests I noticed he'd put the boat back into the boathouse the wrong way round, not that that mattered. But it was when I was cleaning the cottage I noticed something very strange. Mr Myles and whoever came with him left all of the things in the cottage untouched. People usually move the chairs a few inches to get a better view of the TV or put the occasional table between the armchairs that sort of thing. Not a problem if they do of course, they are my guests.

But then I noticed other things. The rubbish in the bin wasn't anywhere near the amount I'd expect from two people spending four days at the cottage. And I always read the electric and water meters after a letting and the amount they'd used was about one days worth. There's no mains gas at the cottage just electricity. The days in November are usually nice and dry but it gets very cold at night. You'd need the heating on. I'm pretty certain Mr Myles and his companion stayed only one night although he'd paid for four. He didn't write anything in the visitors' book so perhaps he didn't like the place or perhaps some emergency cropped up at home and he had to leave early".

All this information was relayed to DI Ruby Scott.

A couple of days after Mrs Anand's interview with the constable from Llanwrst two of her regulars were on their way to the cottage for a week's stay. Mike and Pauline Stanway from Liverpool rented Mrs Anand's isolated cottage every year during the Spring season. They both worked long hours in the city Mike as a train driver for Merseyrail and Pauline as a nursing sister at an NHS hospital. Seven days in the peace and solitude of Snowdonia before the main tourist season started was something the middle aged couple always looked forward to. They hiked, they cycled, they took Mrs Anand's boat out onto Llyn Brenig. And all this less than an 80 minutes drive from their home in Liverpool.

The colony of pike living in Llyn Brenig were oblivious to the arrival of the Stanways. For sixteen months their needle sharp teeth had firstly been tearing away at the inedible, tasteless, black cocoon which had appeared at the bottom of their domain. Next their teeth tackled the equally inedible fabric beneath until their efforts were rewarded and the feeding frenzy began. It kept them well fed through two long, cold, Welsh Winters.

Immediately after breakfast on the third day of their stay at the cottage the Stanways went sailing on Llyn Brenig in Mrs Anand's boat. They sailed from the jetty attached to the boathouse toward the centre of the lake. It was a still, sunny, cold day with a cloudless blue sky. They could have been the only people on Earth. It was an exhilarating feeling until Pauline noticed something appear from beneath the surface of the water and float alongside the boat. Then a second similar item emerged from the icy water and started bobbing about. Pauline had spent many years working as a theatre nurse and thought she recognised what she was seeing.

"Mike !" Pauline shrieked "come here and look at this" Mike joined his wife and stared into the water

"It's a bit of a dead sheep" Mike suggested

"With black hair? So it's the black sheep of the family? I'm going to scoop these bits up in my hat". Pauline did so. "Mike I think this is human. It's scalp and hair, look there's another bit just appeared"

Mike rushed to the other end of the boat, leaned over the side and started retching.

"Pull yourself together, Mike. Dial 999 and ask for the police, I'll gather up any more bits that appear". But nothing else emerged from the depths and when Mike and Pauline noticed a police jeep making its way along the east side of Llyn Brenig they turned the boat back to the shore to meet the constable. It was the same constable from Llanrwst who had interviewed Mrs Anand.

"I'm a nursing sister with theatre experience" Pauline explained "and I'm pretty sure this is human tissue. These three pieces appeared on the surface of the lake while we were sailing". The constable took an evidence bag from inside his jeep, put on a pair of rubber gloves and gingerly extracted the three items from Pauline's now sodden hat. He used his radio to contact Llanrwst police station and reported the possibility of a body in Llyn Brenig.

The sergeant at Llanrwst arranged for the tissue samples to be sent by courier to the forensics laboratory at Risley in Cheshire and contacted the North Wales Police Underwater Search Team based at force HQ in Colwyn Bay. Early afternoon a team of four divers arrived at Mrs Anand's cottage. Pauline Stanway was there to meet and greet. Before entering the cold water the officers asked for cups of hot tea which Mike was instructed by Pauline to prepare and serve.

"We were in the centre of the lake when the tissue reached the surface. It's a still day and the water's calm so I suggest you start your search at the centre of the lake" Pauline advised the experienced divers her professional flair for organisation and for issuing orders momentarily taking over. One of the officers half way through easing himself into his diving gear gave a mock salute and said "Sure thing, ma'am". Realising what she'd done Pauline squealed with laughter and handed around biscuits.

Meanwhile back at his police station the constable who had attended the earlier call-out was phoning DI Ruby Scott of Mid Land Police.

"DI Scott? This is PC Elis Parry from Llanrwst police. I interviewed Mrs Navya Anand and sent you my report about her holiday cottage. I hope it was of some use to you"

"Thank you PC Parry it was very revealing but has made a complex matter more complex"

"Sorry about that, ma'am but something's just happened at the lake adjacent to Mrs Anand's cottage. It may be unconnected to your case but I thought I'd mention it. I attended a call-out this morning made by the couple renting the cottage this week. They were sailing on the lake when they saw what they think is human tissue floating on the surface. The woman picked it up in her hat. We've sent the bits off to Risley for analysis and our divers are at the lake now to see if there's anything else down there"

"PC Parry, please let me know the results of their search the moment you hear".

Ruby left her office, entered the main CID room, brought her team together and told them about this latest bizarre development. A detective constable was tasked with contacting the Forensics Lab at Risley, informing them that a DNA sample was being sent to them today by Mid Land Police and requesting would they please check to see if it matches the tissue samples on their way from North Wales Police. The DNA sample from Mid Land Police related to Carl Ramsey.

The police divers at Llyn Brenig worked until sunset that day and found nothing. They returned at 10am next morning and after tea and biscuits once again entered the waters. It was another sunny, still day. They had noticed that even on calm days such as this the water had a slight north westerly drift so concentrated their search on an area south east of the centre of the lake. Early afternoon they found it. It took all four divers to bring their discovery to the surface. It was the remains of what had once been a fully clothed human body which had been wrapped in some sort of thick, black plastic then weighed down with house bricks with holes in them which had been attached to the package with domestic electric cable.

PC Elis Parry in Llanrwst made another phone call to DI Ruby Scott in Repton Magna.

The remains were transported to the forensics lab at Risley, Cheshire. There it was discovered the fish in the lake had stripped the carcass to the bone. The ears, eyeballs, lips and tongue had gone as had the genitals and most of the internal organs. The bones bore scratch marks which were assumed to be fish teeth marks. Cause of death was not possible to determine but it was observed the back of the skull had been fractured. The indentation didn't appear to be deep enough to be fatal. The DNA from the bones and scalp specimens matched the DNA sample provided by Mid Land Police. There was a 99.9% certainty Carl Ramsey had been found.

In Chester the next day morning coffee at the home of Mr and Mrs Ramsey was interrupted by the ringing of their doorbell. It rang slightly too long. Mr Ramsey opened the door and admitted to their home two uniformed, unsmiling police officers, a man and a woman.

Before adding 'murder' to the list of charges against DC Peter Guild his boss Detective Inspector Alan Church checked the duty log of Dainford police station for the four nights Friday 8 November to Monday 11 November of the year before last. DC Guild had been on duty each night but, DI Church thought, there was nothing preventing his driving to Llyn Brenig during his time off duty which would have been during the hours of daylight to help his sister manoeuvre Carl Ramsey's body into the boat and then into the lake. It was a grim task Laura King certainly didn't manage on her own. Carl Ramsey had been a heavy, sturdily built man. Proving Peter Guild's involvement was another matter.

In the third week of March DI Alan Church from Dainford, DCI Graham Radway from Blackbird City and DI Ruby Scott and Det Sgt Meredith Wynne were reviewing the case in Ruby's office in Repton Magna police station.

"Interviewing Peter Guild is a waste of time" Graham started "he robotically repeats 'no comment' to every question we ask him even when his solicitor is present. The worrying thing is the Crown Prosecution Service are saying we've got nothing strong enough to make a case. On what we have got they say there's no chance they'll bring anything before a court. All we've got is speculation and circumstantial. And if we sack him the CPS say he's probably got grounds for wrongful dismissal and a huge compensation claim. Max Graden will do his nut. Again"

"Have we checked Peter Guild's bank account?" Meredith asked

DCI Radway answered this point saying "Yes we got a Court Order to do that. Nothing doing. Just his police salary going in and the kind of day to day expenditure you'd expect"

" 'Phase 2 completed'" pondered Meredith Wynne "after Laura King had plundered the bank accounts and vanished she sent just that one short text message to her brother, nothing else"

"What are you getting at, Merry?" his boss Ruby asked

"I'm wondering what Phase 1 was. If we presume Phase 2 was the bank accounts and her disappearing act what was Phase 1?"

"I've been saying for months there's something else going on here we're missing. Laura King and 22 Station Road, it keeps coming back to the same starting point. WHY?" Ruby shouted banging the table with both her fists and making everyone jump "what is it about that property?"

"I'm wondering if I've been a fool" Meredith responded "our PC Andy Edge who owns the property has been saying all along there was nobody in the ground floor flat and I dismissed his concerns and now I'm recalling some other worries Andy had. Remember he reported his grandma's white van had been stolen? Then a bit later on he mentioned he'd noticed paintings and objets d'arts had disappeared from his grandma's house. I didn't take any of that too seriously at the time either"

"Benefit of hindsight, Merry. Did Andy actually use the words 'objets d'arts' ?" Ruby Scott asked mischievously

"No, boss, what I think he said was 'pictures and stuff'. The point is though he was talking about things that had happened at 22 Station Road before he'd even decided to convert the place into two flats. We've never linked all these things together"

"Understandable" DI Church joined in "there is no obvious link, what we've learned about this month is fraud or money laundering on a vast scale and the murder of Carl Ramsey. I think we should have a word with PC Edge, see if he remembers anything else odd happening before the building got converted into flats"

"I agree. I'll have a word with the Inspector in charge of Uniform Mrs Prisha Gayan and ask her if she can spare Andy for half an hour" Ruby said adding "but I think it should be just Andy, you and I, Merry, keep it as informal as possible, tea, biscuits, calm quiet chat"

"And no banging the table, boss"

PC Edge was on duty and between call-outs. Mrs Gayan agreed Andy could be spared for an hour. Ruby had arranged three chairs in a semi circle around an occasional table on which were cups of tea and a packet of biscuits, about as relaxed as she could make it. She started

"First, Andy, thanks for sparing us a bit of your time. This is an informal chat about 22 Station Road, we're interested in the period between when you inherited the property after your grandma died up to when the lettings started. I want you to think about everything that happened chronologically and see if you can remember anything that struck you as odd no matter how trivial it seems. Think it through, what happened first?"

"Well let's see, I got back from Australia in November four years ago. I certainly remember Audrey Hinstock settled grandma's affairs surprisingly quickly after my return. Then early in the following year I got my builder mate Simon King to look over the place. It was while we were looking around the house I noticed some of grandma's pictures and ornaments had gone. Oh yes, then something I didn't expect happened. Simon got a locksmith in and had all the locks changed to the house, I'd forgotten that. I think he did it early on in the building work"

"Did Simon say why, Andy?" Meredith asked

"He seemed a bit more concerned than I was about grandma's stuff disappearing and said as the house had stood empty for a while it was a precaution. Now that's made me remember something else. I'd had a set of keys to the house for many years but thinking about it I didn't come across any other house keys when I was emptying the place, just some small keys like drawer or bureau keys. So what happened to grandma's house keys? She must have had at least two sets. Anyway after the locks had all been changed Simon gave me a set of the new keys and kept a set for himself so he and his builders could get in every day to do the conversions. I didn't visit the site much while the work was underway. Then in the Summer of the year before last the work was all finished and the lettings started"

"Andy can you remember which flat was let first?" Ruby asked

"Not really. I remember Spring & Fall got tenants very quickly, surprisingly quickly but of course they only had one of the flats to think about because the estate agent Carl Ramsey contacted me and said he wanted to rent the first floor flat himself. He moved in first, well obviously because as we now know nobody ever did move into the ground floor flat, something I suspected all along"

"Sorry about that, mate, I thought you were worrying unnecessarily"

"Yeah right. Anyway the rest you know. Carl disappeared and Laura King became the new tenant of the first floor flat"

"Did you think that was odd, Andy?" Ruby asked

"Well I'd engaged Spring & Fall to handle everything to do with the lettings and they just told me they'd got a new tenant, Laura. Oh ! I've just remembered something else although it's a bit trivial. Mention of Laura reminds me that Simon told me Laura had been annoyed about Carl Ramsey jumping in to rent the first floor flat. Apparently she wanted it herself. Simon and Laura bumped into each other one day on Market Repton High Street and had a chat. They've remained on good terms. Anyway Laura told Simon she was annoyed both flats had been let as she wanted to move up from Birmingham to cut out all the travelling"

"So Laura King was annoyed about Carl Ramsey moving into the first floor flat, even though we now know it was Laura who'd started renting the ground floor flat using the name of the late Selwyn Myles" Ruby slowly recapitulated

"But surely there's no reason why Laura King would kill Carl Ramsey just to get his flat? She'd stayed there with him, they were lovers at some stage" Meredith observed

"So it seems Laura King wanted the whole of that property to herself and we keep coming back to the same question 'why?' " Ruby asked

"I don't think I can help you with that ma'am" Andy Edge said adding "it's not as though there's any buried treasure there" and his words hung in the air silently for a moment.

"This is all very helpful, Andy. If you think of anything else tell me or Merry straightaway". Andy finished his tea and biscuits and went back to what he considered to be proper policing with his apprentice Mike Perez who told him excitedly

"While you were at your meeting Andy the sergeant told me to go out on foot patrol on my own for the first time. Guess what? I arrested somebody !"

"What for, Mike?"

"Indecent exposure in the shopping precinct. Mrs Gayan came down to the custody suite to congratulate me. That's the second time she's done that. After the CID told her about that Spanish translation I did for them she thanked me for that too"

"Yeah I like Mrs Gayan. She's fair and reliable. She'd make a good Chief Constable but the problem is she knows too much about policing"

"What was your meeting about, Andy?"

"It's connected to the same case as the Spanish document you translated, Mike. Some mystery about my late grandma's house. I dunno what's going on, it makes my head spin thinking about it"

"The lads say you're dead rich, Andy. Did your grandma leave you a fortune?"

"I'm beginning to think it was more like a curse".

Ruby Scott and Meredith Wynne were still talking about what Andy had just revealed. Ruby was summing up "....so Andy's grandparents were antique dealers, after his grandma died some of their paintings and other items disappear from 22 Station Road and then the locks get changed and Andy never found his grandma's keys. I think we can guess what 'Phase 1' was all about, Merry"

"If that is the case, boss, some of that stuff must have been eye wateringly valuable. But why kill Carl?"

"Sooner or later Carl Ramsey would have realised there was nobody in that ground floor flat. Perhaps Laura couldn't risk his saying something about it. Perhaps there were millions of pounds at stake".

CHAPTER 33

Goodbye

In the following month Mid Land Police HQ in Blackbird City received the information they had requested from the banks in the Isle Of Man, The Channel Islands, Gibraltar and the Cayman Islands. The accounts to which Laura King had transferred vast amounts of money over several years were called -

Esperado (Isle Of Man) Ltd
Esperado (CI) Ltd
Esperado (Gibraltar) Ltd
Esperado (Cayman) Ltd

A detective put 'esperado' into Google Translate and discovered it means 'eagerly awaited'.

The accounts had all been opened twelve years earlier and showed a history of significant deposits ranging from £5000 to over a million pounds. Few withdrawals from the accounts had been made so the credit balances kept rising until over the period from late February to early March of the current year the accounts were systematically emptied and the huge credit balances transferred to one single bank account in Panama City. It was a company account called Esperado (Panama) Ltd. A detective learned from Google that the UK does not have an extradition treaty with Panama.

A detective constable was set to work to go through the formal procedures to obtain the names of the directors of the companies in the Isle Of Man, the Channel Islands, Gibraltar and the Cayman Islands and also the dates when these companies were formed. Everybody knew there was no point attempting to do this for the Panama company. The British territories which had cooperated with the detective's request albeit slowly and reluctantly eventually revealed that all the companies had been incorporated twelve years earlier and that they all had the same directors :

Brian Atchley
Ben Hinstock
Laura King

Despite going through all the proper official channels no cooperation was forthcoming from the banks in The Bahamas, North Turkey and Singapore. Nobody was surprised about that although it was assumed similar transactions and transfers were also being made through those countries.

Detective Chief Inspector Graham Radway telephoned DI Ruby Scott and told her of the latest developments.

"So now we know where the money went to, well at least where it went to when it left the UK. Company bank accounts in the usual tax dodge offshore places. It is very interesting that the companies' directors don't include Peter Guild and Audrey Hinstock. Also interesting is the fact that the offshore bank accounts were opened and the offshore companies incorporated twelve years ago, the year when Laura King joined the Lapley & Hinstock practice"

"Graham, concerning Peter Guild either he's not involved and we have got it all wrong or it's been contrived to conceal his involvement"

"With the financial malpractice it's a possibility but the murder of Carl Ramsey and the disposal of his body isn't something Laura King managed on her own. Furthermore if he's not involved in any of this why keep saying 'no comment' in response to all our questions? But there's something else about Peter Guild, Ruby, and you're not going to believe this"

"Try me"

"At my last interview with Guild his solicitor insisted we either charge him with something or return him to full duties. I've been consulting with our Human Resources division to see if we have any grounds to sack Guild without having to pay him a fortune in compensation. HR expressed surprise I was asking this as Peter Guild had resigned from the force over a month ago. He gave the required 30 days notice period and was removed from our payroll at the end of last month, March.

HR assumed he'd told his bosses and colleagues at Dainford that he'd resigned. Of course nobody bothered to check. Of course there was no cross referencing between HR and Internal Conduct And Discipline. Guild had told nobody he worked with that he'd resigned and didn't even tell his solicitor. So all the while we were interviewing him (or I should say listening to him saying 'no comment') he was quietly working his way through his thirty day period of notice. And now he's disappeared. But we had taken the precaution of confiscating his passport so he's still in the UK"

"My belief threshold holds no limits where this case is concerned, Graham. This resigning secretly couldn't have happened when we were a small county constabulary. Everybody knew everything in those days. So although we can't prove anything I take it we're assuming Peter Guild was somehow involved but I wonder how he gets his share of the proceeds?"

"I think we'll continue to assume he's Laura's accomplice hence the contrived fake interview with a non existent Selwyn Myles which I suspect they worked on together"

"When you say he's disappeared what do you mean exactly, Graham?"

"I mean he isn't at home and we don't know where he is. His solicitor said we had no grounds to continue holding his passport and insisted we return it to him but Guild had disappeared before we could do so"

"They're running rings around us, Graham. Of course he may have just gone on holiday somewhere in the British Isles. He's got grandparents in Dublin remember, if he's gone there by ferry he wouldn't need his passport just photo ID. His police ID card or driving licence would do the job"

"Possibly. But I'd like to knock his door down to check his flat, see if clothes and toiletries have gone but Mr Posh Lawyer said if we attempt anything like that it'll be compensation time"

"Is he a posh lawyer, Graham?"

"King's Counsel no less from a big firm in Birmingham. Now I wonder how a detective constable can afford the services of a KC? Anyway I'm finishing for the day and going off home, how about you, Ruby?"

"Looking forward to my midweek meeting with Mr Arthur Guinness"

"Give him my regards".

In Market Repton Ian Fall was locking his office. Wednesday nights he used to have a few pints straight after work with his friend and business partner Carl Ramsey. Ian hadn't been into The Golden Lion pub on the High Street since Carl had disappeared. He had received a telephone call the previous month from Det Sgt Wynne informing him Carl's remains had been located. On an impulse Ian walked into The Golden Lion. He would have a pint and think about Carl. At the bar, pint in hand, looking for a suitable table Ian saw a face he recognised although he couldn't remember the man's name. The man was sitting alone at a table. Ian walked over.

"Hello, I'm Ian Fall from the estate agency on the High Street. Sorry, I know you from somewhere but I've forgotten your name"

"Hello, Mr Fall. I'm Ray Proudfoot. My wife was Tina Proudfoot, you know......."

"Of course, I'm so sorry, Mr Proudfoot"

"Call me Ray. Would you like to join me?"

Ian sat at Ray's table saying "I haven't been in here since my business partner Carl disappeared"

"I haven't been in here since Tina died. We used to call in every Friday evening straight from work"

"I knew Tina of course because we do a lot of business with Lapley & Hinstock. Correction, I should say we used to do a lot a business with Lapley & Hinstock"

"The police haven't arrested anybody I understand" Ray said

"Sorry, about Tina or Carl?"

"Both. Do you think they're connected, Ian?"

After a long pause Ian said "I haven't thought about it. It's hard to see a link but we're both looking at this from our own point of view and from our own personal loss. If there is a wider picture I can't imagine what it is. Are the police in contact with you over Tina, Ray?"

"I have a personal liaison officer who phones me every three or four weeks. She's sympathetic but basically just says 'sorry I've nothing to tell you' in the nicest possible way"

"Ray, have you heard one of the partners from Lapley & Hinstock has disappeared - Laura King?"

"Yes, it's the talk of the town. There's rumours flying around about embezzlement, fraud you name it"

"I've heard those rumours too. Something odd happened today, Ray. There's only two of them left now at Lapley & Hinstock - Brian Atchley and Audrey Hinstock. Well today their offices didn't open, the place remained shut up and in darkness all day. I noticed from my office across the road that people kept turning up for their appointments, couldn't get in, hung around for a bit looking puzzled then wandered off, so it looks like an unexpected closure"

"Perhaps they've done a bunk too. Do you think we should tell the police, Ian?"

"Let me think. It might be nothing. Tell you what, Ray, if the office doesn't open tomorrow I'll phone that Detective Sergeant Wynne at Repton Magna police station and let him know. Don't see what more we can do"

"Fancy meeting up for a pint again sometime, Ian?"

"How about same time next week, Ray?"

"Suits me". The two new friends exchanged phone numbers.

Next day Ian Fall noticed the offices of Lapley & Hinstock again remained unopened. He had business cards for Brian Atchley and Audrey Hinstock. He rang their mobile phone numbers, there was no reply. Brian's card also showed a home landline number. There was no reply from that either. Ian still had the card Detective Sergeant Meredith Wynne had given him when DS Wynne had asked him to email 'Selwyn Myles' about the occupancy of the ground floor flat. Ian called DS Wynne and told him Lapley & Hinstock's offices had unexpectedly closed. DS Wynne reported this turn of events to his boss Ruby Scott who rang her boss DCI Graham Radway whose response was

"This has the potential to get some major media interest. The body in the lake already has of course but just as a murder story. I'm going to speak to the Chief Constable about this latest development and get someone from our press office ready to start fobbing off any unwelcome questions. Look, Ruby, can you and Meredith Wynne reinterview Brian Atchley and interview Ben Hinstock and ask them about these offshore bank accounts. And see if you can find out why the offices of Lapley & Hinstock have closed. I'm going to start some damage limitation here".

So Ruby Scott and Meredith Wynne drove north to Market Repton and to the home of Brian Atchley. It was a traditional semi detached house within walking distance of the town centre. Well maintained, tidy garden, clean windows, tasteful curtains, no-one at home. The couple living next door had been neighbours of the Atchleys for over 20 years. They informed the detectives that Mr and Mrs Atchley had gone on holiday to the Canary Islands for two weeks. The neighbours were unaware that the Atchleys had sold their house fully furnished online and would never be coming back.

Ruby and Meredith ascertained that Ben Hinstock lived on the northern outskirts of Repton Magna. They called on him next having earlier telephoned him to ask could he please spare them some of his time. Ben Hinstock Junior was now aged 73 and years spent at a desk had taken their toll. He had the same unhealthy rotund shape as his daughter Audrey and hunched shoulders. They could not tell how tall he was because he did not get up from the dining room table throughout their interview. He had in front of him a cup of tea, a digestive biscuit and a glass of whisky. The detectives were not offered refreshments. He seemed more like 83 than 73 but did have alert, intelligent looking eyes. Ruby and Meredith had been admitted to the house by Mrs Hinstock as she exited to take their dog for a walk. Ruby introduced herself and Det Sgt Wynne and started their discussion.

"Mr Hinstock are you aware of the recent disappearance of Mrs Laura King?"

"I understand she's not at home, that doesn't mean she's disappeared"

"Are you aware that Mrs King had been passing significant amounts of money through the bank accounts of deceased clients of Lapley & Hinstock?"

"You arrested and questioned my daughter in connection with the matter. I believe she did mention to me the nature of your enquiry"

"Do you know where your daughter is now, Mr Hinstock?"

"Yes"

"Would you mind telling us where she is?" Meredith asked recognising the lawyer's irritating tendency to answer questions literally

"She's in Portsmouth staying with an old university chum for a couple of days"

"So she'll be back to re-open the office?" Meredith continued

"The office is closed?"

"Yes, unexpectedly it seems. We've had reports clients are turning up for appointments and finding the place locked and in darkness"

"Where's Brian Atchley?" Ben Junior asked

"According to his neighbour Mr and Mrs Atchley have gone on holiday"

"Somewhere sunny I expect. Brian likes warm, faraway, exotic places. I'd rather sit in the garden"

Ruby resumed the questioning with "Mr Hinstock we understand you are a director of several overseas companies" but when Ben Junior remained silent Ruby realised he was waiting for a question so said "Mr Hinstock are you a director of one or more overseas companies?"

"I am not and never have been a director of any company neither in this country nor anywhere else"

"Company regulatory authorities in the Isle Of Man, the Channel Islands, Gibraltar and the Cayman Islands have provided us with the names of the directors of several companies of interest to us and those companies' records show Ben Hinstock as one of the directors. Do you still maintain you are not a director?"

"I repeat I am not a director of any company and never have been"

"Can you account for why your name should appear as a director?"

"The name does not relate to me. It was probably my late father Ben Senior"

"Do you know why your father would be a director of several overseas companies?"

"All the places you mention conjure up images of financial wrong doing, tax dodging and money laundering. Let's face it what other reason could there be for going to any of them? Unless of course you go to the Isle Of Man for the TT races"

"Sorry, what do you mean, Mr Hinstock?"

"My father was a crook"

This extraordinary statement momentarily silenced both Ruby and Meredith as each thought of their next question. Eventually Ruby asked

"What sort of wrongdoing do you believe Mr Hinstock Senior was involved in?"

"I think he persuaded selected rich clients to sign Lasting Powers Of Attorney in favour of Lapley & Hinstock when they made their wills. Nearly always those clients would also name the firm as executors of the will. So then he'd have full control over the client's finances both before and after they die. I think he then used their bank accounts as the temporary resting place for the proceeds from the sale of…...er…...well…. items which came into his possession. Then I believe the funds were transferred out. If you've uncovered overseas bank accounts I presume that's where the money eventually went"

"Are you aware of the implications of what you're saying, Mr Hinstock?"

"Not really but then my father's dead, I'm retired, I didn't benefit in any way, played no part in any of it, inherited next to nothing under my father's will and live here in this modest house with my wife and my dog"

"But how can someone who's died still be listed as a company director?" Meredith asked

"Presumably the same way someone who's died can still have an active bank account. You simply don't tell the company or the bank that the person has died" Ben Junior said explaining the obvious

"Where would the records be now for the cases your late father worked?" Meredith asked

"My father died sixteen years ago. We used to store closed files for 20 years in a fireproof vault in the cellar beneath the offices. Then they went off for destruction. When we started to run out of space I made the decision to reduce the period to 15 years. I believe it has since been reduced again to 10 years. There'll be nothing left from my father's time"

"We will need to discuss what you've told us with our senior staff, Mr Hinstock. We may need to speak to you again". And with that they departed. On the short drive back to Repton Magna police station Ruby asked

"How much of that did you believe, Merry?"

"A few weeks ago I'd have said it was all totally unbelievable but now.....well, why would he lie? And he offered us all that information in an informal interview, not under caution. There's something very clever about all this, boss. They probably know perfectly well Mid Land Police haven't got the resources to investigate anything on this scale. I know we've referred it to the national Serious Fraud Office but they're only interested in the biggest of the biggest frauds where hundreds of millions are involved. I worry this case won't be big enough for the SFO so it ends up with nobody investigating it"

"Ben Hinstock Junior is hardly living a life of luxury is he? No sign of unaccountable wealth there. When we get back to the office I'll speak to Graham Radway and tell him what we've just learned. We've got Audrey Hinstock's smartphone number haven't we? Get onto our IT lot, Merry. Ask them to run a location trace, let's see where she really is".

Meredith did so. Audrey's smartphone was in Portsmouth.

Two weeks later in late April Peter Guild walked into Dainford police station to clear his desk, empty his locker, say goodbye to his colleagues and invite them all to the local pub for a drink. His UK passport was returned to him.

Meanwhile in Market Repton the offices of Lapley & Hinstock still hadn't reopened. Meredith Wynne asked his IT department to run further location checks on the smartphones of Audrey Hinstock and Brian Atchley. No signal was located. Meredith rang each phone and heard recorded messages saying the number called had been discontinued. He reported this to his boss Ruby Scott suggesting he go immediately to the homes of the two, Ruby agreed.

Meredith accompanied by a trainee detective constable drove northwards to the home of Brian Atchley in Market Repton. The house looked exactly the same as it had when he visited two weeks earlier with his boss. There was no-one at home. Meredith knocked on the door of the next door neighbour he'd spoken to before who said

"We can't believe it. They've gone for good, disappeared. Sold the house fully furnished on the internet. We've been friends and neighbours for over 20 years. My wife is terribly upset about it, you know, going off like that and not saying a word to us. First thing we knew was when a removal van arrived and a new couple started moving in".

Meredith and his colleague drove back to Repton Magna and visited Audrey Hinstock's flat which was in a converted mill on the banks of the River Repton within walking distance of the town centre and the police station. Meredith heard exactly what he was expecting. The new owner had moved in two weeks ago having bought the place fully furnished online.

CHAPTER 34

Meet Murder, My Angel

There had been no history of heart problems. Most days Mrs Marjorie Edge felt fine but other days the warning signs were there. Marjorie wasn't a worrier but always a thinker and a planner so thought it prudent to finalise her end of days plans. One day in September she made two appointments, one in the morning with a funeral director and the second in the afternoon with those helpful solicitors on Market Repton High Street.

She bought for herself a 'cremation without ceremony' having first heard of this arrangement after David Bowie had died the year before. Marjorie didn't believe in a god nor an afterlife and saw no point in expecting what few friends and relatives she had to sit in a draughty church listening to the words of someone they had never known.

Marjorie had already made a will with Lapley & Hinstock naming them as executors and had signed a Lasting Power Of Attorney also in favour of Lapley & Hinstock. She didn't want her sole beneficiary, her grandson Andrew, to have to handle the issues her colourful past had created. Sensible and useful up to a point Andrew had never displayed the kind of talents which would be needed here. Marjorie had learned that Lapley & Hinstock had. During a meeting with Miss Audrey Hinstock Marjorie gave instructions on how she wanted things to go.

Two months later in the November of that year after Marjorie had gone to her final resting place (even though she didn't believe in such things) Audrey wasted no time in starting to carry out her client's wishes. Marjorie had supplied a list of the 30 most valuable items in her home including paintings, jewellery and small sculptures which she wanted Lapley & Hinstock to sell on behalf of her estate. Given the method in which many of the items had been acquired it would be inadvisable to advertise them or place them into a public auction. Marjorie had accordingly added against each item the name and contact details of individuals who may be approached and invited to purchase with a suggested sale price. Individuals who were all specialist collectors and who would not ask challenging questions about an item's provenance.

Using a set of keys Marjorie had thoughtfully supplied for them Audrey Hinstock, Laura King and Brian Atchley visited 22 Station Road on what Brian had amusingly called 'a works outing'. They carefully went through Marjorie's list, identified the 30 items and placed them into three large lockable chests in the surprisingly clean, damp free cellar. Their plan was to start the sale process with the initial approaches to the potential buyers before Andrew Edge returned from Australia.

Apart from the 30 most valuable items for which Marjorie had identified individual potential buyers she had negotiated a deal with one of her long term Birmingham antique dealer contacts for the remainder of her small but modestly valuable portable possessions. These were placed into Marjorie's white Citroen Berlingo van and driven to their destination by Laura King.

The white van was then given to a career criminal and thug-for-hire Lee Parker of Birmingham. Mr Parker had never done a day's honest work in his 34 years. Laura had become aware of his existence through legal colleagues engaged on criminal prosecution or defence work. The defence side always seemed to be more effective than the prosecution side where Mr Parker was concerned and he'd never served a single day in any prison. His one positive trait was that once paid to do a job he could be relied upon to carry it through. So Laura gave him the white Berlingo van and mentioned she might one day have a task for him. She also gave him one of her business cards and asked that he keep her informed should his mobile phone number ever change. Her dealings, for the present time at least, with Mr Parker concluded Laura returned to her flat in Birmingham thinking of a song sung in some theatrical legal setting but she couldn't recall its source -

'All thieves who could my fees afford relied on my orations
And many a burglar I've restored to his friends and his relations'

Back in Market Repton the solicitors correctly guessed that Andrew Edge would engage Spring & Fall to handle the sale of 22 Station Road. They were the only estate agents in Market Repton, but the best outcome as far as they were concerned would be Andrew's deciding to convert the house into flats. This would mean a long delay before the property came onto the market.

Laura King had already started dating Carl Ramsey and it was she who suggested to Carl that 22 Station Road would make an ideal property for a flats conversion. Carl in turn suggested this to Andrew Edge on his first visit to Spring & Fall Estate Agents. It was a useful coincidence that Laura's ex husband Simon King was Andrew's closest pal and the efficient Simon also saw the property's potential for the lettings market. So the building work started and this was good news for the three solicitors. At first they still had access to the property after Simon King and his builders finished their work each day so were astonished when they discovered the meddling builder had had all the locks changed. The sale of Marjorie's collection, by its nature a slow job, had to be suspended for well over a year until a new plan was put into place - Laura King renting the first floor flat and their helpfully deceased client Selwyn Myles, whose bank account they were manipulating, renting the ground floor flat which would give them unhindered total control of the building and its works of art.

But then they were angered to learn Carl Ramsey had helped himself to the tenancy of the first floor flat. With millions of pounds at stake the decision was made to remove Carl, permanently. They made a plan and called it 'The Send Off'. Swindling, embezzlement and fraud had been traits of Lapley & Hinstock's senior staff since 1923 when Audrey's great grandfather co-founded the firm but nobody had ever been murdered up to now.

The trio had all agreed Carl had to go and any misgivings about the physical unpleasantness and mess of murder were countered by thoughts of the money involved and what it would bring the three of them. The big problem they all agreed was the disposal of the body. Laura sought advice from her brother Detective Constable Peter John Guild following which the plan was put into action.

At 6pm on Thursday 7 November, two years after they had dealt with Marjorie Edge's post mortem arrangements, Carl Ramsey returned to 22 Station Road from his day's work. He intended being at home only long enough to change his clothes and collect his kitbag. Then it was off to Dainford FC to deliver his coaching session. Audrey Hinstock and Laura King were waiting inside the darkened ground floor flat with its door slightly ajar. Laura had had a set of keys for the new locks since she in the guise of Selwyn Myles had become the tenant of the ground floor flat. When Carl walked past the door on his way to the stairs Audrey stealthily crept up behind him and brought a lump hammer down onto the back of his skull. Audrey was not in the habit of carrying a lump hammer around in her handbag. The hammer had been purposefully left in the cellar by Laura King on one of the occasions when she'd been staying with Carl.

The blow was meant to stun, not to kill. Carl's skull cracked and he crumpled unconscious to the floor. The two women carried a tub of water out of the ground floor flat and manoeuvred Carl's limp body to its edge. It was essential he still be alive, his lungs had to be full of water. They held Carl's head under the water until he stopped breathing. They held his head under the water for another five minutes to make sure. Then they wrapped the body in multiple layers of strong, thick black plastic sheeting left in the cellar by the roofers. The only personal items they removed from Carl's pockets were his smartphone and his keys. They destroyed his smartphone. They dragged the wrapped body into the ground floor flat and left it there until the late afternoon of the next day, Friday 8 November. After finishing work on that following day they transferred Carl's body into the boot of Audrey's car, locked the flat and the building and set off on their drive to Mrs Anand's remote cottage on the east side of Llyn Brenig.

The three solicitors had previously researched locations of remote holiday lettings on lake shores and found Llyn Brenig ideal being in a national park not too far from County Repton. Then they discussed how many days the cottage rental period should be. One or two days was out of the question. Nobody books a remote cottage for one or two days. So it was to be three, four or five days. They decided upon four.

Mrs Anand had been correct. Her cottage had been occupied for one night only. It was all they needed. Next morning at first light Audrey and Laura struggled the body into Mrs Anand's boat, sailed to the centre of the lake, attached bricks using electric cable and pushed the body over the edge of the boat. The bricks had been pre-collected from builders' skips especially for the occasion. Carl's body rapidly sank to the bottom of the cold, dark water of Llyn Brenig.

Meanwhile back at 22 Station Road Brian Atchley had been busy with a mop and a bucket full of a water and bleach solution. Everywhere Carl's body had been was meticulously cleaned multiple times. The hall's Minton tiled floor had made a perfect killing ground. Brian took the precaution of taking the mop and bucket back to his house and putting them into a neighbour's wheelie bin.

Detective Constable Guild knew that it was only a matter of time before Carl Ramsey's disappearance would be referred to his team as a MissPer. He monitored the police computer system and as soon as he saw that Cheshire Police had referred the matter to Mid Land Police he allocated the case to himself. His intention was to delay as long as he could his initial visit to Market Repton to interview Carl's ground floor neighbour (who, of course, he knew didn't exist) and Carl's business partner Ian Fall. Irritatingly this plan was forestalled when he received a phone call from a Police Constable Edge at Repton Magna police station who informed him that he was the owner of the property 22 Station Road and the landlord of the missing Carl Ramsey, a most unexpected and unwelcome development.

He immediately relayed this to his sister. None of them had been aware that Marjorie's grandson and sole beneficiary was a police officer. Laura had in turn reported this news to Audrey Hinstock who said

"Should we be bothered?"

"It's an unexpected thing but I wouldn't say it's a game changer. No we'll work around it. Carry on as planned" Laura had replied.

The contrived interview in the early December of that year between Detective Constable Guild and 'Selwyn Myles' they regarded as a masterstroke. Laura had escorted her brother into the ground floor flat and they sat at the table to invent a convincing story. 'Selwyn' described Carl as a perfect neighbour but went on to tell an intriguing story of comings and goings in the early hours of the morning all of which was complete fiction. Adding times to the lies about Sunday mornings "Carl comes back in a taxi around 2am and at 2.15am goes off in a second taxi" made it sound all the more convincing.

But the best bit of all was the one part of the story which was true. Carl had already mentioned to Laura his recurring knee problem. Years earlier it had prevented Carl's becoming a professional football player. It got so bad in that Autumn that Carl struggled to get up the stairs to his flat. Then one of the footballers at Dainford FC had given Carl some 'ludicrously strong painkillers'. When DC Guild asked 'Selwyn' for his opinion on what Carl might be up to 'Selwyn' quickly replied 'drugs' even suggesting the police search all the lockers at Dainford FC.

Immediately after the fake interview DC Guild closed down the MissPer case and passed the matter to Repton Magna police who deal with drug crime. Significant amounts of police time and money were then wasted on a fruitless drugs enquiry. But the whole nonsense was given a degree of credence when one of the football players admitted supplying Carl with the 'ludicrously strong painkillers'. While all this was going on attention was diverted from what really was underway at 22 Station Road.

So the sale of Marjorie Edge's works of art resumed without the risk of Carl Ramsey in the first floor flat witnessing all the comings and goings. Legal work to revoke the tenancy agreement of the first floor flat had been started as soon as they decided to kill Carl. By the time Andrew Edge became aware of the need to get the tenancy revoked work on doing so was already well underway. This time they made sure Laura became the new tenant. The moment the legalities had been completed Laura walked across the High Street to Ian Fall, signed and paid.

CHAPTER 35

Wondrous Stories

Brian Atchley and Audrey Hinstock were descendants of the co-founders of Lapley & Hinstock. Brian was a nephew of the last of the Lapleys and Audrey was the great granddaughter of Eric Hinstock. After Samuel Lapley and Eric Hinstock founded the firm in 1923 they entered the area of embezzlement by accident. By the late 1920s they had built up a portfolio of wealthy local clients happy to have these clever, qualified, young men available to give them legal advice.

One of these clients was a Mr Murgatroyd, a rich, elderly recluse whose only relative was his brother in the west of Canada. They did not keep in touch with each other save for an annual exchange of Christmas cards. Mr Murgatroyd had made a will naming Lapley & Hinstock as executors and leaving his money, his house and its contents to his brother. When Mr Murgatroyd died the attempts of Messrs Lapley & Hinstock to comply with the terms of their late client's will presented them with a problem. The brother in Canada had had no family of his own and had moved from his last known address. Canadian lawyers were approached but failed to track down the missing potential legatee.

Lapley & Hinstock sold old Mr Murgatroyd's house and all its contents and placed the money raised into a client account under their control along with all the money from Mr Murgatroyd's bank account which they arranged to have closed. Ten years later when nobody had come forward to claim the money Messrs Lapley & Hinstock decided they'd keep it for themselves, it might be a technical embezzlement but they decided to call it a victimless crime.

Lasting Powers Of Attorney became a speciality just before and during the second world war. Thousands of County Repton men made their wills before going off to play their part in the conflict and the unmarried men felt reassured to know that the reliable, local solicitors would take care of their affairs should they regrettably not make it back. Into this situation came the turmoil created by an entire continent of people uprooted and moving, offices, homes and documents destroyed in bombings, inheritances going unclaimed and Lapley & Hinstock finding themselves with a vast sum of money at their disposal.

After 1945 when the citizens of County Repton slowly resumed their normal lives very few took the trouble to investigate the legal and financial affairs of their lost relatives. Those who did found Lapley & Hinstock obliging and efficient. Those who didn't never saw a penny of their departed relatives' cash.

Samuel Lapley died of liver failure in 1953 after years of rich food and excessive drinking of the finest wines and single malts his clients' money could buy. Eric Hinstock's son Ben (Ben Senior) joined the firm to replace him. After Eric retired Ben Senior ran the firm on his own until the late 1970s when two things happened. His son Ben Junior joined the firm and Ben Junior's daughter Audrey was born. A problem became apparent almost immediately - Ben Junior was not interested in the finer things in life. His life revolved around his baby daughter, his dog, his garden and his wife. All he wanted to be was a regular, reliable, trustworthy, small town lawyer.

Brian Atchley arrived at the practice at the age of 29. Both Ben Senior and Brian had inherited their ancestors' appetite for the finer things in life especially where someone else's money was paying for them. At last Ben Senior had a reliable partner in crime.

Fifty years had to pass before the firm had another estate to administer as lucrative as Mr Murgatroyd's had been. Miss Nika Anrepiy was the last survivor of what had been an immensely wealthy Saint Petersburg dynasty. At the first mention of the word Bolshevik the entire family moved west taking their money and their treasures with them. First to Paris then to London and lastly to avoid the Blitz just before World War Two started the two remaining Anrepiys, Nika and her widowed mother, moved to what was to be their final home in a small village in County Repton.

The Anrepiys were originally clients of Eric Hinstock until his son Ben Senior took over their affairs. Nika's mother died in the 1960s leaving everything to Nika. When Nika died in an expensive care home twenty years later there was no-one left. Believing herself to be descended from Cossack stock (and being quite right about that) she left her entire estate to a variety of UK horse charities. While still of a sound state of mind Nika had signed a Lasting Power Of Attorney in favour of Lapley & Hinstock. Sadly there was a long history of hereditary mental instability in the family of which Nika was well aware and fearful.

When Nika entered the care home Ben Senior arranged for her house to be sold having firstly removed from it the vast collection of jewellery which had been handed down through the Anrepiy generations. Many of the items had been hand made for the family by three of imperial St Petersburg's most renowned jewellers Bolin, Hahn and Keibel.

After Nika's lonely death in the care home Ben Senior prepared the final accounts for her estate. The horse charities were all sent generous cheques but the final accounts undervalued the estate by several million pounds - the money which would eventually be raised disposing of the jewellery collection plus the £450,000 from the sale of the house. But Ben Senior and his then junior partner Brian Atchley had a big problem. Neither of them had any idea how to sell the magnificent collection of gems in Ben Senior's possession at the best possible prices.

Then George and Marjorie Edge moved from Birmingham to Market Repton and attended an appointment with Ben Senior. An understanding was reached, they could be mutually useful to each other. Over the following two years using their contacts in the USA, Birmingham's Jewellery Quarter and within the antique dealer community George and Marjorie sold all of Nika's jewellery for a sum exceeding £10 million. Their commission was a modest 5%.

Most of the money was raised in the USA and Ben Senior arranged for a client bank account to be opened for himself in the USA through one of their associated American law firms. The American proceeds were paid into that account. The UK proceeds were placed into several bank accounts including the main business account of Lapley & Hinstock, the individual bank accounts of Ben Senior and Brian Atchley and the bank accounts of their clients which the solicitors had control of through Lasting Powers Of Attorney.

Once all of this financial activity had been completed Ben Senior then decided to step down from full time work. He bought a multi million dollar apartment in Palm Beach Florida which he and his wife lived in for six months of each year from October to March. Their granddaughter Audrey was a regular visitor. Back in County Repton for the other six months of the year Ben Senior kept in touch with Brian Atchley and acted as a part time consultant to Lapley & Hinstock as and when needed.

Several times over the Christmas and New Year holiday period Ben Senior and his wife had their granddaughter Audrey stay with them at Palm Beach. During the first such visit after the start of her law degree course in Nottingham Audrey told her grandparents about her new friend Laura. During her visits to Florida Audrey had experienced the luxurious lifestyle of her grandparents and realised this was not financed by the usual small town lawyer activity. Audrey wanted a taste of this for herself. Ben Senior introduced Audrey to the concept of what he called victimless crime. He told Audrey about old Mr Murgatroyd from way back in the 1920s, about Nika Anrepiy and about George and Marjorie Edge and how useful they could be.

Audrey outlined her future plans to her grandfather. She wanted to make as much money as possible in the shortest amount of time. Ben Senior was happy to give her all the advice she needed. After law school Audrey's seemingly mundane two year contract with a firm in Manchester specialising in family, land and inheritance matters taught her about preparing watertight, unchallengeable legal documents. Ben Senior was happy and sad. Happy because he had in Audrey a natural successor and sad because he realised it would eventually be the end of the line for Lapley & Hinstock.

Both Ben Senior and his wife died of natural causes within twelve months of each other. Ben Senior was 85 when he died. Audrey inherited the apartment in Florida. Ben Senior left only a modest sum of money to his son realising there was no point in leaving a fortune to an heir whose idea of a good time was spending a few rainy days in an inexpensive boarding house in Aberystwyth. The bulk of his fortune was left in trust to his granddaughter Audrey provided she become a partner in Lapley & Hinstock and remain so for at least ten years.

Brian Atchley was the executor of the wills of his late partner and his wife. After complying with the terms of their wills Brian 'forgot' to mention to the bank that Ben Senior had died so his account remained open and useful. Brian mentioned this to Audrey when she and Laura joined the firm four years later. Audrey had said "It's what he would have wanted" and laughed until she cried.

Brian meanwhile had been marking time. With the unimaginative and unambitious Ben Junior as his partner there was little other choice. But Ben Senior had briefed Brian about Audrey and promised Brian that when Audrey and possibly her friend Laura joined the firm he could expect innovation such as the firm had never seen before. Brian had been careful to avoid any ostentatious displays of wealth living in a modest semi detached house and cultivating an image of a slow, middle aged, pedantic, reliable solicitor. His appearance suggested a man whose major interests might include cardigans and lawnmowers. It was cleverly done. With his share of the proceeds from the Nika Anrepiy event Brian had bought for himself and his wife Betty a luxurious apartment on Paradise Island, Nassau, Bahamas.

Ben Junior eventually retired and left the firm to spend more time with his dog, his garden and his wife in that order. In that same year Audrey and Laura arrived at the firm. Within a matter of weeks companies and corporate bank accounts for them had been set up in the Isle Of Man, the Channel Islands, Gibraltar and the Cayman Islands. Brian Atchley, now the senior partner, already had a US dollar bank account in Nassau, Bahamas. In a fitting tribute to her late grandfather Audrey suggested Ben Senior be named as one of the directors of the companies they had set up.

He had been dead for four years by then but after all nobody ever checked up on these things and his still-open bank account could be used as one of the channels to fund the corporate accounts.

Over the next 12 years all of these accounts were used as resting places for funds liberated from clients by the dynamic new regime at Lapley & Hinstock. With internet banking now firmly established manipulating funds around the world had never been easier. The UK banks played their part by closing branches, doing away with the need for any of their staff to have banking qualifications and introducing what they called 'customer service' meaning a call centre in a foreign country.

Brian Atchley had been overseeing the investments and bank account of Mrs Mary Montgomery-Gradbach since Ben Senior's retirement. When she died in AD2000 Brian 'forgot' to tell her bank and her pension payers about the wealthy lady's demise. Brian sent to her next of kin a 'final statement of affairs' on what seemed to be the finalisation of her considerable estate. Of course none of the family thought to check that her bank had been told of her death. It was taken for granted that her efficient solicitor had done everything. After that it became one of the essential go-to bank accounts for handling the money Brian embezzled from his clients' estates.

Brian, Audrey and Laura all knew there was a time limit on their activities. Brian already had a retirement home in the Bahamas ready and waiting but Audrey and Laura had no intention of waiting until they reached retirement age to start to live their lives of luxury and excess. The three of them mutually decided that all of their fraudulent internet banking transactions would be done by Laura alone and only on her computer terminal. Their thinking was that when the financial malpractice was eventually uncovered Laura with her dual nationalities and choice of passports would vanish first. With nothing to link immediately Brian and

Audrey to the wrongdoing they could remain in place long enough to close down the business and transfer out any funds Laura hadn't managed to, firstly to the company accounts in the British overseas territories and then finally to the Panama company account. They each had their individual escape plan ready. It was a matter of waiting to see which event would trigger the start of the end.

Then one late September afternoon Marjorie Edge walked into the offices of Lapley & Hinstock to keep her appointment with Audrey Hinstock. Marjorie told Audrey of her final arrangements and what she wanted her to do.

CHAPTER 36

Getting Away With It

After her meeting with Marjorie Edge in that September four years earlier Audrey had spoken to Brian Atchley and Laura King and briefed them on what Marjorie had asked them to do on her behalf when the sad time came. Disposing of art and other treasures was an area of activity with which they were all unfamiliar but they had Marjorie's list of the items involved, potential buyers to contact and suggested sale prices. They would simply follow Marjorie's guidance. They were not expecting the news of Marjorie's death to come as soon as it did.

They would have to manage two sales. The sale of Marjorie's items they called 'Phase 1'. 'Phase 2' when it eventually became a necessity would be the disposal of everything else including Lapley & Hinstock's premises.

Their time scale for the sales was thwarted by Simon King changing all the locks at 22 Station Road and then Carl Ramsey moving into the first floor flat. Once Carl was out of the way and Laura installed they brought Marjorie's items, 30 in total, out of the cellar and into the ground floor flat. They did not want to have to take potential buyers down into a cellar.

They split the list between them so ten items each to sell. Marjorie had highlighted the top three, they allocated themselves one each :

Number One

At midnight on 31 December 1999 when the fireworks were exploding over Oxford to welcome in the new Millennium robbers were breaking into the city's Ashmolean Museum. They had been tasked with stealing just one thing - Cézanne's painting 'Auvers Sur Oise' then valued at £3 million. The robbers were successful. The painting was delivered to the woman who commissioned the theft. Her mansion near Worcester was burgled the following night by a gang of small time thieves from Birmingham. The Cézanne was amongst the things they snatched at random in their raid. Back in Birmingham the lads had no concept of what they had on their hands so they asked around and heard about George and Marjorie's antique shop. They were very happy with the £6000 cash they were given. Many years later a man from Qatar visited the ground floor flat and paid Marjorie's asking price of £6 million.

Number Two

In 2011 the British Museum 'lost' a Cartier diamond ring then valued at £750,000 presumed stolen. Five years later the museum reported its disappearance to the Metropolitan Police who decided it was too late to start an investigation. During the following years the ring changed hands many times each time selling for a small fraction of its value, basically it was too hot to handle. It passed through Birmingham's Jewellery Quarter like a cursed version of pass the parcel until someone remembered that efficient couple the Edges. But hadn't they retired many years ago ? Through the antique dealers grapevine George and Marjorie became aware they might be of service and bought the ring for £200,000. The ring remained in their possession for well over a decade and then a lady from Monaco arrived in Market Repton, visited the ground floor flat, inspected the ring and paid Marjorie's asking price of £2,200,000 to her representatives.

Number Three

In the late 1970s the Scottish painter Jack Vettriano was starting what would turn out to be his immensely rewarding career. His early works were sold around Edinburgh for between £50 and £100. A visitor from Birmingham visited a car boot sale in Musselburgh in 1979 and paid £65 for an original painting in the artist's usual and haunting style. In one of their last house clearances before retiring George and Marjorie became the owners of the painting. A man from County Galway visited the ground floor flat in Market Repton and paid Marjorie's asking price of £825,000.

The other 27 items fetched far more modest amounts ranging from £4,000 to £45,000 and their total raised by the time the sale ended was £661,500.

Overall total raised on the 30 items £9,686,500.

Audrey had negotiated a commission of 17.5% so the split was :

£8,039,795 into the estate of Marjorie Edge (executor Audrey Hinstock)
£1,646,705 to the three solicitors.

The money was spread around the client accounts they were manipulating, later moved into one of their overseas corporate accounts and finally transferred to Panama.

"Phase 1 completed a bit later than expected" Brian had said

"And a lot more profitable than expected. Just under ten million pounds" Audrey had replied.

With their Phase 1 sale completed the three solicitors decided on a pause to allow 'the dust to settle'. The trigger for their 'Phase 2' as they had already discussed would be Carl Ramsey's body being found or Selwyn Myles's real identity being revealed or some issue involving Andrew Edge.

Andrew Edge was they agreed the least likely trigger. With 22 Station Road no longer a factor and the rents being paid regularly on his two flats there was or so they thought no longer anything there to draw Andrew's interest. Andrew's concern about the apparent absence of his tenant 'Selwyn Myles' they dismissed as a temporary issue. Should the need arise Laura could at any time use the email address she'd created to feed all manner of stories through to Ian Fall or Andy Edge about how the talented Mr Myles had been engaged on yet another time consuming overseas railway project.

Selwyn Myles had been a worry. They had made a serious error on his identity with everyone assuming he was a white man. But his widow in South Africa had made no further contact with them following the apparent satisfactory finalisation of his estate and as that was well over four years ago they thought it unlikely his phantom tenancy and the continued use of his UK bank account would be their trigger.

So they considered the eventual discovery of Carl Ramsey's body would most likely provoke the end game.

Actually it was none of the three. The foiled attempt by Laura King to use Mrs Mary Montgomery-Gradbach's Barclays Bank account to transfer £15,000 to their Bahamas corporate account triggered the start of the end. Laura of course had been unaware the bank had put a block on the account. The three solicitors agreed it was time to cut and run. So Laura emptied the other 7 client accounts she had been running for the past twelve years and via their collection of offshore accounts the funds had reached their Panama corporate account. Exit Laura.

Two of the 7 accounts to which Laura still had access related to living clients of Lapley & Hinstock, one working overseas and the other to a person incapacitated from running their own affairs. Both owned decent properties in County Repton. Brian Atchley had the bright idea of inviting overseas buyers to invest in the British property market on a 'buy to let basis' with 'guaranteed returns'. Undervaluing the two properties to attract quick sales both were bought unseen through the internet by a property investment company in Luxembourg for a total of £690,000. Brian naturally did all the property conveyancing work in record time. The money was transferred into the still open bank account of the late Ben Senior, whence to their Gibraltar corporate account and finally to their Panama corporate account. A few weeks after Mrs and Mr Atchley had permanently left England a removal van arrived with new tenants ready to move into one of the houses only to find its owner still in residence and unaware his property had been 'sold'.

Audrey Hinstock meanwhile had been busy seeking buyers for the property 27 High Street, Market Repton RE15 8AH which Lapley & Hinstock had occupied since 1923. A law firm called Repton Legal Services with existing offices in Repton Magna and Dainford jumped at the chance of expanding into Market Repton especially as it would be into the premises of a long established and respected firm. They paid £740,000 for the building and the book of clients. That money also ended up in the Panama corporate account.

Then it was time for Audrey and Brian to disappear. With both their homes and cars already sold and the proceeds in the Panama corporate account their escape plans were put into action. A Google search had revealed the best way to travel around the world without drawing attention to oneself - travel alone and with minimum luggage.

As Audrey's father Ben Junior had told the detectives Audrey had indeed been visiting an old university chum in Portsmouth. When she left her friend's home she threw her smartphone into a builder's skip and paid cash for a one way foot passenger ticket on the Portsmouth - Bilbao ferry. Once in Spain Audrey made her way to Madrid and then westwards across the Atlantic.

Mr and Mrs Atchley as their neighbour had told Detective Sergeant Meredith Wynne had gone to the Canary Islands. But they were there for only two days not two weeks. Then they flew to Lisbon and on to their home in the Bahamas via the USA.

A few weeks later meetings were taking place at two very different bars in two different continents. Brian Atchley, Laura Guild (as she was now known) and Audrey Hinstock were enjoying cocktails in Moon Bar at the five star Cove Hotel on Paradise Island, Nassau, Bahamas. It was the first time Brian and Audrey had seen Laura sporting her natural short, black, slightly wavy hair. They were seated around a table and had made sure no-one was within earshot. It was also the first time they had met since their departures from England. Laura was speaking

"…...so all the money at our disposal now rests in our corporate account in Panama City. I've emptied the buffer accounts in Gibraltar, Cayman and everywhere else. The question now is do we close all those buffer accounts, close some of them, leave one open…...what do you think?"

"Close them all" Brian suggested "they've served their purpose and we've capitalised everything we can, there's nothing left in Britain"

"Agreed" Audrey added "closing them would also produce a dead end for anyone trying to find out where we are. Did you manage to close all the individual clients' accounts, Brian?"

"Laura had of course emptied all the client accounts but I found that I had to leave them open because of the difficulties of closing them. It would have involved a phone call to each bank. The on-line banking system wouldn't let me close the accounts. So the 8 accounts are all still open. We suspect that Mrs Montgomery-Gradbach's account has been blocked by Barclays but as far as I know the other 7 accounts remain open and available. They're no use to us any longer and any attempt to use or even access one of them would leave an electronic footprint we wouldn't want.

The last time I looked which was back in the office when I tried unsuccessfully to close them online I noticed the state pension for Ben Senior was still being paid into his account every four weeks. He'd be well over a hundred years old now. Somehow I forgot to close his account when he died and I also forgot to report his death to the Ministry Of Pensions. Shows what a hopeless executor I was. The total state pension accumulated in the account over the years up to the present time was £147,409.60. The final transaction I did from my tablet when I was in Lisbon was to move it all to the Gibraltar account and then into our corporate account in Panama"

"I wondered what that was. Well done, Brian" Laura said

"Grandad would love all this" Audrey added "I agree with Brian. We must never attempt to access any of the accounts ever again. But I wonder if the Department Of Work And Pensions will keep paying grandad's state pension forever?"

"Not our problem" Laura offered "but everything at our disposal is now in one place in our Panama corporate account as we'd planned. There's $9,000,000 US dollars......." Laura stopped speaking as a waiter approached and asked if they'd like fresh drinks. For Brian it was another Manhattan, a Singapore Sling for Audrey and a Lemon Drop Martini for Laura, then their business resumed.

"Like I was saying nine million US dollars rounded down to the nearest hundred thousand. We'll be keeping the Panama corporate account open and the Panama company will remain 'in business'. If we're all in agreement I'd like to pay a million Euros into my brother's Irish bank account and split the rest equally between the three of us. What do you think?"

"Fine by me" Brian agreed "John played his part with advice on disposal of the body, maintaining the Selwyn Myles fiction and keeping us updated with every move the police were making. It wouldn't have gone so smoothly without him"

"OK with me too" Audrey said continuing with "is John permanently in Ireland now, Laura?"

"Yes. He sold his flat in England and bought a place near grandma and grandpa in Dublin. The irony is he'll eventually qualify for a UK police pension ! You couldn't make it up !"

After the three had stopped laughing Brian asked "So where are you two going next?"

"Laura & I have that meeting in Panama City to attend then I'll be off to my apartment in Palm Beach for a few months. You're both welcome there any time and of course, Brian, that includes Mrs Atchley. The apartment is available for you when I'm not there. I can leave the keys with the concierge"

"Thanks, Audrey. Betty loves Palm Beach. It's not essential I be at the meeting in Panama City is it?"

"No, Brian. Laura and I will go. So what about you, Laura? Any long term plans?"

"My long term plan is not to have a long term plan. I don't think we need worry too much about keeping ourselves just in countries with no extradition treaty. With all the funds at our disposal now in US dollars alone we've got the only global currency everybody accepts"

"And who would start the extradition process? Our helpful former clients are either too daft or too dead to bother and the UK police haven't got the resources anymore. Here's to the Police And Crime Commissioner" Brian added and the three, laughing, raised their glasses in a mocking toast.

"That's reminded me" Laura spoke again "...my Birmingham contacts tell me nobody has reported us to The Law Society yet. We're all still allowed to practice law !"

Audrey nearly choked on her drink before asking "And what about you, Brian?"

"I'm going home now. Our apartment is within walking distance of this bar".

Thousands of miles away on the same day Ian Fall and Ray Proudfoot were enjoying their now weekly 6pm Wednesday session in The Golden Lion, High Street, Market Repton. It was a cold, wet, windy day. They got their first pints from the bar and took them to a table. Ian had his back to the door and when the next customers arrived accompanied by a blast of cold air Ray said "Simon King the builder has just walked in. Do you know him, Ian?"

"Yes I know him well. He's the on-call builder I use for any problems arising with my let properties"

"I don't like the look of the guy he's with, he looks like a bruiser"

Ian turned around to see who Ray Proudfoot was looking at and laughed. He realised it was the first time he'd laughed out loud in The Golden Lion since Carl had disappeared.

"It's funny you should say that. When Carl first set eyes on him he described him as a 'right thug'. Actually he's one of my clients, Andy Edge, Police Constable Andy Edge"

"Sorry, Ian, I didn't realise. He just doesn't look the type you'd like to come across on a dark night"

"Simon might think differently. I'll invite them over and introduce you". With a shouted greeting and a wave Ian invited Simon and Andy to join them and the introductions done the four men got down to some serious chat and drinking.

Next time the door swung open it was to admit two women - Councillor Mrs Hilda Judd and her friend Mrs Boyce-Harmon.

"On a day like this I think we need something warming, dear. Fancy a B and B?"

"Perfect, Hilda. Oh look there's Simon King. I'll just have a quick word with him about a job I want him to do for me"

"Two brandy and Bénédictines, please" Hilda asked the barman and once served went to join her friend who was by then chatting to the four men

"Hello, Simon. Hello, Ray" greeted Hilda "is this a regular session for the four of you?"

"Probably will be from now on at least when Andy isn't on duty" Simon replied

"Of course, you're Marjorie Edge's grandson aren't you. Terrible business what those so called lawyers were up to for years and nobody suspected a thing. Did you know Simon and I played a major part in their downfall? I'm sure he'll tell you all about it. I've just been to the offices of Repton Legal Services who've taken over. They've had their frontage painted in a hideous shade of yellow. I've told them it's quite unsuitable for our conservation area and will have to be changed. There's a table free near the fire, dear. Let's take our drinks over there"

Once seated at their own table Hilda and Mrs Boyce-Harmon continued a conversation they'd started earlier ".....my husband will be here any minute now, we'll ask him what he's found out" and on cue the pub door opened again and a wet and windswept Mr Judd arrived having walked from his allotment. He got a pint of best bitter from the barman and after saying hello to the four men joined his wife and Mrs Boyce-Harmon.

"So what have you got to tell us?" Hilda immediately demanded barely giving her husband chance to sit down

"Er…..well, we've decided to extend the rhubarb forcing season and…....."

"Stop !" shrieked Hilda "I'm not interested in your rhubarb forcing, I want to know what you and your daft cronies have found out about that plot of land adjacent to the allotments. That's what I asked you to do"

"Sorry dear I forgot to mention it"

"I'm sure you all gather up at those allotments just to drink that disgusting home made cider…......"

Things were returning to normal in Market Repton.

CHAPTER 37

Come Undone

On a pleasant Wednesday morning in early Summer Michael Ryder's normally enjoyable early morning drive to work was interrupted. Michael, aged 57, lived in Kidderminster, Worcestershire and was the head groundsman at a golf and country club situated adjacent to the A456 road to the west of Kidderminster. Michael's regular-as-clockwork journey to work was 5am to 5.20am and it was usually a daily pleasure. He rarely saw any other traffic on the road and during the leisurely drive Michael went over in his mind his tasks for the day ahead. Work days always started with breakfast with his workmates in the club café, something else to look forward to.

But on this particular Wednesday Michael's breakfast was to be delayed. Just south of Bewdley, Worcestershire, a bridge carries the A456 over the river Severn. It's not a particularly attractive or historic bridge just a functional river crossing. Just before he reached the western end of the bridge Michael noticed a panel of the bridge's fence had been demolished. It hadn't been like that when he'd driven home the night before.

Michael stopped his car adjacent to the damaged fence, got out of his vehicle and looked down into the River Severn. He saw what looked like a Range Rover lying on its side in the shallow water close to the riverbank. The water was level with the upended side of the Range Rover so the river had filled the car and was flowing through it. Michael pulled his phone from his pocket and called the emergency services. A policeman from Bewdley was next on the scene followed a few minutes later by a fire and rescue vehicle also from Bewdley. After giving his brief statement to the policeman Mr Ryder was back on his way to his work and to tell his colleagues about the river incident.

It was a complex job. Two police divers had been summoned and reported the driver's body was still in the vehicle held in place by the seat belt. The airbag had not deployed, there was no-one else in the car, the divers were asked to remove the body. The fire and rescue team spent most of their shift removing the Range Range from the river.

The drowned body was that of a man whose wallet was found in one of his pockets. His driving licence was inside his wallet and identified him as Mr Lee Parker aged 38 and showing an address in Birmingham. His smartphone was also recovered from the scene. The post mortem subsequently found neither alcohol nor drugs in his bloodstream. Cause of death was drowning, it was unclear what had caused Mr Parker to veer off the road, crash through the bridge's barrier fence and plunge into the water. There was no sign anyone else had been in the car with him or that any other vehicle had been involved. The police accident investigator would only speculate that maybe Mr Parker had fallen asleep at the wheel or had been taken unwell.

The owner of the Range Rover had woken up on that Wednesday morning to find his vehicle missing. He reported its theft to the West Mercia Police.

As a matter of routine the constable from Bewdley entered Mr Parker's details into the national police database. It revealed he was a 'person of interest' to several police forces including West Mercia, West Midlands and Mid Land. The name was referred to West Midlands police as the late Mr Parker had lived in their area. Given his long criminal history the assumption was that Mr Parker had been carrying out a theft-to-order, Range Rovers being one of the most targeted vehicles for this type of activity. Someone must have driven him to the vehicle's location the night before but the police were not going to use their limited resources investigating that.

There were few expressions of sympathy at the demise of the career criminal and hitman. Over 20 years of crime and not a single conviction was some sort of record in itself. The only people likely to miss him would be the defence solicitors for whom one long gravy train of legal aid had finally hit the buffers.

Also as a matter of routine West Midlands Police obtained a court order compelling Mr Parker's smartphone service provider to supply details of all activity on the phone requesting, given his history, that this be for the past 12 months. The arduous procedure then commenced of cross referencing the phone's incoming and outgoing caller record against the police national computer database to see if any other names of interest were revealed.

Any such names are listed with the name of the police force interested and the name of a contact officer. Eventually the number registered to Mrs Laura King came up in the log of incoming calls to Mr Parker's smartphone. The contact officer was shown as Detective Sergeant Meredith Wynne of Mid Land Police who was seeking information about Laura King in connection with murder, fraud and absconding. A routine report was made to Sgt Wynne showing the date and time of Laura King's calls to the deceased.

"So Laura King phoned this now deceased Lee Parker twice on the day Tina Proudfoot was killed" Meredith Wynne was explaining to his boss Detective Inspector Ruby Scott "first at 2pm then at 6.10pm. Now I ask myself why she would be in touch with a scrote like Lee Parker?"

("What?")
("Is it done?")
(" 'course")
("Where's the van?")
("Torched it……..")

"The implication is that she was arranging Tina Proudfoot's murder before Tina took any action on the financial goings on she'd uncovered. But I wonder how Laura knew what Tina had found out?" Ruby pondered

"It's guesswork of course but I'd say from computer logins which always leave an electronic footprint. It's like our system. Anyone can see who last accessed a record, from where and precisely when. The day Tina Proudfoot was killed was also the same day a burnt out Citroen Berlingo van was found round the back of the railway station and let's remember it was a Citroen Berlingo van which disappeared from 22 Station Road while Andy Edge was in Australia a few years ago. By coincidence Andy Edge attended the fire incident"

"So do we tell Ray Proudfoot?"

"I think so. It's that word we have to use nowadays 'closure'. But Andy tells me he is now a regular drinking buddy of Ray Proudfoot. Might be less distressing for Ray if Andy broke the news to him"

"OK, Merry. See what Andy thinks about it".

CHAPTER 38

Small Town Boy

"Something's still bothering me, Merry"

Andy Edge, Mike Perez and Meredith Wynne were sitting around a table in the canteen at Repton Magna police station.

"Is it about speaking to Ray Proudfoot about what we think happened to his wife?" Meredith asked

"No, it's not that at all" Andy responded "as I meet Ray regularly in the Golden Lion it's better coming from me. But I'll visit him at home, it won't be a conversation suitable for a pub"

"So what's the problem, Andy mate?"

"The rents are still being paid on the two flats in Station Road"

"Now that is weird. Where's the money coming from?"

"This is another worry. It's coming in from some overseas bank every month. Of course it gets paid to the estate agents Spring & Fall like it always has. I asked Ian Fall to find out from his firm's bank where exactly the money comes from but the bank said they can't disclose where in the world it's coming from because of the Data Protection Act. It puts me in a bad place, Merry, because there's a possibility it's proceeds of crime.

I've mentioned it to my boss Mrs Gayan and she said I should ask Spring & Fall to stop transferring the money into my bank account. I've done that now and I took the fed rep Chloe Gibbs with me so my chat with Mrs Gayan was witnessed and recorded. But the problem's still there, Merry. Jeez, will this nightmare never end?"

"There's no proof it's proceeds of crime and as far as work is concerned you've done everything you can do to cover your back, but have you thought about what you're going to do with the Station Road house long term, Andy? You don't want to leave it standing empty for too long"

"Yes. I'm going to sell it, Merry. I've already asked Ian Fall to put it on the market. I've had enough of all this endless intrigue. Ian reckons it'll fetch around £625,000 either selling the two flats separately or the whole building sold as a buy to let"

"Either way you could retire comfortably on the proceeds" Meredith suggested

"Please don't retire yet, Andy" Mike Perez joined in "not while I'm still a proby"

"No I won't be quitting yet but I just want to get all this behind me. I've also decided to sell my house here in Repton Magna. Ian Fall says a traditional semi within walking distance of the city centre should sell very quickly"

"So where will you live, Andy?" young Mike asked

"I've accepted an invitation Simon has put to me many times"

As Ian Fall had correctly predicted Andy's house in Repton Magna sold within two weeks. Not being part of a property buyer/seller chain helped. Andy had lived alone in the house for 20 years but it contained little he was attached to. The only item of furniture he took with him to Simon's home in Market Repton was the antique bureau he had removed from his grandparents' house.

On the day of the move Meredith Wynne drove Andy's car the 12 miles north to Market Repton while Andy rode there on his motorcycle. His last glimpse of his former home was the Spring & Fall For Sale board with a red banner added across it saying 'Sold subject to contract'.

A buyer was found for 22 Station Road within two months. The asking price of £625,000 was paid. Andy didn't care who had bought it or what they intended to do with the property. As soon as the sale legalities had been completed the rental payments on the two flats stopped. Nobody ever discovered where the rent money had been coming from.

CHAPTER 39

A Room With A View

Audrey Hinstock and Laura Guild next met in Panama City. They had arrived on different days and from different compass points into Panama and met in The Peacock Alley, the cocktail bar adjacent to the lobby of the city's Waldorf Astoria Hotel where they had booked a suite for a few days.

"Do we have a day and a time for the meeting, Laura?"

"3pm tomorrow. It's a short taxi ride from here. Where did you go after we met Brian in Nassau, Audrey?"

"I stayed in Nassau for a few days and then I went to Havana where I met someone we both know from our time in Nottingham, Joanna Brooks, remember her? We keep in touch through Facebook, I saw she was in Havana and we arranged to meet up"

"Yes I remember her. And after our time here where will you be going next?"

"The apartment in Palm Beach. The Atchleys will be coming over for a couple of weeks in June. Then Joanna Brooks later in the year"

"And what if Joanna asks you how you're financing it all, what will you tell her?"

"I'll say that I inherited the apartment and a lot of money from grandfather which of course is true. What have you been up to since we last met?"

"I took a beach holiday in Costa Rica. I thought the Spanish classes would come in useful but nearly everybody there speaks English. It's full of Americans"

"So like here then. Laura, have you thought about what we're going to have to do when our current passports expire? I know you've got both UK and Irish passports but what happens when they need replacing?"

"I'll cross that bridge when I come to it, just try the obvious path first. I'll go to the British and Irish embassies here, start the replacement process and see how far it goes. I don't know if the UK police have access to passport records or if some kind of flag has been put on our records as wanted in connection with enquiries. Why? Is it something that concerns you, Audrey?"

"Yes. My passport has less than 18 months to run. I've done some research about getting a Panama passport. We have a registered company and its linked bank account here and have had for years. That's a good start. Then all you need is a home address here and that's not a problem because property is cheap in Panama City. Then they'll give you citizenship if you keep at least a million US dollars deposited in one of their banks. I'll do that"

"I'll bear it in mind. You know, Audrey, I've been living this life of idle luxury for less than three months and I'm already getting bored with it. I'm going to have to think about another challenge soon".

Next day at 2.40pm the two women got into a taxi outside their hotel and asked the driver to take them to their destination. At 67 storeys The Point apartment tower when it was completed was the tallest building in Latin America. Visible from nearly every part of Panama City its luxurious residences have 360 degree views across the city, the bay and the Pacific Ocean.

They entered the building and approached the concierge. Laura said to him "Buenas tardes. Estamos aquí para visitar el apartamento cinco, cinco, cero, uno por favor". The concierge phoned through to apartment 5501 and its owner granted permission for the two visitors to be sent up. The apartment occupied the whole of the 55th floor. They got out of the lift, walked through a door which had been left ajar for them and stepped into the apartment's cool, air conditioned vastness.

A slim woman approached them, her heeled shoes clicking on the marble floor. A woman who looked to be in her early to mid seventies but who was actually 85. Her clothes looked, but only looked, simple. Her short straight hair was expertly sculptured to the shape of her head. A woman with one grey eye and one blue eye.

"Hello, Marjorie. You're looking well" Audrey said extending her hand in greeting

"Thank you. It's probably a lot to do with that feeling you get when you realise you're untouchable, beyond any law. Let me show you both around. The views are breathtaking but I love just staring out across the Pacific Ocean"

Marjorie showed her two accomplices around her home which surprisingly had very little artwork. Each room had just one painting, large, colourful and abstract, a contrast to the creams, whites and pale greys of the walls, ceilings and floors.

Whilst on their guided tour they met one other person, a Panamanian man Marjorie introduced as Jorge and who seemed to be in his early sixties. Jorge was in the kitchen squeezing limes.

"3pm is not too early for a Daiquirí is it?" Marjorie enquired

"Not for us it isn't" Laura replied

"Jorge will bring them to us in the terrace room with a few nibbles. We'll talk and watch the ocean. The sunset from here is an unforgettable experience. So tell me, what triggered the endgame?"

Before either had chance to answer Jorge entered the terrace room with three well shaken Daiquirís and a small selection of savoury nibbles on a tray and placed them before the three women before quietly withdrawing.

"Not something we expected" Laura began explaining "one of the client accounts we'd been using for many years suddenly got blocked by Barclays Bank, then we learned from my brother that the police were planning a raid on our offices. I put my escape plan into operation"

"And left Audrey and Brian to face the music?"

"Not at all, Marjorie" Audrey joined in "it was part of the plan. We'd arranged it to look like only Laura was manipulating the bank accounts. We knew the police would raid our offices but we didn't know precisely when. Laura's policeman brother wasn't able to find that out for us. On the day the police arrived Laura had already vanished and I got to the office to find Brian putting on a superb act of confusion and dithering. We were both interviewed and had our computers checked by the police IT experts who, of course, found nothing. While all the attention was on Laura Brian and I emptied the remaining accounts, capitalised everything we could lay our hands on and here we are"

"I haven't heard any news about it and there's been nothing on the internet which is odd considering it must be one of the biggest and longest running frauds Britain has ever seen when you take into account Ben Senior's activities. George & I fenced that Russian woman's jewellery collection for over £10,000,000 at least thirty years ago" Marjorie said

"I think you mean found discerning buyers, Marjorie" Laura added and the three of them laughed

"Yes and our names don't appear on any 'Wanted' posters" Audrey continued "we think it's all been hushed up probably because of the huge embarrassment it would cause. The banks have kept accounts open for people who common sense should tell them would be dead, the police haven't got the resources to do anything about it and they have the added awkwardness of one of their own feeding us information, although they can't prove it. Also The Law Society would find themselves having to explain how such a thing could possibly happen and go on happening for decades. Your man knows how to make a good cocktail, Marjorie. These are better than the ones we get in the Waldorf Astoria"

"Jorge is a good cook too. I'll ask him to bring fresh drinks. So what's next for the two of you?"

"A life of leisure for me" Audrey responded

"Me too at the moment but I can't hang around cocktail bars in five star hotels forever. Soon I'll have to look around for something else to amuse myself" Laura added

"Well you're in the right place. There must be more dodgy money sloshing about here and more crooks per square mile than anywhere else on Earth and I include present company"

They were still all helpless with laughter when Jorge brought the next platter of drinks and some of his homemade nibbles. A few moments of smug, self satisfied silence followed as they ate and drank. Laura had noticed during their walk through Marjorie's home the absence of any personal touches. But here in the terrace room she noticed on a small side table two framed photographs of Andrew Edge. One was a head and shoulders well composed photograph and the other had Andrew and Marjorie standing side by side, photographs perhaps taken by George. One day within the next few years Andrew will do a routine online check of his bank balance and see that a credit of over £27,000,000 has appeared. He will panic but will eventually be reassured by the bank that the entry is correct.

Audrey resumed the conversation "Now you've heard our stories, Marjorie. Tell us what happened to make you quit England". There was a pause while Marjorie considered where to begin.

"George and I were always aware there was a chance our past would catch up with us. It would be difficult for anybody to produce enough evidence for any court to convict us but some of the people we've, how can I put it, engaged with over the years aren't the sort of people who'd go through the courts anyway. The higher end of the antiques business isn't all the genteel affair you'd think from the cosy teatime TV programmes. There's some pretty ruthless people out there.

We'd kept in touch with our friends and contacts in the Birmingham antiques community and the Jewellery Quarter and visited them frequently after we'd retired to Market Repton. 'Market Repton' ..... how strange that name sounds now spoken here 55 floors above Panama City. By the time George died most of them had retired too so I started visiting them more frequently. I think it was the first Christmas after George died I started to learn things I didn't like the sound of. 'Someone's been asking around about you and George' one of my friends had said adding something like 'I don't know who it was but he seemed quite anxious to get in touch'. That sort of thing. The more of my acquaintances I visited the more I heard. That's when I started thinking about my future.

I was staying with a friend in Birmingham for a few days just before Easter in the year of my fake death, we were doing the tour around of people we'd known, all very pleasant reminiscences and chit chat with sherry when someone took me aside and said 'there's a man from Canada been asking around about you. I told him you'd long since retired and left the area but I didn't have your contact details. He gave me one of his business cards and asked me to contact him if I ever met up with you again. He seemed very persistent. Said he'd been trying to track you down for a year or two when he could spare the time to come to England. Here's the card he gave me'.

So she handed me his card and it said 'Adrian Cork Business Consultant' with his phone numbers, email and an address in Toronto. I guess he wanted the Klimt portrait back several decades after he accidentally gave it to us. Now that would have made an interesting day in court !

I realised straight away it was time to organise my departure. The rest you already know as you were involved in the arrangements. I bought the cremation plan and timed my 'death' for the period when Andrew was in Australia. When you hear someone has died how often would you ask 'can I see the death certificate?' - never, of course. As you've both realised from your years at Lapley & Hinstock nowadays hardly anybody checks anything any more. The banks and other institutions have made themselves almost uncontactable unless you possess the patience to try to understand what a foreigner in an overseas call centre is trying to tell you.

When Andrew returned from Australia it was all over, I'd gone. I'm sure he was impressed with how quickly you sorted out my estate, Audrey. My son, daughter in law and Andrew all knew I'd bought the 'Cremation Without Ceremony' arrangement but again who would ever think to check with the cremation company that the arrangements had actually been carried out? Nobody ! You just accept what you're told in such matters"

"We did think about what we'd do if Andrew asked about a death certificate" Audrey said "but we are acquainted with enough villains in Birmingham to know where to get one forged. But Andrew didn't ask"

"Of course he didn't. What was the cause of my death going to be?"

"Heart failure"

"Obviously and always acceptably meaningless"

"I miss my grandson. How are things between him and Simon?"

"They seem to be better than ever now. One of the last things we noticed before we departed from Britain was that Andrew has put up for sale through Spring & Fall estate agents both his house in Repton Magna and number 22 Station Road. We guess they'll be living together" Audrey replied.

Changing the subject Laura asked "What time does the sun set?"

"The light starts to go around 6.30pm" Marjorie replied "it's 5 o'clock now, if you've not made any plans for this evening you may as well stay and watch the sunset from here. You won't get a better view"

"We have no plans for this evening or any other evening" Laura replied

"Jorge makes a very fine herb omelette".

So they stayed and enjoyed Jorge's excellent light supper and then the two murderers and the swindler opened a bottle of wine and shared it watching the sun set over the Pacific Ocean.

Marjorie broke their silence asking "Do the two of you ever wonder how we were allowed to get away with everything we've done?"

"The interesting thing is, Marjorie" Audrey explained "it's actually easier than ever to get away with fraud nowadays if you plan carefully and stay focussed. Successive British governments have introduced quango after quango, regulatory bodies, industry regulators and so-called watchdogs all disparate and working independently of each other. And they don't work efficiently because they're headed by budget minded accountants and staffed by target chasing box tickers. Then they introduce well meaning legislation which actively prevents all these bodies coordinating their work. The Data Protection Act is one of the best examples and one of the greatest allies any serious fraudster could hope for. No one is allowed to tell anyone else what they're doing"

"Look at our area of work" Laura added "we're supposed to be part of a justice system but actually Britain doesn't have a genuine justice system. It has a legal system which operates mainly for the benefit of the people employed within it. What we've been up to hasn't wrecked anybody's life but had we been caught and brought to trial do you really think we'd have been sent to jail? No way ! Struck off the solicitors' register and an insignificant fine imposed and that would be the end of it"

Marjorie was of course unaware of the wrecked lives left behind in Market Repton.

Audrey took up the theme "Yes I agree with Laura about sentencing. There's little deterrence anymore to most kinds of criminal activity and the wrong doers know this. Sometimes you'd think the courts, especially the magistrates' courts, were encouraging the people appearing before them to go out and commit further crimes. Imposing laughably small fines that don't get paid, community service that's not done and driving bans on youths who've never passed a driving test or held a licence in the first place. It's like a Carry On film !"

Laura resumed "And it's not just weak sentencing. We have a Crown Prosecution Service mainly concerned about its budget, millions spent on Police And Crime Commissioners nobody wants and the last job advert I saw for Mid Land Police was for a person to maintain and expand their social media presence".

By now the sun had set leaving a deep orange slash of colour across the horizon. Their drinks and snacks were finished and the alcohol had muted further conversation. They had said all they had to say.

When it was time to go Marjorie escorted Audrey and Laura to the lift. After their farewells and just as the lift doors started to close Marjorie said enigmatically

"When shall we three meet again....?....."

Acknowledgements

I would like to thank all the people whose real life anecdotes over several decades have found their way into this story.

Also the residents of one particular small town whose fascinating habits inspired several aspects of the tale.

In a perverse way I owe a debt of gratitude to the Covid lockdowns of 2020 and 2021 for providing me with the spur to sit down and start writing.

Finally thanks to Marius Ganea Photography for realising the front cover design.

Printed in Great Britain
by Amazon

37764267R00175